Her R~~~~ ~~~~ss M~~~~el of ~~~~ ~~~~r of five previous books: *The Serpent and the Moon: Two K~~~s for the Love of a Renaissance King*; *Crowned in a Far Country: Portraits of Eight Royal Brides*; *Cupid and the King: Five Royal Paramours*; as well as the first two titles in the Anjou trilogy.

For more than twenty-five years, the Princess has pursued a successful career lecturing on historical topics. She lives with her husband, Prince Michael of Kent, in Kensington Palace in London.

www.princessmichael.org.uk

Also by HRH Princess Michael of Kent

*Crowned in a Far Country: Portraits of Eight Royal Brides*

*Cupid and the King: Five Royal Paramours*

*The Serpent and the Moon: Two Rivals for the Love of a Renaissance King*

The Anjou Trilogy: An Historical Novel

*The Queen of Four Kingdoms (volume I)*

*Agnès Sorel: Mistress of Beauty (volume II)*

*Quicksilver (volume III)*

# Quicksilver

*Her Royal Highness*
Princess Michael of Kent

Constable • London

CONSTABLE

First published in Great Britain in 2015 by Constable
This edition published in 2016 by Constable

A CIP catalogue record for this book is available from the British Library.

ISBN 978-1-47212-307-7 (paperback)

Typeset in Palatino by SX Composing DTP, Rayleigh, Essex
Printed and bound in Great Britain by CPI Group (UK) Ltd, Croydon CR0 4YY

Papers used by Constable are from well-managed forests and
other responsible sources

MIX
Paper from
responsible sources
FSC
www.fsc.org FSC® C104740

Constable
is an imprint of
Little, Brown Book Group
Carmelite House
50 Victoria Embankment
London EC4Y 0DZ

An Hachette UK Company
www.hachette.co.uk

www.littlebrown.co.uk

*To my two Freddies – my brother and my son – who are both blessed with the erudition and intelligence of their ancestor, Jacques Coeur, the subject of* Quicksilver

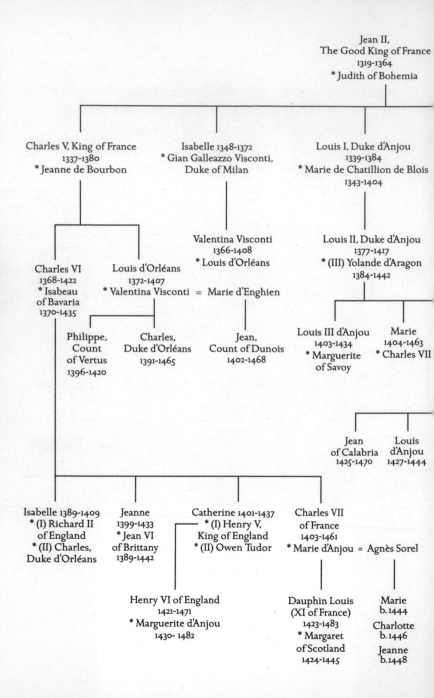

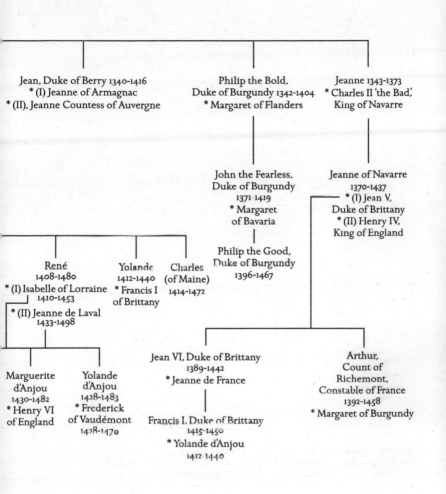

Jean, Duke of Berry 1340-1416
* (I) Jeanne of Armagnac
* (II), Jeanne Countess of Auvergne

Philip the Bold,
Duke of Burgundy 1342-1404
* Margaret of Flanders

Jeanne 1343-1373
* Charles II 'the Bad',
King of Navarre

John the Fearless,
Duke of Burgundy
1371-1419
* Margaret
of Bavaria

Jeanne of Navarre
1370-1437
* (I) Jean V,
Duke of Brittany
* (II) Henry IV,
King of England

René
1408-1480
* (I) Isabelle of Lorraine
1410-1453
* (II) Jeanne de Laval
1433-1498

Yolande
1412-1440
* Francis I
of Brittany

Charles
(of Maine)
1414-1472

Philip the Good,
Duke of Burgundy
1396-1467

Marguerite
d'Anjou
1430-1482
* Henry VI
of England

Yolande
d'Anjou
1428-1483
* Frederick
of Vaudémont
1428-1470

Jean VI, Duke of Brittany
1389-1442
* Jeanne de France

Arthur,
Count of
Richemont,
Constable of France
1392-1458
* Margaret of Burgundy

Francis I, Duke of Brittany
1415-1450
* Yolande d'Anjou
1412-1440

THE ROYAL
FAMILY OF FRANCE
AT THE TIME
OF THIS STORY

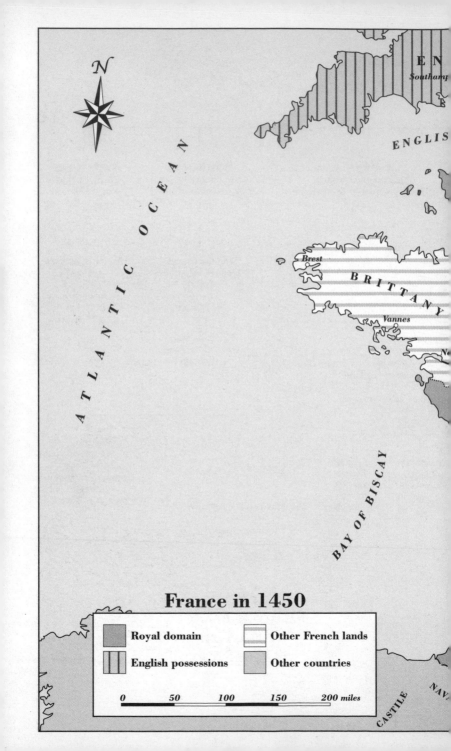

**France in 1450**

| | |
|---|---|
| Royal domain | Other French lands |
| English possessions | Other countries |

0    50    100    150    200 miles

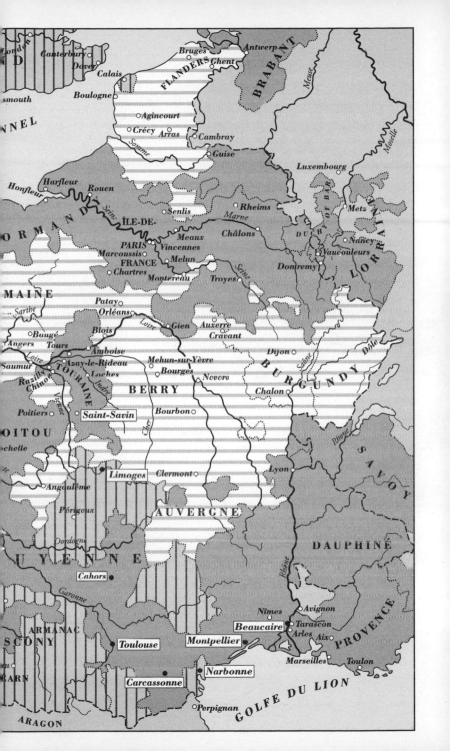

# Foreword

By the mid fifteenth century, the merchant Jacques Coeur of Bourges was said to be the richest man in the kingdom of France. He was the owner of the largest fleet of armed merchant ships in the Mediterranean, and financed King Charles VII's army in its efforts to push the English out of France and Normandy to Calais. In other words, a man to be reckoned with.

His achievement was all the more remarkable in view of his humble beginnings.

Jacques was born in Bourges in 1400. His father, Pierre Coeur, was a successful furrier who imported and sold the best furs in the sovereign territory of Berry, a royal province situated in central France. Yet the family was neither well connected nor influential. If the continued English invasion and alliance with the Burgundians had not forced the deposed and unrecognised dauphin Charles to flee Paris and move to Bourges in 1418 with his followers, even a man of Jacques Coeur's intelligence and ability might not have had the opportunities that came his way and enabled him to make his fortune.

# Chapter One

*France, early fifteenth century*

'*P*apa! Wait for me! These skins are so heavy, I can't keep up,' pants young Jacques as he struggles to stay with his father, but his legs are short and the load he carries is heavier than usual.

'You're doing well,' says Pierre Coeur, stopping to let the boy catch up and patting his head. 'We're almost there.'

Pierre is a furrier to royalty among other illustrious patrons, and young Jacques is accustomed to following his father carrying pelts. But today is special – it is his first visit to the Duke of Berry, his father's most important customer in their town of Bourges, capital of the duke's sovereign state. The uncle of King Charles VI of France, the duke is one of the greatest connoisseurs of the era. Pierre Coeur's commission is to supply his royal patron with the delicate stomach skins of martens with which to line his clothes – the elderly duke suffers greatly from the cold and damp.

'Welcome, welcome, my good friend,' calls the duke as Pierre and young Jacques enter the castle's high-vaulted central hall, the boy almost tripping over the long-tailed skins he carries as his eyes travel upwards. 'Aha! I see you have brought me not only furs, but a live young marten itself!'

Jacques blushes; he is indeed swaddled in the soft furs, some over his shoulders, others cradled in his arms and hanging to the floor.

'Shall we skin him too?' jokes the venerable man as he greets Pierre Coeur warmly.

The boy notices the easy familiarity between this august royal personage and his father and is amazed. While the two men discuss the season and trading, and the furs are unravelled from him, Jacques begins, a little tentatively, to turn on the spot where he stands and gape in awe at his surroundings. As his father makes his presentation, the good duke sees the boy's inquisitive glances and urges him to wander about his great chamber.

'Go, lad, and look around; feast your eyes on all the things exotic and beautiful I have spent my life collecting,' he says with a wave of his hand.

Before they arrived, Pierre asked his son: 'How much do you know about the Duke of Berry, our royal overlord?'

'From the teachers at school I heard he was the third son of King Jean II, who gave him the sovereign province of Berry.'

'Yes, good. And who was King Jean?' Jacques thought

his father was beginning to sound like a schoolmaster, but he supposed it was all part of learning to become a tradesman.

'King Jean was succeeded by his eldest son, King Charles V.'

'Good,' said his father again. 'And what did he have to do with our duke?'

'When our last king captured Poitou, he gave the territory to his brother, our Duke Jean, so that he could join it to his provinces of Berry, Auvergne and Touraine.'

'Yes,' sighed Pierre, 'you have learnt well. Further, you should know that added together, Duke Jean's provinces represent a large part of central France.'

'Does that mean he is very rich?' asked the boy, wide-eyed, and his father noded:

'The richest man in France.'

They walked on in silence for a while, and then Pierre added:

'Our good duke owns many palaces, châteaux and mansions, and spends his time commissioning the great artists of the day to fill them with glorious creations. Many of his palaces are depicted in his famous illuminated manuscript, *Les Très Riches Heures du Duc de Berry*. I am telling you this because today you will have your first view of one of the most remarkable collections of our time.'

A curious and observant lad, Jacques now stands absorbing the perfection of all he sees. With a clasping of hands, his father's business is done, and the duke turns to the boy, his arms folded.

'So, my young friend, what do you like best in this great chamber?'

Somewhat to the duke's surprise, Jacques replies at once, pointing. 'Why, Monseigneur, I am very curious about that shield there, high on the wall.'

'Pierre, my friend, this boy of yours delights me,' says the duke with a hand on the father's back. Then, turning to Jacques, 'I bought it from a trader, who told me it came from a great battle the ancient Greeks lost long, long ago to the Persians, at a place called Thermopylae. Have you heard of it? No, I am not surprised. Still too young for Greek lessons. What are you? Six? Seven?

'Thermopylae is famous in history as one of the most heroic stands made by a small force against an enormous army. Although the Greeks – soldiers who came from Sparta, in the south – knew they could never defeat such overwhelming numbers, still they fought with all their might to the last man. It is said that even their enemy was impressed, and wrote poems and songs praising them. I find that having one of their shields on my wall gives me courage when I need it,' he says with a smile at Pierre who can see that the duke takes such pleasure in his possessions, he even enjoys sharing his knowledge with a young and unimportant child.

Walking home, Jacques asks his father more about Duke Jean.

'Well, my boy, you have now met one of the most generous and learned patrons of the arts in our country. Duke Jean is also known as a host who entertains lavishly and often, not only his peers, but also the artists he admires and considers his friends. Yes, I know that is rare in any patron, let alone such an illustrious one,' and Pierre adds proudly: 'You did well today my boy, the duke was clearly taken with you. From now on you can come with me whenever he summons me.' They walk on in silence for a while. 'You see, our duke is a compulsive collector. He is celebrated throughout our country and beyond for the exquisite quality of his many residences and their contents. In particular, his libraries are filled with wonderful books and illuminated manuscripts.'

'Like the one you told me about? *Les Très Riches Heures*?' asks Jacques.

'Oh yes, that's the most famous, but he commissions one after another, their bindings in silk, velvet or red leather, with small gold or silver fastenings studded with pearls and precious stones, and sometimes covered in the most delicate enamel work. Our duke is a man of great knowledge and discrimination, and has the forethought to place orders with the most famous contemporary artists, as well as collecting the works of the great masters.' Jacques can tell his father is deeply impressed by his royal patron.

Pierre looks down at his young son and wonders how much he has taken in. He knows that Jacques is intelligent, and seeing his interest, he decides that in future he will nurture the boy's appreciation and knowledge with visits to his important clients, so that he can observe and learn from his surroundings.

'Papa, is it true what they say in the town? That our duke's palaces are as grand and glorious as those of the Duke of Burgundy, his younger brother?'

'Yes, my boy, I believe that is true, although I have never personally been to the famous court of Burgundy. But

Duke Jean's insatiable interest in all that is of the highest quality does not stop with his patronage of the arts, you know.'

'What else does he collect?' asks the inquisitive boy.

'I was told by his secretary that the duke's library contains forty-one histories, thirty-eight romantic works of chivalry and many religious works and bibles. There are extraordinary volumes depicting flora and fauna, astrological treatises and three mappemondes. Among his manuscripts are Marco Polo's *Book of Travels* and Nicolas Oresme's *Fleur de la terre d'Orient*. Most especially treasured by the duke is a beautiful psalter filled with paintings of the Apostles and the prophets.'

Pierre can see that the list is not of real interest to his son. 'Oh, and he also collects rare animals – ostriches, dromedaries, chamois and bears – which at times he takes with him on his journeys to his various palaces. Perhaps if you are good ...'

And it happens. One day, when his father's business is concluded, the duke takes young Jacques to his private zoo, telling him the history of the strange creatures in the large enclosures, and of the distant lands whence they came.

'You may have noticed that the emblems on my coat of arms are bears and swans,' he says, and the boy nods. 'And you have seen their likenesses on many of my possessions.' Again the boy nods. Then he shows Jacques the two large black bears he keeps in the deep dry moat around his castle in Bourges, which roar as he tosses food down to them from the ramparts. Seeing the boy shake, he takes his hand and leads him to the lake, where he can see a number of swans and their cygnets. 'So you see, my young friend, my family is both strong like the bear and beautiful like the swan. But do not imagine the swan is gentle. He is a vicious bird and could break your arm with a single blow from his wing.'

These visits to the Duke of Berry are Jacques Coeur's first sight of true luxury and of craftsmanship in works of art, and they plant in the boy the seed of a lifelong desire to search for the exceptional and the beautiful.

Over time, he is permitted to wander throughout the duke's many palaces and mansions, accompanying his father to wherever his patron is residing. He marvels as they walk past tapestries emblazoned with great coats of arms, scenes of battles or stories from the Bible; embroideries from England and Florence, gold brocade from Lucca; enamels, porcelains, silver and gold dinner services, and much more.

One day the duke asks him, 'Jacques, my boy, from among all the wonders you see in my palaces, what do you think is my most prized possession? You have no idea? Then I will surprise you. It is my collection of precious stones.' This does indeed come as a surprise to the boy. 'Italian and Jewish dealers in particular know my taste and present me with the rarest and the best. My collection of rubies is considered exceptional, one alone weighing two hundred and forty carats!' With a flourish he produces the large stone from deep inside a pocket of his wide robe. He shows it to Jacques and then allows him to hold it up to the light. The boy is transfixed by the glowing red facets within it and holds his breath in wonder, until his awestruck appreciation induces the duke to clap his hands! 'Oh my boy, you will be a connoisseur like me one day, I predict it. Your reaction equals mine when I first gazed into this stone's blood-red prisms. Next time you come, I will show you more of my treasures.'

With each visit to Jean de Berry's exquisite salons, Jacques notes and absorbs not only the glamour, but also the workmanship of the hangings, paintings, carpets and beautiful objects of every kind. Sometimes, when the duke sees him admiring something, he tells him all about its background.

'This silken carpet I saw you caressing on the table just now was brought to me by a trader who swore it came from Egypt. He said it had been wrapped around the young Queen Cleopatra when she was brought secretly to Caesar and then unrolled at his feet! I didn't believe a word of it, but he was so charming and the carpet so fine, I could not resist. You know the story, don't you?' Jacques – open-mouthed and wide of eye as usual whenever the great man speaks to him – does not, and the duke takes great pleasure in the telling of Cleopatra's tale, all the way to her placing an asp on her breast and dying from the snake's poisonous bite …

There are many opportunities for Jacques to go along with his father to the other great houses Pierre visits with his quality pelts; but of equal importance to his future is what he learns at the stalls of the moneylenders and changers of Bourges. The city is situated in the centre of France, with the river Yèvre and several canals running through it for ease of transport, and the streets are busy with people going about their business with a certain sense of urgency, yet gaiety too. Merry exchanges pass among the tradesmen; women ask each other about their various young ones or the illnesses of the older generations; hawkers call out their wares. The leather tanners' pits, with their distinctive odours, are full of jolly workmen; the narrow lanes throng with the sellers of ribbons and bolts of cloth – some fine for ladies' dresses, others wool dyed in darker colours.

It is a friendly society and open, visitors are marked out by their different clothing, and many people greet Jacques. Already he has quite an eye for the girls, always accompanied by their mothers or nurses. Although the streets are dusty and often muddy, the citizens look well dressed and tidy, as do those riding mules or in donkey carriages, transporting goods to warehouses. And there are plenty of those. Bourges is a commercial city containing such a mix of cultures and nationalities that coinage is brought in by traders and visitors from all corners of the known world.

On arrival in Bourges, travellers and merchants go to the eastern part of the city, where there are some twenty or thirty little booths for changing the currency they carry. As Jacques follows them from stall to stall, he notices how the rates vary depending on demand; who comes to which stall; the coins that are true in silver or gold content; which promissory notes are trustworthy and which dealers have the best reputation. With his gift for rapid mental calculation, soon he is able to advise his father on how to benefit from the varying rates and take advantage of sudden alterations in exchange.

Pierre Coeur is renowned in Bourges for his knowledge of the fur trade. He pays his creditors promptly, so is always welcomed by the assorted moneylenders, and

Jacques watches them watching him. They know that he only buys the best and sells well.

One evening after their meal, Pierre keeps Jacques at the table once it has been cleared and his young brother sent to bed. 'Come, my boy, I want to teach you what being a successful merchant is all about. Quality and demand,' he tells him, 'are the two factors necessary to make a profit in any trade.'

Jacques sits quietly on his chair and listens, the fire still glowing in the hearth and the great clock ticking.

'You see, my son, there is no point in having something wonderful if no one can afford it or wants to buy it, so demand is essential, though this can also be created with clever promotion. Then a good trader must consider quality. Sell only the best to connoisseurs, or they will not return. You *can* sell inferior goods, but solely to those who cannot pay or are ignorant of quality.'

Young Jacques says little, but he learns these and indeed all his lessons well. Although he has an older half-brother, his mother's son from her first marriage, Jacques is the brightest of the three boys, all educated by the good monks of the Sainte-Chapelle in Bourges. From an early age he wears the tonsure, the small round patch of hair shaved from the centre on the back of his head. It is hoped by his parents that at least one of the boys will enter the priesthood.

It is normal practice for the eldest son of a merchant family like the Coeur's to follow in his father's profession, becoming apprenticed to him when he reaches the age of fourteen. But Jacques' ambitions are greater than just trading furs. Sitting regularly with the money-changers, he meets traders from all over the Mediterranean, men who salve their loneliness with stories of their home cities. He hears about Florence, Siena, Milan, Venice and Genoa; he learns the names of the great families of these cities, merchants, bankers and military leaders: the Médici, the Albrizzi, the Bardi among others. In this way, he acquires the language of the traders, and the sure knowledge that trade is the key to earning great riches and living like the merchants about whom he has heard tell, their lives equal to those of great princes.

And yet France is not a country at peace. There are continual invasions by the English from their land of Normandy in the north, and frequent aggressive skirmishes between the two warring factions of the court of King Charles VI – the Orléanists, led by the king's devoted brother Prince Louis; and the Burgundians, who follow their duke. The Duke of Burgundy leans towards the English on account of their commercial contacts in Flanders which he needs. The attacks on one another's followers often result in serious disruption to trading.

Nevertheless, during the first quarter of the fifteenth century there is a great artistic flowering in France – in painting, architecture and literature. This is due to the patronage and guidance of a number of *grand seigneurs* like Duke Jean of Berry and the fabled court of Burgundy. Living in Bourges, Jacques becomes aware of the artistic developments around him, and through the kindness of Duke Jean he is able to seek out the best among the local craftsmen to teach him how to judge their creations.

'Ah, young Jacques – yes we have heard of your visits to our great duke. So you want to know how his glassware is made? Come.' And he is taken into the dark barn with the hot cauldrons, and the glassmakers show him how it is done, twisting and turning the bubble of molten glass at the end of a tube, blowing down the pipe to enlarge it, shaping here, twisting and cutting there, until he witnesses the perfection of the finished work. 'Now go and see how cloth is woven,' they say with a laugh and send him on his way.

Jacques learns how brass is beaten, and how carpets are made. Best of all, he watches the potters turning their wheels, making shapes out of clay with their hands, then standing the finished cups and vases to dry in rows on shelves – and they let him try it too. His visits become regular, and he is greeted with a merry 'Hey, Jacques, come back to know more? Touch the quality of this then,' – or of something else. Born with an eye and a feel for excellence, he learns quickly, knowing that all this will be useful one day when he achieves his ambition – to become a great merchant.

## Chapter Two

$\mathcal{B}$y 1416, Jacques Coeur, a strapping lad as old as the year, is employed in a very junior post at the Royal Mint in Bourges. While taking his son with him to the various courts, it has become clear to his father that finance and figures are the boy's talents, added to his quick intelligence and calm and persuasive manner in dealing with people. Pierre notices how Jacques has a natural gift for finding the essence of a person – whether he would be a client or not – and soon his own dealings with a number of his father's important clients seems to qualify him for this first position. Somehow, although he says little, he manages to say the right thing at the appropriate time – to entice, or console, or just be friendly. Best of all is his talent for rapid mental calculation. This, added to his experience of observing and helping Pierre to profit from the money-lenders without anyone feeling badly done by, gave him the opportunity to be taken on at the Mint of Bourges.

*

The youngest of the team at the Mint, but possibly the strongest, Jacques allows himself to be teased by his colleagues about his energetic bodybuilding: 'And how many times did you run around the square this morning, young Coeur, *and* carrying a full pail of water in each hand, no doubt? Was it fifty? More?'

Jacques smiles – it's a daily joke. 'Oh, at least fifty, maybe more,' he replies. 'Healthy body, healthy mind' is his mantra, and although they laugh, his colleagues do rather admire him. Having had to carry great loads of hides and skins at his father's warehouse since he was a young boy, Jacques has grown strong, and he does not want to lose that.

Although he is always good-natured and polite, Jacques is a silent type, far more so than the others at the Mint, who freely exchange details about their private lives. He listens, smiles, but never offers information. It is something he learnt from accompanying his father to the houses of his wealthy patrons – pay attention and absorb, then offer what they want or need. It is one of the reasons, he realizes, why his father is trusted and well liked, although Jacques could see quite early on that Pierre's trading could be more effective. Yet together, father and son added to the family income by being alert and astute at the money-changers' booths, and soon after Jacques' twelfth birthday the family was able to move into a larger house in a better district, by which time Pierre Coeur had become known as the leading furrier in the city.

Jacques' half-brother is three years his senior, and they are firm friends, as he is with his younger brother Nicholas.

At the dinner table, current events are always discussed, and in this way he is able to piece together the political situation in France and in particular at the French court, the seat of government. Pierre, like the heads of most local families, likes to expound to the attentive boys.

'Our good King Charles tries hard, when sane,' he says with a sorrowful face, 'to keep the peace between the two fractious sides of his family: his own supporters, the Orléanists, and those of his cousin the Duke of Burgundy, whom the people call "Jean-sans-Peur" – Jean the Fearless.'

'Why is he called that – I hear he is a monster!' blurts out young Nicholas.

'That he may be, and not ours to judge,' replies his father, 'but the people of Paris are behind him and against our king's brother, Duke Louis d'Orléans, who I have had the honour of meeting with our own duke here in Bourges, when I found him to be a very fine and admirable gentleman indeed. The Parisians even turned against our dear Duke of Berry for loyally siding with the king his nephew. They ransacked his beautiful mansion, the Hôtel de Nesle in Paris where I once had the honour of calling on him and plundered and burnt his château just outside Paris. You young ones won't remember, but just four years ago, the Burgundians besieged our city of Bourges!'

'Oh yes,' says Jacques, 'I remember it well. You told us then, Papa, that it was because our good duke had not joined either faction and that he had to seek refuge in the cloister of Nôtre Dame. It's true, isn't it, that it was only due to his skill at negotiating that our city, *his city*, was spared from destruction?'

Pierre looks at his son with a mixture of amazement

17

and admiration. 'Yes, it is true, and the citizens of Bourges will never forget their duke's intervention, which saved both their lives and their property.'

One year later, during another evening spent at home by the fire, Pierre tells his wife Marie how frail and sad he found their duke when he called on him that day, and how he brought up the topic of the Battle of Agincourt, fought and lost two years ago in 1415.

'I think our dear duke is not long for this world, which saddens me more than I can say. I believe he has never recovered from losing so many of his family and friends on that terrible day.'

He turns to the boys. 'Jacques, you were barely fifteen, not yet old enough for the army, but certainly old enough to understand the horrific consequences of France's defeat by the English.'

Jacques lowers his head in shameful memory. How he wishes he could have gone with his older brother to join the army and fight for his country's freedom, to finally push the English all the way back to Calais. It was a miracle his brother returned even though he was not used as a soldier but with the transport wagons. He remembers how everyone believed it would be a certain victory for France, with the English outnumbered at least five to one, and most of those laid low with dysentery.

'The best of the youth of France died on that day,' Pierre says, looking grim, 'and I thank the Lord you *were* too young, or I am sure I would have lost you too. How grateful your mother was when her eldest returned – it was a miracle in our eyes. When our enemy, King Henry V, saw

that he had not enough men to contain the prisoners captured by the English for ransom, he gave the chilling order
"No prisoners"'. His voice now a whisper, 'that all should
be killed, their hands tied behind their backs, their throats
slit – the scions of our great houses among them. The only
aristocrat left alive on the field that dreadful day was the
young Duke Charles d'Orléans.'

'Two men had fallen on top of him, hadn't they?' pipes
up Nicholas. 'And the English only saw he was alive when
the dead were lifted off him! And then King Henry said he
must be kept locked in the Tower of London for all his
life!' The look on his father's face makes the boys realize
they have said enough and must leave the table now.

Pierre Coeur is aware how much his beloved patron
suffered on learning of the many deaths in his own family,
his sovereign territories and throughout the country. Their
king was deranged and could not fight; his cousin, the
Duke of Anjou, too ill; and his uncle, their dear Duke Jean,
too old and frail. The children could see their father's
thoughts were with his patron.

'Yes, it's true – we lost the golden youth of France in our
disastrous defeat at Agincourt, and so many our dear
duke had known and loved.'

It is no more than a month later that he gathers his
family at the dinner table and with tears in his eyes tells
them:

'Agincourt and its aftermath has proved too much for
our beloved duke. What I feared has come to pass. Jean de
Berry, one of the greatest humanists and connoisseurs of
his time, who has greatly enhanced our city and all his
sovereign lands, has died, surely of grief.'

'So who will be our duke now, since he has no children?' asks Jacques.

'I hear he has left his entire estate to his great-nephew Charles, our poor mad king's third son. As you know, he is now the dauphin following the deaths of his two older brothers.'

The boys look at one another. They have all heard the story of how these royal princes were poisoned – and by their uncle, the Duke of Burgundy, the man they call Jean-sans-Peur.

# Chapter Three

At the age of sixteen, and with a steady income from the Mint, Jacques Coeur dares to plan for marriage. For some years he has been observing the daughter of their neighbour, Lambert de Lodepart, the Provost of Bourges, a most influential citizen and a former valet to the late Duke of Berry. Marcée is a few years his junior, and extremely shy – which he likes. Their courtship has been painfully slow, but Jacques has decided that no matter what it takes, she will be his wife. Year after year he has contrived to leave his father's house when she leaves hers, return home from school when she does, go to church with his family when she goes with hers. Of course she has noticed him, and he has even caught her watching him from her window, the lace curtain pulled back a touch.

Marcée is more pleasant to look at than pretty, except when he sees her shy smile and it reaches her merry blue eyes. Is she intelligent? He has tried to find out through school friends, but no one knows – her family are socially superior to his and they do not really mix within the neighbourhood.

Naturally, Jacques' mother has noticed his interest too. 'My boy, I often see you looking at our neighbour's daughter Marcée – isn't that her name?'

Jacques blushes and stammers: 'Mama, I want to marry her. Can you help me speak to Papa? He is so conscious of our inferior social position, but if we two are agreeable, should that matter? I will work hard and make her proud of me, I promise.'

'Darling son, does she know you like her? That you want to marry her? Have you spoken to her? To her family?'

'No, but she has seen me looking at her, and she smiles at me when we meet by our gates when leaving or returning home.'

His mother laughs. 'That's hardly a basis for a marriage, you know. What do you have to offer her? Yes, you have a steady job, but she comes from a very comfortable home. '

'Mama! How can you be so cruel? You know I am in love. You must help me! Please talk to Papa.'

A few evenings later, Pierre asks Jacques: 'Your mother tells me you have it in mind to marry our neighbour's daughter, and you want me to ask her father for permission to call? Frankly, my boy, although I am sure that you will do well in the world, in view of the considerable difference in our social standing, I must warn you that I am doubtful of success.'

To Jacques' relief, his father agrees to ask, and to the surprise of both father and son, the Provost agrees to their visit.

The young gallant will never forget this first formal meeting, naturally prearranged. He knocks on his neighbour's door and, accompanied by his father, is ushered into the front room. While they wait, Jacques looks around, noticing the plush chairs with their crisp white cloths on top of the headrests; the green crystal glasses standing on a sideboard together with a jug covered with a thin cloth edged with beads – no doubt to keep out flies. He looks at the pictures on the walls: family portraits of rather grim men and women, and one or two of flowers. There are books in a low bookcase. These interest him: *The Lives of the Saints*, and several books of Greek and Latin classics. Does she read Latin or Greek? he wonders. He hopes not, since his own humanist studies have not gone so well. Mathematics, now, but girls are not interested in maths …

After what seems an age, Marcée enters, followed by her father. Jacques finds himself tongue-tied, twisting his hands until his father comes to the rescue.

'My dear neighbour,' he addresses the Provost, 'would you be so kind as to show me the books in your library?' These are at the other end of the parlour, and the two men head that way. With a slight movement of her hand, but no word spoken, Marcée invites Jacques to sit on a high, hard square seat with a leather cushion. She sits on another beside him, smoothing her dress, eyes cast down modestly.

Hesitantly, Jacques begins, clearing his throat. 'Mademoiselle, we have lived alongside one another most of our lives.'

'Yes,' she replies shyly.

'And I have watched you grow into a most lovely young lady,' he continues, gathering courage now.

'Yes,' she says again, still looking down at her dress.

'I have asked your father for permission to call on you in the hope that we might talk more and get to know one another better.'

'Yes,' she says once more. By this time, Jacques is getting a little desperate, sure that his father and hers will leave the bookcase any minute.

'Perhaps we could walk together after church one Sunday?'

Again all she says is a soft: 'Yes.'

Jacques does not get another word out of her that day, but the following Sunday, the two families sit near one another in church, and slowly, to his relief, he discovers that Marcée can speak.

He has been falling in love with this girl for a number of years. She appeals to him in every way – her demeanour; her open, pleasant face; the way her eyes light up when she smiles at her siblings, though not yet at him. Of average height and strong build, Jacques wonders if she finds him appealing. He contemplates his own face in the polished metal plate hanging in the bathroom: square jaw, straight nose, intense blue eyes and thatch of light brown hair. Secretly much of his efforts to become strong are aimed at being her protector in some way, as well as for himself – who knows when he will need strong arms and a strong back? One thing he does know for certain and for that he prays fervently each night – that Marcée Lodepart will find him worthy of her.

One day as they walk back from church, she says, 'Jacquet' – she is the first to call him by this nickname – 'Jacquet, I hear it said that I would be marrying beneath my station if I were to accept your proposal.' He holds his breath, dreading her next words. 'But I think we could be very happy together.'

Jacques is overwhelmed with relief. Not only does he want her as his wife for her appearance and her good sense, but, he has to admit, this marriage will enable him to greatly advance his career. Marcée's grandfather served as Master of the Royal Mint at Bourges, so union with the Lodepart family would give him an entrée into an altogether higher level of local finance.

It takes Jacques a further two years to convince Marcée's family that he is indeed worthy of her, and in 1418 they are wed. Naturally, he knows he has married above his station, but by now, he has fallen deeply in love.

That same year, the Burgundian faction, allies of the English and followers of the young Duke 'Jean-sans-Peur' of Burgundy, take over Paris. The dauphin Charles is rescued in the middle of the night by the capital's Provost, an ally of the powerful royal family of Anjou, who brings him in haste to Bourges. A staunchly monarchist city, Bourges welcomes the dauphin as the heir of their late, beloved Duke Jean of Berry.

In his shrewd way, the eighteen-year-old Jacques Coeur begins to observe the dauphin. He sees a lad of fourteen, lacking in confidence, fearful after his hazardous flight from Paris, certain that his two elder brothers were poisoned on the orders of his cousin Jean of Burgundy, who covets the throne. Only he, the third dauphin of the reign, stands in the duke's way once the half-mad king, his father Charles VI, dies.

The young prince holds just one winning card: Yolande d'Aragon, Duchess of Anjou, known as the Queen of Sicily – that being the senior of her many titles – his future mother-in-law. Yolande's only involvement in Sicily is to provide the means for her eldest son, Louis III d'Anjou, to reconquer his inheritance. Her importance in the dauphin's life is her immense power and wealth as the widow and regent of her late, beloved husband, the king's cousin, Louis II d'Anjou. Charles VI knows and trusts her, as does his queen, Isabeau.

Yolande understands the queen's anxiety in her husband's presence. She knows about his sudden attacks on his servants and anyone in his orbit; his filthy habits and his cruelty when a fit overtakes him. In her sympathy, and in response to Isabeau's plea for help – 'one king's daughter to another' – she found and placed a girl of her choosing from Anjou by the king's side to comfort him, since his queen was no longer willing.

Through Yolande's intercession with his mother, the ten-year-old dauphin, an unloved thirteenth child and, at the time, the third surviving son of the king, was betrothed to Yolande's eight-year-old daughter Marie, and came to live with her family at their mighty castle of Angers in Anjou. These were happy years for the boy, and young Charles came to love and respect Yolande, whom he referred to thereafter as his *bonne mère*.

Now installed in Bourges, his splendid inheritance from his great-uncle Jean of Berry, the dauphin has still no one to sustain him; he is without direct funds until there is peace and his newly acquired administration is set in order. Nor does he have a clear future, since the English have conquered most of his country. But for the Queen of Sicily and her family, Charles has no friends or supporters he can rely on, no entourage to guide or advise him.

It does not take Jacques Coeur long to realize that it must have been Yolande d'Anjou, in her position as the widow of the senior of the royal dukes, who persuaded the childless Duke of Berry to appoint the dauphin as his heir. For the past five years, Charles has been financially dependent on Yolande since his betrothal to her daughter; she knows better than anyone how badly he needs his uncle's inheritance to establish himself and survive.

Some months later, Jacques is informed that the formidable Queen Yolande about whom everyone speaks in hushed awe, is in Bourges, has heard of his services to the late duke and indicated that she would like to meet him. Together with about forty gentlemen of all ages, he is summoned to the royal palace. Although he has not been there since the year before the duke's death, he feels quite at ease within the imposing interiors he has known since childhood. And yet he experiences the same tightening of his throat as he gazes in wonder at the magnificent tapestries lining the walls, while the silk carpets under his feet make him feel as if he is floating on air.

As Jacques enters the Great Chamber, he is struck at once by the presence of the imposing Queen of Sicily, standing tall, slim and erect in her black and white mourning robes, quietly surveying the company from her podium. Lost in admiration, he feels a hand on his arm, and a handsome young page addresses him in a voice of liquid honey: 'Sir, am I correct in believing that you are Jacques Coeur, who is employed at the Royal Mint?'

Nodding, Jacques is led before the strikingly beautiful Queen of Sicily, and instinctively bows low before her. Her smile is the more charming for being slightly crooked, he notices, and the warmth of it reaches her eyes. Standing near her is a nervous lad, twitching slightly; Jacques recognizes him as the dauphin Charles.

'Would you mind if I sit, Monsieur Coeur? I have been standing all day and I am fatigued.' The queen motions him to come near, as though their conversation is not intended for everyone. Watchful by nature, Jacques notes how Queen Yolande's every gesture, no matter how small, is designed to reassure the dauphin, who constantly shifts his position but never strays far from her side, like an anxious levrette or greyhound.

'I have wanted to make your acquaintance,' she says, their eyes now level, her chair on the raised platform, 'because I have heard such interesting things about you. Now that I have met you, I can see that you are a young man who will go far,' she says smiling warmly, 'and I would like to hear of your progress. I understand you are working at the Royal Mint in Bourges?' Jacques stammers that he is. 'But I also hear that you are a merchant at heart, and have it in mind to travel along our Mediterranean coast?' Again he stammers that this is his plan, though he wonders how she could know. 'Be sure if ever you come to my port of Marseilles to inform me well in advance. If I am there, I would like you to tell me of your experiences on your travels; if not, I will appoint someone trustworthy to meet with you.' Another warm smile, and Jacques knows his audience is over.

He leaves her presence with a deep sense of admiration, and a perception that he will meet this remarkable lady again. But why did she summon him? he wonders. Had she really heard of his services to the late duke? They were hardly substantial, just delivering pelts and conversations – but what conversations. Sometimes he believes that all he knows came from the lips of that dear, wise man. No, there is something else – almost as if he was being interviewed for a position of some kind. He noted how her strength of character almost radiates from her, and all Bourges knows of her support of the dauphin Charles.

It is the same young page, introducing himself this time as Pierre de Brézé, who accompanies him to the door of the chamber. What fine features he has, thinks Jacques, and an almost magnetic presence in one so young. He resolves to find out all about him, this Pierre de Brézé, and of his connection with the Anjou family, which is clearly a familiar one. The lad cannot be more than twelve or thirteen, and yet already he has such confidence and maturity in his approach to strangers.

As he leaves, Jacques thinks to himself: if I am to go far, as the Queen of Sicily says, then so will this dazzling young page of hers.

# Chapter Four

The following year, in September, the Armagnac faction, supporters of the king's murdered brother, Louis d'Orléans, take their revenge on his assassin. The Duke of Burgundy, together with a small group of his followers, is set upon and killed on the bridge at Montereau. The brutal murder of his father persuades the late duke's son and heir, Philip, to attach his army, the strongest of all the French ducal forces, to that of France's enemy, Henry V of England. It is a terrible time, and the worst of it is that the dauphin Charles appears to have played some part in the Duke of Burgundy's death.

When the news reaches Bourges, the citizens are stunned. Not long afterwards, the terms of the shocking Treaty of Troyes has them reeling further. Made in 1420, five years after the battle of Agincourt, it seals the final settlement of France's indemnity following the English victory. Princess Catherine, a daughter of King Charles VI, is to marry their conqueror, England's King Henry V, and their son will be proclaimed the ruler of both countries. It was Queen Isabeau who signed the Treaty in place of her ill husband and under pressure from the new Duke of Burgundy. The dauphin, traditional heir to his father's throne, is disinherited and the kingdom of France is given to England.

Charles VI , France's king, is known to be insane most of the time while Queen Isabeau lives a confused existence. Having lost the support of her murdered brother-in-law Louis d'Orléans, in her terror she turned for succour to his murderer, the Duke 'Jean-sans-Peur' of Burgundy, and did his bidding. Now he too is dead and she accepted the instruction of his son the new Duke Philip. The result? Only the territory south of the Loire – Berry, Touraine, Poitou, Anjou, Provence, Orléans and Lyons – is left out of England's possession. This is all that remains of France, a dismembered country given to the enemy.

The death of Pierre Coeur two years earlier has left a great gap in Jacques' life. Pierre was not a clever man, but he was an honest one, and he taught his sons patriotism, a sincere loyalty to their king and country. In his absence, Jacques turns to Marcée's father, the Provost Lodepart. Seated in his large salon, refreshments on several small tables, candles lit and his hunting dogs sleeping by the fire, Jacques moves away from the other members of the family, who are playing cards or reading, and turns to the Provost:

'My respected father-in-law, tell me, what do you make of all this? Give me your views on the treaty made at Troyes with the English – I need to understand: where does our duty lie in these confusing times?'

His darling Marcée and the rest of the family come to sit around the fire with the family's elder, and by reputation, the wisest man in Bourges. The same question perplexes them all, and they need to hear from him.

'These are indeed troubling times,' says the Provost, looking at each of them in turn. 'As long as the English are here in force, there is nothing to be done. But in our hearts we are French! How can our conquerors expect us to become subservient Englishmen? Our countries have been adversaries for longer than anyone can remember. Are we to forget and forgive our losses, in particular our recent dead at Agincourt? Is there a family in the country who did not lose a loved one in that slaughter?' His audience nod and murmur in agreement.

'The humiliating terms of the Treaty of Troyes cannot be ignored. But nor can we fight. There is no one left to lead us, nor do we have an army to defend our ailing king and country.' And he shakes his head, looking down at his hands.

Later that night, in their own home, Jacques and Marcée discuss the problem. 'Dearest wife, I am a Frenchman! And the father of one, and soon another,' he smiles, stroking Marcée's round stomach. 'What does the future hold for us now that we have a family?'

'Your father made plain when we married that I was to be your sole support and that of our children – he must provide for his sons now.' Marcée, like Jacques, has always been a woman of few words. 'Are we not happy, you and I, dear husband? Do we not have enough with your earnings at the Mint, especially with your promotion following our marriage?'

Jacques holds her – she is so very dear to him, and capable – but he knows they do *not* have enough, not with the family growing as it is and prices rising daily due to the general uncertainty and widespread lack of confidence in the population about the future.

'Now that our dauphin is to marry Marie d'Anjou, the Queen of Sicily's daughter, I am sure their flourishing court based here in Bourges will attract wealthy courtiers and bring more trade and prosperity to our city, which will help us all, dear husband,' says Marcée with confidence. Marriage and motherhood suit her, and she relishes another imminent birth.

The more Jacques has travelled, the prouder he has become of France – of the verdant countryside, the land's production and the potential for trade and commerce. When he could disregard the civil war, and for many – at least in the cities – trade continued, it has made him love his country even more fiercely than before. The shock of the humiliating terms of the Treaty of Troyes makes him determined to use his success as a merchant not only for the good of his family, but also to find a way of restoring to France her kingdom.

Although still employed at the Mint, Jacques has begun his trading business in earnest, and it has not taken him long to attract attention. His energy, financial acumen and intelligence impress many, and it is generally considered that he has a promising future. At present, most of his merchandise is bought and sold within France, but his burning ambition is to become a real merchant trader, one who brings goods from outside the country to sell at a profit. That, however, will have to wait. No one would fund such a quest at this time of uncertainty, since he would need to travel not only widely within France, but more importantly, to the Near East. It is there he believes he can find the commodities that would be the most profitable to trade at home.

When the dauphin arrived in Bourges in 1418, there were four major monetary authorities issuing coinage in France. By 1422 the system has stabilized, but there are still at least a dozen mutations of the coinage. One day, a colleague approaches Jacques: 'I hear you are about to be a father again. Can you afford it?'

Jacques looks down at his hands. 'My trading business is doing well, and yes, I can manage. Why do you ask?'

'You often mention your wish to trade with the Near East and the lack of someone to finance your journey there. I could help, you know – in fact we could help one another.'

'But we work long hours as it is,' answers Jacques, 'and I doubt there is more we can do in these troubled times. The Mint is fulfilling all the orders we get, and I would need much more interesting stock for my trading business to expand.'

'No, my innocent young friend, we can make money easily by other means.'

He explains the scheme to Jacques that his colleagues all know but need him to join them. It takes several further weeks of argument and the gathering pile of unpaid bills at home, the birth of his third child, and despite Marcée's efforts but clear needs, that finally tip the balance for his co-operation.

Their position in Bourges as mint masters – providing the local coin – makes them partly officials, partly independent

QUICKSILVER

operators. They are trusted to mint the coinage correctly, but it is not difficult to issue coins with a little less than the ordained weight of precious metal. To his everlasting shame, Jacques and his colleagues exploit the system for their own profit.

Put simply: temptation and greed overcome Jacques Coeur's moral principles. Most people they know are taking advantage of any way they can find of making a fast profit. That is no excuse, and young fools that they are, they imagine they can enrich themselves without detection.

With so much dishonesty in the city's financial exchange, inspectors are brought in to check the Mint. This is something the young mint masters did not expect. Jacques arrives one morning to find the doors open and a number of official-looking strangers talking earnestly with two of his colleagues. When they see him, his colleagues call to him to join them. 'Jacques, these gentlemen have been sent by the Paris Mint to check the silver content of our coinage. You understand the figures better than any of us. Do please enlighten them that all is in order.'

Jacques blanches. All is not in order, as he well knows – just as they do. He bows to the strangers. 'Gentlemen, what is it that you require of us?' he asks hoping they are merely passing through.

'Everything,' answers the senior of the four inspectors: 'We want to make a random choice of coins to melt and test for silver content.' This is the worst scenario Jacques can imagine. 'Leave us now and we will make our inspections alone. Your colleagues have seen our papers and know we have the necessary authority.'

Jacques leaves with his colleagues, their faces equally

pessimistic. The inspectors would have to be complete amateurs not to be able to see within a short time that any coin they choose to melt is short on silver content.

Nor does it take long for the inspectors to discover the false dealing. The following day, Jacques and his colleagues are called to account to none other than his father-in-law, the Provost of Bourges. This is their salvation – he would not send his beloved daughter's husband to gaol, and for her sake, he hears the case in a closed session. But the shame and indignity of even this modified exposure of his dishonesty teaches Jacques a valuable lesson. Since his ambition is to become a merchant trader, he needs to have a good reputation. *Thank God my father is not alive to see this* passes through his mind.

To his great relief, Marcée's parents stand by him, and little of the affair is known outside their circle, but he can see their disappointment. Even his beloved wife cannot face him for a while, and that is the worst punishment of all. There is a system of royal pardons in place, instituted to give young offenders another chance, and through the intercession of his father-in-law, this saves him. But the shame remains embedded within him, and he vows then that he will make his fortune using his wits honestly and honourably, to gain for himself, his family and his country what they all need.

Due to connections made through his in-laws, slowly Jacques comes into contact with the royal court, and with those courtiers and staff who have followed the dauphin to Bourges. Some have come for their own benefit, others through patriotism: financiers, officers and magistrates among them. As more and more wealthy followers arrive to settle in the relative sanctuary of Bourges, Jacques' long-held dream of trading with the Orient comes closer to reality.

On 2 June 1422, the wedding of the dauphin Charles and Marie d'Anjou, daughter of the Queen of Sicily, takes place in Tours. Jacques Coeur is among the many merchants from Bourges who travel to the city to support the couple on this grand occasion. He knows some merchants there and is curious to hear what they have to tell him now.

'Well, my friend, as you know, any merchant is delighted when there is such an influx of visitors with money in their pockets,' one fellow tradesman tells him happily, 'and this wedding is important because our dauphin needs to be seen by more of his people. His union with the daughter of our neighbour, the widowed sovereign Duchess of Anjou will strengthen his position   certainly in this part of his territory.' Jacques can see that the dauphin will also need a great deal of support from the French people if he wants to become accepted as their king.

During the celebrations, which are to last for three days, he is surprised when Queen Yolande sends for him. The queen has been resident in her territory of Provence during the past two years since their meeting and probably not fully conscious of developments at the court in Bourges. Jacques finds her still as overwhelmingly and grandly beautiful, her face calm, almost expressionless – just a slight smile that barely reaches those fathomless blue eyes. He is pulled out of his reverie when she gives him her hand and says without preamble: 'My dear Monsieur Coeur, I am pleased to see you, because I know

I can rely on you to give me your honest view of the courtiers surrounding my son-in-law in Bourges.'

Jacques is somewhat taken aback at the bluntness of her
question, yet his native curiosity is on full alert at all times.
He is well aware of the make-up of the dauphin's entourage, but he is a young man of twenty-two in the presence
of one of the grandest ladies of the time. Can he tell her
truthfully? Yes, he decides, I must.

He clears his throat. 'Madame and Majesty, may I speak
freely?'

'That is why I asked you, Monsieur Coeur. I am relying
on it,' she replies pleasantly, but he can hear the razor's
edge in her voice. He takes a deep breath.

'Then I must tell you, Madame, with respect, that there
is no limit to the corruption and dissipation of many of the
courtiers in the close circle around the dauphin. I fear I
must also include in this damnation the dauphin's own
lack of self-belief, let alone self-restraint.' With the last
word, his courage slips a little, and he finds himself looking
down at his feet.

'Please tell me more. I would like to know in greater
detail what goes on here,' her voice insistent.

He clears his throat: 'Madame, I fear there will always
be those around the dauphin capable of bringing out in
him the fickle and devious.' It is the nature of his character, thinks Jacques. 'Time and again when I have been at
the palace I have heard the courtiers whose company he
keeps, tempting him.'

'In what way?' she says firmly. Again he takes a deep
breath. He knows he must reply as much as he is certain
she is the only one who can help their future king.

'I heard one say recently, "Sire, you have not visited my mansion for some time. I have not only some excellent hawks just arrived for the hunt, but three young ladies from Paris you might also enjoy pursuing", and then laughter in which the dauphin joined.

'"Why, my good friend," he answered "and do you have a particular hunt in mind, perhaps by firelight in that cavernous great hall of yours? And a captive prize for the hunter to stalk?" This is followed by more laughter and banter, Madame. It is this kind of thing, which happens often, that dismays me.'

'Can you give me any more examples?' replies a tight-lipped Yolande. Jacques hesitates, and she adds a little more softly, 'If I am not fully aware of what goes on here, I cannot be in a position to put it right. You do understand, don't you?'

Again Jacques knows he must reply and honestly.

'Madame, there was an incident at a party held recently in the house of one of the king's friends in Bourges. It seems that the daughter of our baker went to the palace with pastries, and by chance the dauphin saw her and asked for her to be included in the gathering he was attending at a house where, had her parents known, she would not have been permitted to go. A number of young rakes attended; all had too much to drink. The girl was taken to the top floor by the dauphin to "look at the view," or so she was told. There was a struggle; the girl was heard crying, "No! No!" and somehow she fell off the balcony on to the hard ground below. Seriously injured, she died shortly afterwards.'

'What did you do with this information?' asks the queen quietly.

'Madame, all I could think to do was tell my wife.'

'And what was her reaction?' Yolande almost whispers.

'To my surprise, she was stalwart, almost angry, Madame. She said, "What did the silly girl expect? Why did she resist? Once there, all she had to do was give in to his obvious desires, or she should not have gone in the first place." She thinks the dauphin is a man of deep deliberation and thoughts that no one can read; that he has good intentions and bad, and what he needs is someone to lead him like a timid dog on a rope and feed him little treats. But once he is let off that rope, who knows where he will end up.' Jacques pauses, fearful of having said too much.

'And do you agree with this dire conclusion?' the queen asks softly and without any change of expression. Instinctively Jacques knows that she is too intelligent for him to risk obscuring the facts. He pauses, and then replies:

'I believe that many of his courtiers are of the opinion that they have no future after the Treaty of Troyes was made binding two years ago. Instead of supporting their disinherited dauphin, they compensate by seeking profit and entertainment wherever and however they can.'

Perhaps Yolande is unsurprised by what he tells her. She gives no indication; merely thanks him for his frankness and for his offer to be of service to her should she ever need it.

To his surprise, the next day Jacques is summoned to the palace again. Will she ask me what I have done to support our young prince? Precious little, I fear, he mutters to himself. When he enters the Great Hall, Queen Yolande is standing in the centre of the cavernous room, speaking to the dauphin.

'Ah, do join us, Monsieur Coeur – I want to present you to my son-in-law.' As Jacques executes a deep bow to both, she says, 'I wanted the two of you to meet without a great crowd, to allow you the opportunity to talk quietly. I am confident that my son-in-law can use your services, especially during my long absence from court while based in Provence with my eldest son. As the well-informed merchant I know you to be,' she adds lightly, 'you are surely aware that Louis is planning another attempt to regain his throne of Naples and Sicily?' At this Jacques Coeur smiles slightly – of course he knows! 'And I am sure that my daughter, the dauphine Marie, would enjoy visiting your splendid warehouse in Bourges.'

Refreshments are brought – chilled mint tea served in tall, slim Venetian glasses, perfect on a hot June day. While Yolande takes the opportunity to speak with the staff, the two young men exchange pleasantries, all the while assessing one another with their eyes, though betraying nothing. Jacques is three years older than Charles, and this slight edge of experience shows. Now that they have met through the Queen of Sicily, it will be considered quite normal for the dauphin to call the merchant to attend him at court whenever he pleases. It occurs to Jacques that Yolande has told the dauphin to use the merchant often as an advisor and keep him near; that this would be a wise move 'in view of some of the things she has heard.' *I wonder if the dauphin will obey when she is far away*, he muses to himself.

Three days later, Queen Yolande leaves Tours to return to Provence, her two young children there, and her duty to her eldest son currently between Marseilles and

Calabria gathering support for an attempt to regain his kingdom of Sicily. The same day, Jacques Coeur departs for Bourges in the train of the newly married royal couple and their entourage. During the journey, he meets Queen Yolande's second son, René d'Anjou, Duke of Bar, and his wife Isabelle, the heiress of Lorraine. René is well built, Jacques notes, though not fat, with a pleasantly round, laughing face, merry eyes, and a wild thatch of red hair. Isabelle is quite the opposite, as slender as her mother-in-law, with a thick flaxen plait hanging down her back showing a little below her veil since she is riding, and clearly enjoys the sport. Her complexion is fair and her rings, to his professional eye, are superb – no doubt a gift from Queen Yolande since he knows her father has none such. Their mounts are also of the first quality – yes, he has heard that the duke's stable at Nancy is well stocked with full-blooded Arabians.

'My dear Jacques,' René addresses him mischievously, 'if I may? My mother insists that we come to you in Bourges on our next visit there. She has told me of your fame as a magician, and that you possess the famous Philosopher's Stone! That you can turn base metal into gold and frogs into princes! Is it true, or was she teasing me as usual?'

'My Lord, I fear she was teasing you.'

'Aha! You see, Isabelle – I told you that she swore I was really a frog, and only through her intervention with a witch in Anjou did I become a prince. I believed it for years!' and they all laugh.

René continues: 'We are actually based at my father-in-law's court at Nancy, but will return soon to Bourges to spend some days with my sister there. My mother speaks highly of you.'

'My Lord René, in that case I would indeed feel greatly privileged if you and your lady would honour me with a visit to my little warehouse when next in Bourges.' And they smile gaily at one another in recognition: Queen Yolande has told each about the other, and with merit.

René takes his leave, spurs his horse and rides – a little too fast – up the line. Jacques grins – he has heard that this enchanting young pair is a delight to their companions and everyone they encounter. He will think of a suitable gift for them to commemorate their marriage.

It is at this notable time in the history of Bourges that the flourishing young merchant Jacques Coeur forms a partnership with two brothers called Goddard, whom he has known since childhood. The pair is similar – of medium height, well-built through exercise, their faces pleasant without being striking in any way and their eyes shrewd but honest. Their ambitions are similar to those Jacques has nurtured for so long – to venture more energetically into international trading, buying and selling goods in the Mediterranean countries and even as far as the Levant. All three realize that this goal may take them some time to achieve, but as long as the royal court remains based at Bourges, they have a ready market for luxury goods.

That same year, 1422, the luck of the French turns. On 31 August, the victorious English king, Henry V, dies of dysentery, leaving only a baby son to inherit his throne and that of France. Barely two months later, in October,

France's sad, mad King Charles VI follows his English nemesis to the tomb.

In Bourges, a messenger arrives at the court with the news that Henry V's brother and regent in Paris, the Duke of Bedford, on receiving word of the French king's death, has left his brother's cortège to continue to London while he himself hurried back to Paris. On arrival, he immediately proclaims his late brother's baby son the new King of France as well as England; and notices to that effect are to be posted in all the main towns of the country.

The reaction in Bourges is passionate – 'Our dauphin Charles should be king!' is heard from every side. 'Ours is a French monarchist city,' the Provost tells his son-in-law. 'What will happen now, I wonder?'

'Sir, I hear the Queen of Sicily has arrived back in our town, and that gives me reason to believe she will encourage the dauphin to declare.'

'I think you may be right, my boy, I think you may be right,' says the old man with a worried smile.

With the acknowledged son and heir of the late King of France already a grown man of twenty, strong, visible and able to lead his countrymen, the long regency required for the English baby king is unlikely to appeal to the majority of the French. Charles, encouraged by his family and advisers, agrees that it is worth taking the chance of ignoring the conditions of the Treaty of Troyes. Surely the people will not accept Henry V of England's son as the heir to the throne of France?

On a rise of higher ground overlooking Bourges, the majestic cathedral of Saint-Etienne is packed, celestial music soaring into its tall, narrow, flamboyant arches. With his family around him, all wearing the formal black robes of court mourning, and the solemn Gregorian chant resounding in the great space, the dauphin and his family attend a commemorative High Mass for the life of his father, the late King Charles VI.

Jacques Coeur and Marcée are among the congregation on that memorable day. When the Mass ends, they watch the royal family rise from their chairs at the front of the congregation and process slowly down the centre aisle. Charles is flanked on his right by Yolande, wearing her crown as Queen of Sicily and to give him more credibility, she has donned her full regalia. She walks beside him, tall and regal in black velvet, rows of her famous pearls hanging from her neck to her knees. As they proceed solemnly towards the great door, Charles holds aloft the hand of Marie, his wife, on his left, bowing every few rows to the citizens on either side. When they pass him, Jacques is struck by the fervour on the face of his young monarch, and glancing at Marcée, he can see that Charles has made a similar impression on her.

Behind the trio of Yolande, Marie and Charles, there follows René and his wife Isabelle, also both in black velvet court mourning – she too with pearls and he with a black cap, a white feather fastened with a brooch flashing in the candlelight of the dark interior. The royal party halt outside and stand across the length of the top of the cathedral steps, facing the massed citizens beneath them. The clarion call of a dozen silver trumpets silences the crowd.

The royal herald, standing tall on a stone plinth, with the Valois arms on the front and back of his brightly coloured ceremonial tabard, calls out in a loud voice: 'The king is dead. Long live the king!' Then Charles steps forward, and in a strong, loud voice proclaims himself 'the rightful heir of my father by grace of my official investiture as his dauphin.' The trumpet fanfare rings out again, and in the square below, the traditional shouts of 'Noël!', 'Monjoie!' and 'Vivre le roi!' resound as the people of Bourges throw their caps in the air and their arms around one another.

With great dignity, the newly self-proclaimed Charles VII descends the steps with his wife and mother-in-law, followed by René and Isabelle. As they depart the cathedral precincts, Jacques turns to Marcée and declares: 'There goes a king I am willing to serve!'

# Chapter Five

*A* year after the marriage of Charles VII and Marie d'Anjou, on 3 July 1423, she gives birth to a son in Bourges, the new dauphin Louis. To their joy, Yolande arrives in time for the birth and the christening. How the city celebrates – as indeed does all of free France.

Ever since they returned to Nancy following the wedding celebrations in Tours, René has wanted to take Isabelle to visit his sister Marie in Bourges. Business calls his mother back to Provence soon after the christening, and since she is anxious to know how her daughter is coping, René promises to return to Bourges for a longer stay. Without the crowds of visitors who came for the little dauphin's christening, it will be a good opportunity to show Isabelle around the city.

Business in Lorraine delays them, and by the time of their return, Louis is sixteen months old. Before long, the little dauphin, waddling like a drunkard, leads Isabelle to his room to show her his toys. Alone with Marie, René tries to persuade her to unburden herself to him, but all he can gather is that Charles is always kind but does not consult her and only wants to keep her constantly with child. Since Louis' birth she has miscarried three times in rapid succession.

After touring the sights, René takes Isabelle to call on Jacques Coeur, who is delighted to welcome them to his warehouse, an unimpressive building on the outside, but inside an Aladdin's cave of treasures. Noting the two giant negro guards on either side of the inner door, Isabelle shivers a little and René laughs. 'Those gentlemen will skin you alive, my darling, if you so much as breathe desire over any of the contents of this magical place. See their sabres? They could shave the finest golden hairs from your cheeks.'

'But I don't have any hair on my cheeks,' flashes Isabelle, pinching her husband in mock anger as Jacques takes them to his inner sanctum. This is a much smaller room, its walls covered in red velvet, which makes them feel as though they are inside a beating heart, safe and warm. The room is subtly lit by tall candelabra of shiny brass holding dozens of candles reflected in the looking glasses on the walls.

'I see you are amazed at the purity of your reflections,' says Jacques. 'These mirrors come from Venice and have a rare silver-mercury amalgam behind the glass rather than polished metal like most.'

Isabelle and René sit down on large cushions covered in red velvet, with small tables standing nearby and on them plates of delicacies and fruit juices. Against the opposite wall there is spread a different feast – one for their eyes: a

long table draped in red velvet and on it the most beautiful *objets d'art* and bejewelled bibelots they have ever seen.
While they take refreshments, Jacques Coeur produces
some of his recent acquisitions: small carved ivory plaques
made in Jerusalem at the time of Christ he tells them; gold
and ormolu ornaments from Byzantium; icons of saints
and of the Virgin from Russia, painted on pieces of curved
wood cut directly from the sides of trees. Then, from the
countless deep pockets of his flowing robes, he brings out
one by one twists of white silk. These he puts on a tray in
front of him in a pile as one would sweetmeats.

How many pockets does he have in his gown? wonders
the practical René as the merchant picks up one of the
twists of silken cloth and opens it slowly, corner by
pointed corner. The way he peels the cloth open reminds
René how his father would peel open the bananas that
came from Aragon with his mother at the time of her marriage. How they thrived in Provence; René remembers
how his father would peel down the sections one at the
time for the amusement of the children.

From within each twist of silken cloth that Jacques picks
up, still rubbing the nut gently in the silk between his
fingers, he pulls back the four corners from the centre
almost as a ritual, and there emerges from each little silken
wrapping a glittering, translucent precious stone, which
he holds up to the light in two fingers. He does the same
with the other twists, and more precious stones appear:
deep-blue sapphires, clear emeralds and blood-red rubies
that glow as if a flame burns inside them – each the size of
Isabelle's smallest fingernail. 'Oh!' and 'Ah!' and more
exclamations of delight come from both Isabelle and René,

who sit transfixed as Jacques produces the dazzling treasures with the skill of a magician. For every stone there is a story, which adds to its fascination. Jacques, a consummate storyteller. He even recounts tales from his many visits to René's great-uncle Duke Jean of Berry, including the story of the shield from Thermopylae. As they say their farewells, René and Isabelle promise to return on their next visit from Nancy.

As the young couple leave Bourges, so does Jacques Coeur, travelling with the two Goddard brothers, merchants like himself and now his partners. With their armed escorts, they head for Marseilles. From contacts he has made during the past years, Jacques has heard that ships arrive there from the Levant carrying wondrous merchandise for them to buy.

Marseilles dazzles the three young merchants. In the huge sweep of the bay, many sailing ships bob at anchor, and even more are tied up alongside the quay. Sailors of all nationalities gather to exchange stories; while some sit playing cards or writing letters home. There are countless inns and shops, all touting for trade, and barrow men selling fruit, vegetables, cheeses and casks of wine and other spirits. The streets are none too clean in places, with sailors dropping debris as they eat walking along. Further away from the quay, the houses and shops become smarter, tidier and more prosperous-looking. Carriages wait outside several doors, and a number have stables at the back. Their lodgings are in a fine old building not too far from the quay but not too near either – the fishermen's catch may be impressive, but the smell can be overpowering.

Jacques has heard that the Queen of Sicily is in the port. He dispatches his messenger, who returns with an invitation for him to dine at her palace. In this hope he has brought with him his finest suit of clothes in green velvet, his hat dark red with ties hanging down on either side. Arriving at the gates on a fine livery hack he is shown into an antechamber to await his hostess. The room is of medium size, and he cannot help admiring the wall-to-wall tapestries of a quality he has only seen at the mansions of the late Duke of Berry.

A rustle of silk and the Queen of Sicily enters, both hands outstretched in greeting. 'Welcome, Monsieur Jacques Coeur, of whom we hear more and more in our port of Marseilles. Louis,' she says, turning to a tall, fair, strikingly handsome young man who has entered behind her, 'this is the man whose help you will need, and on whom you can always rely to deal fairly.' The merchant of Bourges, flattered, bows low – he knows at once that the young man is none other than Louis III, Duke of Anjou.

'Jacques, I hereby place my eldest son in your adroit management.' Yolande raises her hand to stop him speaking. 'I have made my enquiries and I am satisfied. I now know you to be both honest and clever – no better combination exists in a reliable steward.'

'Madame, your Majesty, and my Lord of Anjou, you can always count on me and my people to serve and supply you.'

'Louis, why not walk with Jacques down to the quay and tell him of your hopes and aspirations? You can be frank with this man, for I trust him.' And with a wave and a smile, she glides into an adjoining room.

As the two men stroll down the long pier, Louis turns to Jacques. 'I believe you may know of some of my troubles.'

'Monseigneur, I know your father was the heir of Giovanna II, the last Queen of Naples and Sicily, but that your cousin Alfonso of Aragon also claims that throne.'

'Yes, that is true. Queen Giovanna's family was a senior branch of the Anjou's, and since she had no other heirs, the kingdom became the inheritance of my family.'

'Then by what right does Alfonso claim it?'

'Giovanna was a harridan and capricious. She was really quite a frightful woman by all accounts. She decided on a whim not to leave the throne to the Anjous after all, but to the Aragons instead, and the two families have been fighting over it ever since. It was the reason for my parents' marriage – my Aragon grandmother had had enough of the fighting and suggested to my Anjou grandmother that her son – my father, then a very young duke – should marry my mother, the only child of the King of Aragon, thereby uniting the two families. But Alfonso felt that a woman could not represent her country's claim, and so the struggle continues.

'And your father? Didn't he rule as King of Sicily?'

'Indeed he did, but throughout his nine years there, he was constantly fighting Alfonso, who eventually defeated him on the Peninsula, all the time while betrothed to my mother. She often told us how she would write to him and wait patiently for his reply, which when one came, was always short and rather military,' Louis says with a chuckle. 'Finally, when he returned defeated, they married. Much later she told us as children, she was rather disappointed she would not reign as Queen of Sicily after all.

Nonetheless, she rode to Arles to her wedding in my father's sovereign territory of Provence, and the moment they met, they fell deeply in love,' he sighed, a sigh filled with memories. 'Theirs was a great love. We children felt it all around us. It seemed to envelop us like a magic cloak making us invincible. Their love endured despite many difficulties and another attempt made against Alfonso by my father which also failed. My dear father returned quite ill from that journey and then died in Bourges when I was fourteen. When my dear father died, he made my mother promise to do everything in her power to regain our rightful inheritance.'

*This worthy prince will never succeed*, thinks Jacques. *I have heard much about Alfonso V d'Aragon, and he does not have the heart of Louis d'Anjou, if he has any heart at all.* More importantly, Aragon has financial backing far greater than even the immense fortune left by Louis' father.

'Tell me, my Lord, am I right in thinking that Alfonso has the support of the Pope in Rome?'

'Yes, sadly that is true. And even if I had the backing of the Pope in Avignon, he could never afford to match the funding of the Holy Roman Emperor, who also supports Alfonso. I must trust in my luck and the Lord,' says Louis with a dashing smile. 'Now look at those fishing boats coming in. What a catch!'

Jacques Coeur is as good as his word. He meets often with both Yolande and Louis, and quietly assists them, seeing to all their requirements. He has no doubt that the day will come when the two claimants to Giovanna's throne will arrive at a serious conflict to secure it. The Italian peninsula from Naples down to the toe, plus Sicily – that is a kingdom worth fighting for.

Jacques is certain that the Queen of Sicily will continue to do her duty and raise money, supplies and troops from her various holdings, even though she knows it is a hopeless quest. He can see her love for this eldest son shining in her eyes and others tell him he has grown in the image of her beloved husband – another victim of the Anjou's obsession with their Italian kingdom. Now that they have met, he will keep a careful watch on Louis through his agents. This young man of nineteen or twenty is far too handsome, and his eyes too kind, to defeat the man Jacques has heard Alfonso V of Aragon to be. He will need help, and Jacques will give it where he can.

# Chapter Six

While Jacques Coeur follows in the king's progress to the other cities and châteaux of his domains, he hears about Jeanne d'Arc, the remarkable girl who has come from René and Isabelle's territory of Lorraine. Like his fellow countrymen, Jacques is amazed by the story of how the Queen of Sicily recalled her army of Anjou marching on its way to Marseilles, to meet with Jeanne in Bourges, where the citizens all stared with incredulity at the slight girl who was expected to save their country.

Now Orléans was under siege by the English, and this extraordinary girl in white armour sat on her great white charger on a hill out of arrow range opposite the city, her silk banner with the red cross of Lorraine fluttering in the breeze. The fighting was brutal and bloody, and all the while, Jeanne d'Arc remained each day on her horse on the hill, motionless it appeared to the troops, the sun shining on her so that it seemed she was heaven-sent, an icon to encourage the soldiers.

And inspire the soldiers she did, just as Queen Yolande prayed would happen. Throughout the siege, Yolande, Marie and Isabelle, accompanied by their ladies and others of their entourage, wait each day by the gates of Bourges for news brought by the daily courier. It is René's first time riding to war, and Yolande has asked Pierre de Brézé, her able young equerry, to keep an eye on him. Charles de Dunois who arrived in Bourges with Pierre, had already gone ahead with a company to join the soldiers within Orléans and help them. Yolande frets about her son, but silently, and she and Marie feign optimism to Isabelle, who returns it. Jacques has come back to Bourges in advance of the king. 'These three ladies are made of steel,' he whispers to Marcée. 'They know that the country's fate depends on raising the siege, and yet they are as courteous and gracious to the people of Bourges as if nothing was happening. Now *that* is the stamp of a great lady,' he says almost to himself.

And then a packet arrives from René and they rush to Marie's rooms to read it with Juana, Yolande's governess, who came to France with her from Aragon and whom she sent to Bourges to be with Marie and her son. It does not take long for the contents to be relayed to the waiting court-iers and ladies. Every detail is savoured and repeated until the next packet arrives, sometimes also from Pierre de Brézé to Queen Yolande and with more military detail than René's enthusiastic missives. The wait seems to last an eternity.

Then comes the day of the good news! The miraculous news! After nine days of vicious attacks and counter-attacks, the siege is raised and the city freed. The story seems so unbelievable as to be a miracle, say the rescued inhabitants as they emerge half crazed with hunger. Orléans was beyond hope, and then out of nowhere appeared this apparition, this girl from Domrémy in Lorraine.

Orléans has been saved! The gates are open, the skeletons from within walk out to be embraced by the Angevins. René finds his cousin Charles de Dunois and cannot stop embracing him, feeding him beakers of wine and non-stop chatter. They are joined by Pierre de Brézé who never lets on that his role was to keep René safe on his mother's orders.

At Bourges – oh, the relief! Jacques hears Queen Yolande tell her ladies that somehow she was sure it would happen; after all, who knew better the strength of her army of Anjou? Yet the soldiers, though brave, are basic and uneducated; they needed a leader and Yolande gave them a vision, a mystical personage to fulfil their spiritual needs. These men, and the citizens of Orléans, hail Jeanne as their heroine.

Jacques and Marcée join the crowd as the army arrives back in Bourges with Jeanne at their head. The citizens overwhelm them; there is cheering, shouting and laughter. Refreshments are brought and horses taken away by grooms as the soldiers embrace their loved ones. 'What a sight, Marcée, shall we ever see the like again? Our country saved by this strange, wonderful girl who inspired our rough soldiers?' Yolande is surrounded by her Angevins: she is their sovereign duchess who gave them the Maid to inspire their victory. Jacques sees the Queen of Sicily and Jeanne d'Arc deep in discussion with the captains. After refreshing themselves and their horses, they must move on to Loches and meet with the king. Their plan is long established; their next goal is Rheims and the coronation.

None of the three royal ladies can ride with the army – Rheims is in enemy territory, and progress will be dangerous – but Jacques has decided he will accompany them. True, he is not a soldier, but he is fit and strong and perhaps can be of some use. Many local people and peasantry have flocked to join what is now called 'The army of Jeanne d'Arc', some with horses, and many without. This is a fight for France and they want to be part of it.

The three ladies bid farewell to René, flushed with his success as a soldier, his red hair protruding from his helmet front and back and the light of self-conviction gleaming from his face. 'Take care, beloved son,' says Yolande gently as René leans down from his horse to kiss her hand; Isabelle comes and lays her head quickly on his thigh, and Marie calls, 'Fare thee well, my darling brother, bring me back my anointed sovereign lord.' René bows to them all, and waves to Juana, standing with Marcée. Jacques follows with the other recruits, turning for one final glimpse of his wife and family, their faces a blend of pride and fear.

More successes follow; a tired nation is lifting its head as the army fights its way to Loches to meet Charles VII there. As the king's nearest relative, René joins the Council as they gather to discuss the next step. Naturally they want to pursue the fleeing enemy, taking advantage of the terrorized English soldiers, who, they are told, saw the shining vision on the hill opposite Orléans and believe her to be some sort of spiritual apparition. Afterwards, hearing that Jacques has come to join the army, René seeks him out.

'Jacques, dear friend, with what pleasure I greet you – a soldier! Our merchant of Bourges has become a soldier!' He is so proud of his own achievement that he thrusts it on anyone willing to take the same risks.

As they call for refreshments, they are joined by Dunois and Pierre de Brézé. 'I need to share something with you, my friends,' begins René, 'for I cannot tell anyone else here and I know you will understand. I was in the king's private apartment a short time ago when to everyone's surprise, Jeanne burst in, tears streaming down her face, and threw herself on her knees, begging Charles to stop holding endless councils of war and making plans to destroy the fleeing English. Imagine, she clutched his ankles and began kissing his feet, and begged, *pleaded* with him to advance to Rheims to be consecrated and receive the crown "of which you are worthy"! Those were her exact words. Extraordinary, don't you think?'

'Well?' asks Dunois. 'What did he do?'

René gives his cousin a withering look – this is his story and he is going to tell it his way. 'He looked startled, and then he raised Jeanne from the floor and turned to me, saying: "Your mother – my *bonne mère* as I have anointed her, seeks my anointing and coronation. She has made our great victory possible with her soldiers and her belief in this Maid. If that is her wish, the fleeing army must be dealt with afterwards." Then, gesturing to us all, he announced boldly: "To Rheims!"'

And René sits back with such a strange look on his face that Pierre and Dunois smile. 'So that's the plan!' he says, looking at them expectantly.

Pierre and Dunois both understand René's need for approbation. 'You've done well,' says Dunois with a pat on his younger cousin's back, and Pierre does the same. Jacques knows his place and bows before René.

'My Lord, I hear from all sides the tales of your courage in the battle to relieve Orléans, and most of all from your cousin the Count of Dunois here, who told me he fell into your arms with hunger and fatigue.' He means it sincerely, but René guffaws.

'Fell into my arms like a girl, he did!' And they all smile, happy to be safe and together.

Some days later, the king arrives in Bourges with Jeanne d'Arc and the army. It is a short stop to greet Marie, who is sad not to be joining him for the journey to Rheims for his coronation and what should also have been hers. But the road is full of ideal places for an ambush, and she is much too advanced in her pregnancy. Yolande will remain with Marie and Isabelle, who lightly strokes René's knee and smiles up at him on his charger in loving conspiracy.

Jacques jumps from his horse to embrace Marcée. 'I am going with them, my dearest wife,' he tells her. 'If there is to be a coronation, ceremonial costumes and finery will surely be needed by the courtier knights. Come help me to load a cart with suitable adornments for the grandees!' and they rush off to his warehouse, calling for his staff.

Two days later, the king leaves Bourges with Jeanne d'Arc and the army, as well as a sizeable baggage train, heading for Rheims. Marcée mutters to Juana, 'That baggage train alone is inviting an ambush by the English.

Half the finery of our warehouse is in it! I hope it comes back. My Jacques has suddenly caught the fever of war; and just when our two eldest say they want to go into the Church – at ten and eleven years old! Who will run the business if he does not come back?'

'Marcée, dear friend, I have a good feeling about this expedition. God rides with them and the Maid. We must have faith.'

After no more than two hours' ride, the army reaches enemy territory and the soldiers have to fight their way through a dense wood. From then onwards, they are constantly under attack. Jacques Coeur, bringing up the rear with the baggage train, fights as hard as the others, determined to witness 'the King of Bourges', as Charles has been derided by the English, become the consecrated King of France. Strong and fit, he finds himself able to keep up with the hardened soldiers of Anjou, and they look at him with a certain respect.

His worst moment arrives during the Battle of Patay. The English throw all their force at the French, and set up their longbow men behind stakes to rain down their arrows on the vanguard, which Jacques has joined to be near René, Dunois and Brézé. The English archers are hidden when the French advance nears their position, but they give themselves away with a hunting cry when a stag appears out of the woods. Before the main body of the French army can join them, the two experienced generals, La Hire and Xaintrailles, swiftly lead the vanguard behind the English longbow men. With the archers' only protection the stakes in front of them, they are cut down easily by the French cavalry – a massacre.

It is at Patay that Jacques Coeur experiences the same horror of war mixed with exhilaration that René felt at Orléans – something impossible to forget. *Kill or be killed* goes through his mind. 'We have killed at least half of the English force of about five thousand,' he hears one of Dunois' men say, 'and our own losses are barely one hundred.' A great victory indeed.

When René finds Jacques sitting on the ground under a tree, he joins him. 'Well, my friend, now you too have experienced a real battle. I have a courier about to leave for Bourges – he will take a letter to your wife and family if you wish.'

This lord has so much of his mother's sense of caring in him, thinks Jacques, and he scribbles a quick note to Marcée:

> I was with the vanguard when we came upon the English, and I pray that our sons never have to see such a scene as this. War is a truly terrible thing, and the exhilaration on the faces of the victors is almost as ugly to behold as the dejected expressions of the prisoners, unsure of their fate after the English killed all the captured French at Agincourt.
>
> The hideous screams of the wounded men and horses are such that I wish I could put them out of their misery myself. But we have won, and we are told that the road to Rheims is now open. I have not seen Jeanne d'Arc, but I am sure she is with the king in the rear. Pray for me. J

At their invitation, Jacques rides with Dunois and René towards Rheims. A different atmosphere envelops the army: the confidence of having won a great victory and of approaching their goal. The cartloads of adornments that Jacques has brought for the courtiers are mercifully still intact, and he envisions a splendid ceremony if all continues well.

'Rheims at last!' is the cry from the scouts in front, but the vanguard arrives to see a city barred and barricaded. The army spreads to face the great walls, the king and Jeanne d'Arc now placed with René, Dunois and Pierre in the front row opposite the enormous gates. Jacques is just behind them and can hear much discussion as to the next move: should they send an emissary under a flag of truce to parlay with the captain of the guard, perhaps? And more along those lines.

Suddenly a pale figure on a big white horse, holding aloft a white banner, pulls away from the massed ranks towards the city's walls. It is Jeanne d'Arc, followed closely by her bugler, furiously blowing his horn and kicking his pony. No one moves; all seem turned to stone as Jeanne reaches the walls and rides beneath the heavily armed battlements, archers at the ready above her, an easy target. But no one shoots, and the massed ranks standing out of arrow range hear the shout from the ramparts: 'It's her! She's here! The Maid of Orléans is here! Open the gates, and the Lord is with us!'

Jacques is as dumbfounded as the rest. The gates open, and they ride into a silent, empty city, the windows shuttered and the streets bare. Not even a dog barks.

The army of Jeanne d'Arc moves swiftly towards the cathedral. Everyone knows they have no more than twenty-four hours before the English arrive; they must work fast to achieve their glorious objective. To their amazement, they find the crown still in its traditional hiding place. The other regal paraphernalia has gone, but Jacques has brought wonderful altar cloths of velvet and gold lace; vestments for the clergy and the chalice for the Mass. He runs to find Dunois. 'Where is the holy oil from the monastery of Saint-Rémy that you promised would be here?' he enquires frantically. There can be no ceremony without that vital part.

'The abbot is on his way. Be calm, dear friend.' It is René who reassures him. 'Six of our knights left last night to fetch him and the oil.'

Night is falling and candles are lit; everyone is working – sweeping, dusting, draping, bringing order to the cathedral to make it worthy of the coronation anticipated for the past seven years, since the death of Charles VI.

Exhausted, the band of workers, courtiers, soldiers and the great provider, Jacques Coeur, fall into any bed they can find in a number of abandoned houses. The next morning, everyone rises with the sun to prepare: the horses are groomed to a satin finish; the best from the carts of Jacques Coeur has already been chosen to dress and adorn the king, and the rest is for the courtiers; even the soldiers polish their armour and leave their heads bare. This is not a day for dying – this is a day to remember. As they emerge from their quarters, soldiers and courtiers are a splendid sight. Almost the biggest surprise is the town itself – Rheims has changed its allegiance! Windows are open, as are doors; the populace are dressed in their best; children too are smartly turned out and many are raised up on their fathers' shoulders.

The mounted procession, followed by the foot soldiers, winds slowly and with formality towards the cathedral.

The king sits on a beautiful grey palfrey – he cannot afford to risk one of his prancing stallions on this day when he will wear a crown! – and proceeds under a canopy held by four of his knights, receiving the people's salutations from left and right. Jacques is riding behind Pierre de Brézé and not far behind the royal cousins, René d'Anjou and Charles de Dunois, who are flanking Jeanne d'Arc resplendent in her white armour and on her white horse. The citizens clearly admire the regalia of the procession, calling out their appreciation of particular courtiers and knights, and Jacques feels an inner glow of achievement – yes, he has made this day memorable already. By witnessing the jubilant crowds that greet the soldiers and the royal party with The Maid on this unforgettable day, he is certain that overnight the people of Rheims have realized *this is truly their king.*

The rest of the day passes as if in a dream for Jacques, who quietly sees to every detail. It all goes according to plan: the arrival of the barefoot abbot carrying the holy oil and flanked by four armoured knights, who ride right up the steps of the cathedral and to the altar inside; the cere-mony itself; afterwards, the laying of hands by the king on the sick. How impressive it all is – and then over so quickly to avoid meeting with the enemy, who are said to be coming in great numbers

The return to Bourges is uneventful. Jacques, like most of them, rides in a haze of coronation glory, astounded by all that has come to pass since The Maid entered their lives.

The royal party dismount and enter the city, and the newly consecrated king is formally met by his wife – now Queen Marie – his mother-in-law Queen Yolande, and

René's wife, Isabelle. The two queens in ceremonial dress wear their crowns, and all three ladies curtsey deeply to Charles, now their consecrated and anointed king. He then presents them to Jeanne d'Arc, who falls to one knee to loud cheering from the citizens.

Many bowed low, or cheered, threw caps in the air and generally made merry. Marcée has come to watch the arrival with her family and her older boys – this is an occasion they must remember and will hear spoken of for years to come, she tells them. It is some time before they see Jacques – not being a regular soldier, he had to join the baggage train and accompany the precious contents of his carts. But when they do meet, what embraces there are, and relief mixed with laughter, and questions and talk. Marcée can see the fatigue on her husband's face, but also his pride in having taken part. There will be time to talk – now he must wash and rest!

Not long after their arrival in Bourges, Jacques is informed that Queen Yolande would like to see him, and he hurries to the palace. 'My dear friend Jacquet,' she addresses him with a smile, 'welcome home, and we congratulate you on the success of your mission.' He bows and waits. 'Once again we of Anjou need your assistance.' Again he bows, this time in acquiescence. 'You may recall that I made it clear to The Maid that I must take my army to Marseilles following the king's coronation?' Indeed Jacques remembers well; he has been wondering what will happen now the soldiers are in Bourges and surely hoping to rest after their long struggle in Orléans and afterwards. 'I must now leave with all haste,' Yolande continues. 'Messages reach me almost daily that my son is in great need. Do you have any idea of Jeanne d'Arc's plans? I have advised her to return to Domrémy, or to take up residence in her gift house in Orléans, but she will not answer me.'

'Madame and Majesty, I have seen the Maid enter the city with the king, and have observed the growing army of inexperienced volunteers who flock daily to her standard like sheep to the slaughter, but I have heard no word of her planned departure.'

'No, and that concerns me. My friend – for that is what you have become to me and my family – you and I know that the king is of a fickle nature. He can turn against a professed friend for no reason, and overnight. I have tried to warn The Maid of this, but she will not listen. Can you please try for me? I must leave soon, and I feel so responsible for her. She is just a girl and I put her where she is.'

When Jacques and René meet in the street, they exchange stories of their exploits – or rather, René who tells Jacques of his adventures. Several beakers later, he says suddenly: 'She won't leave. The Maid won't leave. Have you spoken with my mother?' Jacques nods. 'Our army must leave for Marseilles to embark for Naples. What can we do? My brother is desperate for his army, which my mother promised she would send him after the coronation.'

'My Lord René, I have heard that Jeanne d'Arc has been given a large house in Orléans by decree sent by their duke himself from the Tower of London. Why does she not go to Orléans, or home to Domrémy? You have spoken with her?'

'She says she wants to stay with the king and continue to push the English out of our country. It's a noble resolve, but without the army of Anjou ... Look at the undisciplined rabble that has joined her – they are of no use whatsoever, and I doubt the king will hire mercenaries for her.'

'Winter is coming, my Lord, and then perhaps the Maid will realize that without an army, she cannot fight.' But he does not believe it. This young country girl has experienced the heady euphoria of victory and public acclaim, and the taste of it has swayed her to remain with the king, even without the Angevin army. Jacques has seen the light shining out of Jeanne d'Arc's eyes, the light of obsession, and that does not leave quickly or quietly.

The Maid remains in Bourges throughout the winter, and Jacques often sees her with Queen Marie on their way to the cathedral, deep in conversation. He has supplied her with all her commissions, and they were surprisingly many, even a gold mesh tunic to wear over her white armour. The king has been generous and paid for everything, as well as ennobling Jeanne and her family. 'It is right he should do so', Jacques tells Marcée with feeling, but he too is beginning to have qualms about Jeanne's mission.

The people of Bourges are delighted when this extraordinary girl arrives in their midst with their king, but when it would appear Jeanne d'Arc has been 'abandoned by her army', Queen Marie is obliged to explain. *It had all been agreed beforehand; the army has left with her mother for Marseilles and must now finally embark to fight for her desperate brother to save his kingdom.* And the people believe and trust their gentle queen.

King Charles has commissioned Jacques Coeur to provide a quantity of luxurious materials so that The Maid may appear dressed correctly in formal presentation robes when she appears at court. The merchant obeys willingly. Splendid clothes embroidered in gold and silver thread, trimmed with costly fur, arrive at Jeanne's quarters from his warehouses. She feels more comfortable in men's clothes, she states, but if it is the king's wish for her to wear court robes, she will comply. *Is it such a crime for her to wear the current courtly styles the better to play her part?* Jacques asks himself – or, as some at court mutter in their dark envy, *is her love of luxury an indication of sorcery?* How absurd that sounds to a merchant's ears!

Like everyone privileged to meet the Maid, Jacques and Marcée are impressed by her fervour. One day, when Marcée sees Jeanne with Queen Marie, she greets them both, and is struck by the Maid's look of total dedication.

'Dear husband mine, I saw the Maid today as she passed with our queen to visit the poor and followed by the carts filled with food for them. Please give her anything she needs to make her stay more comfortable. I feel she might deprive herself to help others.' And Jacques promises that he will provide Jeanne with more comfort than even Marcée can imagine. In both their eyes, Jeanne d'Arc is someone whose worth is beyond price.

# Chapter Seven

With Marcée and their three children securely surrounded by family members and his business in the safe hands of his partners, Jacques Coeur leaves Bourges, heading south towards Narbonne. He is thirty years old, fit, strong, and sufficiently successful to set out at last on his long-planned voyage of commercial discovery to the Levant. What a relief for him to be able to leave behind the horrors of war.

Riding with a group of travellers, he uses a somewhat different route to the one he has taken before to Marseilles. It shocks him to see the extent of the devastation caused by the civil war: the number of ruined castles, deserted towns, burnt villages, roads and bridges in disrepair; and he is constantly aware of the danger of ambush by robber bands willing to cut throats for a small sum. Famine and plague follow war, and substantial towns have been reduced to no more than a handful of inhabitants. Some fearful townsfolk hide in the forests and woods, which offer a refuge of sorts, and sally forth begging food from the convoy.

Occasionally they meet couriers on the road, and Jacques learns that the Maid spent Christmas of 1430 in Bourges. On his arrival in Narbonne, he finds a letter waiting from Marcèe, full of domestic news, but also describing how Jeanne and her makeshift army of volunteers left Bourges with the coming of spring, and have lost two battles. *Well of course, he thinks. What do they expect? Without the army of Anjou, how can she succeed? She is an icon, not a soldier*. It makes him angry to think the king would allow her to be exposed in this way.

By the time he is ready to sail to the Levant in May, he has received worse news: Jeanne d'Arc has been captured at Compiègne. It seems a soldier hooked the back of the gold chain-mail vest she wore over her armour, pulling her down sharply from her horse. He may not even have realized who she was – the glittering vest was all he wanted. How bitterly Jacques regrets agreeing to her vain commission at the king's expense – and the profit in it for him. Her ransom will be high, but he is never in any doubt that it will be paid.

At the ancient Roman port of Narbonne, west of Aigues Mortes, Jacques embarks on a large galley in the company of other merchants and some pilgrims. His voyage is not intended for pleasure, although there may be pleasure enough to be found; it is an opportunity to learn about the source, quality and cost of the merchandise he would like to bring back to France. His enquiries will be directed towards the nature of the ports, the various means of transporting his purchases, and which of the merchants there are willing to trade with him. Above all, he must establish who is well disposed towards his king and country.

They are a mixed group on board, from various parts of France and even from Aragon and Navarre. There are two Gascons who reek of garlic: 'Take some – chew it and you won't even feel the boat move,' one tells him, swearing that it prevents seasickness. Jacques accepts gratefully, but will wait for the need before he uses it and smells like them. The travellers' quarters are tight and he thinks he will remain on deck as much as possible – the proximity of the goats is a significant deterrent. The meat is certainly guaranteed to be fresh, but the smell …

As well as oarsmen, they have sails, and their galley is armed against pirates and enemy ships. It is a dangerous area, and their ship hugs the coasts of France and Italy before turning south-west towards Sicily. From there they sail across the Mediterranean, arriving at their goal – Alexandria, a Muslim Egyptian port, without incident. Happy to be back on land, and none the worse for his journey, Jacques Coeur leaves the ship to research the city's potential and strike out on his own. He has waited so long to undertake this dream mission that his heart beats fast with excitement and anticipation and he drinks in the sights and sounds like a man come from the desert to fresh water.

What a harbour he finds there, the port of Alexandria filled with a forest of masts on ships of every size and nationality: Catalans, Venetians, Florentines; ships from

Genoa, Cyprus, Syria – all welcome in this city of seventy thousand inhabitants. After some days spent wandering among the crowds of traders, a sea of smiling faces, he travels on alone to Cairo, situated on a hill above the city's port of Boulaq on the Nile, which is filled with even more vessels. Many are the local sailing ships the Arabs call *felucca*, comprising carved wooden hulls with lateen sails. They have arrived from the Red Sea – and some, it would seem, even from India – filled with an astonishing variety of merchandise. There is so much for him to absorb that Jacques forgets home and family, then writes guiltily to Marcée:

> Good wife, I am well and rested from the uneventful voyage. I landed in Alexandria – a haven of divergent products and a future source for me. Now I am in Cairo, where there is much to see among the noisy camel caravans arriving daily after crossing the desert from Syria. They bring carpets from Turkey and Persia; silks, perfumes, amber, pearls the size of thumbs and rubies red as blood. The caravans meet the local sailing boats at the port and off-load on to these their exotic wares. The noise of people shouting, singing and making music, combined with the banging of hammers on metal and anvils, makes for a never-ending, indescribable din. Kiss the children for me and I will write more.

Merchants gather everywhere, offering the most remarkable merchandise Jacques has seen, especially around the sultan's palace. There he examines a profusion of treasures, valuable and rare as well as ingenious. Perfect pearls;

extraordinary precious stones of every colour; intricate beaten gold from the goldsmiths of the Ottoman courts; perfumes of a subtlety so delicious they make his head whirl like the dervish dancers in the square; silks and brocades that dazzle in the sunlight; the softest silken carpets, sometimes threaded with gold and silver. Sultans in large turbans and grand sheikhs in feather-light pale wool robes argue good-humouredly over prices, exchanging hand signals and knowing looks; the strong smell of spices mingles with the heady perfumes.

Jacques speaks none of the tongues he hears around him, but there is an international language of trade involving the eyes, head movements and hand gestures, fingers indicating numbers, and many little beakers of scalding coffee poured from a great height from silver pots with long beaks without spilling a drop – he stares fascinated – until a deal is done. Then he notes how the Egyptian trader clasps the other man's hand in both of his before placing his right hand on his own heart. What a charming gesture, he thinks, and he finds himself warming to the Egyptians with their sunny smiles, white teeth and intelligent dark eyes.

After a little time observing and wandering around, somehow he begins to grasp what is going on and the meaning of the nodding and shaking of the head, clapping of hands or in some cases, one or the other trader receiving a friendly cuff on the back. He is not buying, but he needs to understand prices and determine with whom he will deal when the time comes. Watching the various facial distortions made during transactions is so amusing that at times he cannot help himself bursting out laughing, much to the consternation of those around him.

The banks of the Nile are planted with cane fields, creating something of a screen to divide the various areas of merchandise. The silks and other delicate fabrics must not be too close to the spices and the sugar, or to the many steaming pots, or to the pastry chefs working outdoors. Everyone seems to be staring at something or someone – the Greeks stare at the Nubians, who stare at the Ethiopians, whose huge eyes look hard at the Armenians and the Georgians, and most of all at the Christians, of whom there seem to be more than any other group.

Among these numerous nationalities, Jacques sees many slaves, mostly African, being bought and sold, gold coins clinking in a cupped hand as a deal is done. Then they shuffle off behind a new owner, ankles chained, heads bowed in resignation. Every nationality comes to the caravanserais overflowing with treasures, spices and sweetmeats; men, women, children and animals all for sale; and the budding merchant from Burges concludes that with courage and skill, any conceivable contract could be arranged.

The women are dressed in the most exquisite fabrics – gossamer silks of delicate pastel shades interwoven with gold and silver thread, their silken slippers embroidered with pearls or semi-precious stones. To Jacques' surprise, many local women copy the fashions of the West rather than wearing their own more practical and attractive costumes. *These are the details Marcée would enjoy hearing*, he mutters to himself. *I will write to her tonight.*

He discovers how the local traders categorize the foreigners: the Italians are considered greedy and dishonest;

the Genoese arrogant; the Venetians duplicitous and deceitful. As yet there are no French traders, and with such distinctions in mind, he realizes at once that to conclude business here successfully, he will have to be scrupulously honest, careful and fair in his dealings. The Arabs cannot be fooled – they are more experienced than the Europeans, and far better traders. Furthermore, he can succeed only if he offers them what they want and cannot get from another merchant.

Goods from Europe are in demand, especially leather, but his most extraordinary discovery is that the Egyptians prefer silver to gold. Gold they have in quantity, but not silver, and his mind spins with the unlimited possibilities such knowledge opens up. Having made copious mental notes, Jacques continues on to Syria and arrives at the splendour that is the city of Damascus. To his surprise, he finds remnants still visible of French occupation during the Crusades, faded fleur-de-lys discernible on some of the walls. The city boasts the remains of each of the great civilizations that ruled there – Greek, Roman and Byzantine – and despite the destruction wrought by Tamerlane, this ancient site still remains the crossroads of trade between East and West. There is no fabric as gloriously rich as that which bears the city's name – damask – and every weight and colour of silk can be found here too.

It is in Damascus that he receives news of Jeanne d'Arc's terrible fate, abandoned by the king, then cruelly burnt at the stake in Rouen. *What an ungrateful people we are, when it was she who saved us with her valour and leadership. How could our young king have abandoned her so easily and indifferently? And our great queen who discovered Jeanne in Lorraine, no not our dear little Queen Marie, but her mother, the noble Yolande d'Anjou, my own patroness. Had she really been unable to save her though far away in Provence? Or was she travelling elsewhere and missed the courier? The distance is great, and I am convinced the news of the Maid's capture and trial had not reached Queen Yolande in time for her to act. Surely she would have warned Jeanne d'Arc of the fickleness of the king* ... It is clear to him that the Maid of Orléans, whom all had lauded to the sky, had become dispensable to both king and court. *After all, only great nobles are worthy of ransom*, sears through his mind ...

With a heavy heart he continues his journey, his next destination Cyprus. The island's capital, Famagusta, is the last Latin bastion of the Levant, the furthest Christian outpost. There he is astonished to see the greatest display of wealth he has yet encountered. Every ship leaving the Levant or returning has to pass by the island; merchants and traders, or the countless pilgrims – all must stop there. He goes out of his way to talk to pilgrims on the pier, asking about Jeanne, but many had not much knowledge of The Maid of Orléans – their own journeys long and full of difficulties.

The luxury of the lives of the citizens of Famagusta comes as a surprise and is almost unimaginable. The gems the women wear, the jewels and *objets d'art* the merchants sell: Jacques has never seen the like, not even at the court of the Duke of Berry. The quality of the contents of many of the little dealers' booths – cloth of gold or silver; beaten gold and silver vessels; precious little statues; carved emeralds and ivories; jades of many colours; and a vast range of spices – is such that he is sure no one in Bourges will believe him.

Another anomaly intrigues the merchant: whereas no French aristocrat would sully his family name by engaging in commerce, Italian nobles, led by the Medici, have no such scruples. Nor do the Venetians show any remorse for trading with the 'infidel' – something that is banned by the Pope – and certainly not for selling them arms, and quite indiscriminately.

He can tell that the Venetians are undoubtedly the greatest boat builders; they also hold the monopoly of supplying salt to the Levant – indispensable to the camel trains to preserve their meats while crossing the desert. In addition, they have perfected the art of weaving and dying silks and velvets, and of blowing glass into delicate, beautiful shapes. He recalls how as a boy he would visit the glass-blowers in Bourges so he could become a good judge of quality – and he must admit, the Venetians do it much, much better.

To protect their huge trade with the Levant along the Mediterranean, it seems that Venice employs armed escorts for their merchant ships. They also use the thousands of watchtowers along their coasts not only to observe their own ships, but to levy tax on any other boats putting in to their small harbours for water. And yet to his surprise, Jacques learns that the Venetians are willing to hire out empty vessels to other nations – on condition they do not trade in the same merchandise.

Genoa, the rival republic to Venice, has colonized the area of the Bosporus and the Black Sea, giving it access to the treasures of the Persians and the Muscovites. It soon becomes clear to Jacques that the Genoese far surpass the Venetians in their nautical skills, their knowledge of routes and the making of their own maps, which they keep secret. Furthermore, he learns that they have established themselves in the French ports of Narbonne and Montpellier. Armed with so much valuable information, he concludes that he must find a way of capitalizing on it.

At last a letter from Marcée reaches him.

Dearest husband,

I know Famagusta is your last port, and I am sending this letter in the hope that it will reach you there. I must tell you about our dear Jeanne d'Arc, so cruelly abandoned by the king to a terrible fate. I have heard from Juana that Queen Yolande tried to force our king to send an army to Rouen to rescue the Maid, while she herself sent the money to pay her ransom, but it arrived too late. It seems Queen Yolande was travelling by road to Brittany on urgent business at the time and missed the courier with the news. According to local gossip at home, Jeanne became too imperious for the likes of the court's grandees, and especially the king's arch-bishop, who said she had dared to bypass him by claiming to have direct communication with her saints, which we believe she did. It is a terrible thing that the king, the arch-bishop and her judges have done, dearest husband, and I am spending much time in the cathedral asking for God's forgiveness.

Jacques weeps reading his wife's words, and there on the pier at Famagusta, he vows that should he ever rise from his humble beginnings to great riches and title he will never forget the lesson that Jeanne d'Arc learnt too late and to her cost: *how easy it is to fall from a great height*.

On the return journey, to his regret, Jacques is unable to reach Florence, though at the port of Livorno he hears much talk of the Medici family, and of their head, Cosimo. It fascinates him that such a merchant prince, for whom the arts, diplomacy and politics hold no secrets, is equally dedicated to the pursuit of commerce. What a contrast with the French aristocracy, who will never lower themselves to become involved in their own affairs, and who, as a result, are being ruined by mismanagement.

What he concludes most definitely from his voyage of discovery is that it will not be easy to deal with the Muslims. The Genovese and the Venetians only manage by paying a huge tax on their arrival in the Muslim ports. Christians are despised and not treated well: they are segregated into ghettos, and have sanctions put on their vessels. If they do not pay the enormous duties, their sails and rudders are confiscated.

Although the merchant of Bourges makes many useful contacts for acquiring and selling merchandise, he still faces the problem of how to get his purchases home. He has discovered that the Genoese use the French port of Montpellier because the Pope has granted its citizens a dispensation to trade with the *infidel*. Montpellier, on the other side of the Rhône from Provence, has been ravaged by plague and war. To add attraction to the Pope's dispensation and help repopulate the area, the town's consuls have decided to offer residents six years' tax exemption on mobile wealth. When he learns of this tremendous incentive, Jacques Coeur decides to move the main body of his trading operations to Montpellier but continue to keep a small interest in Marseilles. Provence is the sovereign territory of the Duke of Anjou and with Queen Yolande as her son Louis' regent, it is a part of France which might be useful one day. Until he can afford to build his own ships, he will hire from the Genoese in Montpellier to transport the wares he intends to bring to France from the Near East.

After mulling over all the knowledge he has gleaned from the many new acquaintances made on his exploratory travels, the merchant of Bourges comes to the conclusion that by far the best trading deal he could make in the Levant and the Near East would be to exchange French mined silver for Egyptian gold. It is common knowledge that there are long-abandoned silver, copper and lead mines in the Lyonnais area. Although no silver may leave France without royal assent, if he can get permits to work these mines and find a way for the export of the produce, then serious profits could be made.

As he sails for home in November 1431, more than a year and a half after setting out, Jacques spends his time considering the potential trading options available to him. His expression is always affable, but he keeps his thoughts to himself and talks little with his fellow travellers, who respect his concentration. When the weather changes abruptly, their galley, caught in a storm off Corsica and heavily laden with the valuable goods the other merchants on board have purchased, strikes a coral reef. As people and goods are hurled in all directions, and screaming and panic erupt around him, Jacques becomes ice-calm, rooted to the spot, almost an observer rather than a participant.

They see local people rushing down a hill to board small boats on the shore and row out to rescue them. The change in atmosphere is remarkable – from panic and alarm to almost hysterical relief. But this is short-lived. To the astonishment of Jacques and the rest of the passengers, their rescuers – men with their womenfolk standing ready on the shore with baskets – demand all their possessions, even their shoes and shirts! The captain and the ship's owner are held for ransom, and the rest of them are told they are free to leave, albeit half naked and shoeless.

Inadvertently, Jacques becomes the passengers' leader, and does his best to encourage and cheer them. The next day, the news of their plight spreads rapidly. Soon citizens arrive with rescue boats sent by the local French consul, and all are brought safely back to their own coast, lamenting their losses. In fact, Jacques Coeur is the least inconvenienced – his assets from the voyage are stored safely in his head, and that he has saved undamaged. In addition, through the sharing of this disaster, and the attendant difficulties and discomfort, he has made invaluable friends among the others, some of whom, he realizes, may well prove very useful in his future as a merchant in the Near East.

# Chapter Eight

*P*rior to Jacques Coeur's journey, neither the monarchy nor the people of central and northern France have shown any interest in the commercial riches of the Levant. Up to now, such trade has been in the hands of the Genoese, the Venetians, Pisa to a small extent, the southern French and the Catalans. Naturally audacious and self-confident, as soon as he returns to France, Jacques moves much of his trading activity from Marseilles to Montpellier.

His regular journeys to the Near East continue, and one day in Damascus he meets a member of Duke Philip of Burgundy's household buying spices to ship to Beirut 'Ah, my good sir, are you not the merchant Jacques Coeur of Bourges?' the man addresses him. 'I have heard speak of your travels to the Levant and of the high quality of your purchases.' They exchange greetings and when asked, Jacques informs him that he is there primarily to buy blades. 'I have no doubt you too are aware of their excellence and that they are considered the finest through-out Syria,' he remarks, adding that 'they are polished so fine a man can use one as a looking glass to adjust his turban,' and they both laugh. After taking coffee together, another useful contact is made. The fact that the young Duke of Burgundy has sent an envoy to Damascus to enquire into trading possibilities interests the opportunist in Jacques Coeur.

On another of his journeys, Jacques becomes aware of the Moors' invention of what they call 'Greek Fire' or rockets and on his return, longs to tell his wife. 'Marcée, you will be pleased to hear what I have discovered. Now don't look so miserable when I come home – I am back with you and the family and very satisfied by the way in which you bring them up,' as he gives her a kiss. 'More, I have some valuable knowledge about rockets to pass on to your relation, the Grand Master of Artillery. They look easy to make and not expensive – I must speak with your relation.'

Marcée is a good wife and proud of her husband, whose status and business is growing even faster than his five children. Their house is filled with artefacts he has brought from his travels, which she shows with delight to her neighbours. She is content – her husband is a good man and he more than provides for his family, even if he is not often at home. Their new house is one of the largest and imposing in their neighbourhood, the best in Bourges. What he does on his travels privately, she does not ask. As far as she knows, he is a faithful husband and good to her.

*

By 1433, after some fifteen years as a merchant, Jacques Coeur's trade has expanded to such an extent that he realizes he needs a right-hand man. Jean de Villages, a native of Bourges, came to him as a young apprentice. Intelligent and quick-thinking, he has risen rapidly in his master's esteem and business, and Jacques begins to take him more and more into his confidence. He knows and trusts this young man and has high hopes for him. 'Marcée, dear wife,' he says, 'I know of your acute judgement of the human race. What do you think of our young Jean?'

'Can't you tell I have always liked him?' she laughs. 'And is he not often included in our gatherings?'

Now that Jean has grown to be a man, Jacques notices that Marcée invites him more often to family occasions, and always places him next to her niece Perette, her brother's daughter. 'Jean, my boy,' she says to him one day when they are alone, 'I have noticed how you look at my niece, and she at you. Now don't blush, love is a wondrous thing. I know from my husband that you are a great asset to him, and do well. Would a promotion nudge you to make Perette an offer of marriage, do you think?'

The boy is tongue-tied, but it comes as no surprise when he and Perette announce their decision to marry. Jacques and Marcée are delighted. The wedding celebrations are held in their house, and Jean de Villages is welcomed as a full member of their family as well as the keystone of Jacques' business.

One day Jacques tells him, 'Jean, dear nephew, I have known since the start of my trading with the Levant that I must own ships for my enterprises and not rent them continually from the Genoese.'

Aigues-Mortes is about 2.5 kilometres from Jacques' base in Montpellier and linked to the port of Lattes by a lagoon with canals which enable his ship to reach the sea. 'So that is why you intend to send me to the royal port of Aigues-Mortes,' smiles Jean de Villages. They leave soon afterwards and together install two shipyards there. Jacques has already commissioned a *galéasse*, a Genoese galley, from the shipbuilders in their port. Now he brings it to his own yard for the local shipwrights to copy. When the Genoese hear of this, in their fury they come to Aigues-Mortes and steal the vessel. It takes considerable negotiating skills on Jacques' part, and the might of Charles VII's local authority, to have it returned.

Despite his decision to move his fledgling operation to Montpellier, Jacques builds a fine house in Marseilles, a city not subject to French laws since it is in the Duke of Anjou's sovereign territory of Provence. This gives him the rights of a resident, and therefore he is legally entitled to export precious metals from Marseilles. The dream that he has been turning around in his mind since his first journey to the Near East – the exchange of silver for gold – is slowly materializing.

For a relatively small outlay, Jacques and his Goddard partners buy the concession to four ignored and unexploited mines in the Lyonnais area containing lead, copper and silver. These mines were originally used by the Romans and are known to the Lyonnais people, but due to lack of either finance or interest, they have been left untended for a number of years. Addressing his partners one day, Jacques explains, 'Now that we have had miners explore and examine these mines, I think I understand at least some of the reasons for their having been abandoned.' Seeing that he has piqued their curiosity, he continues.

'Firstly, their exploitation will need a huge investment, and for that we must bring in more partners – I suggest from Lyons. After all, the nearby Rhône will give us easy access from Montpellier.' The Goddards nod in agreement. 'Then we must ensure that the work is made safer and more attractive.' They look bemused. 'Mining is a dangerous business,' says Jacques seriously, 'and I have discovered that since a miner's life is a miserable one, we will only attract good workers and achieve results if we ensure that our men are well housed and fed. A priest will say Mass on Sundays in a chapel I will build near their dormitories. No women can be permitted into the dormitories, nor loud parties or drunkenness.' He can see that the incredulous looks from his two partners are softening into understanding. 'Our factors must be charged to see that the miners are clothed for free and fed a good diet. By that I mean including pork, beef, lamb, bacon, fresh fish as well as salted, eggs, fresh and dried fruit, onions and spices! Their bread is to be made of good quality flour and they are to be offered a decent white wine or rosé to drink.'

'My friend, you are building a holiday camp here!' And they laugh in disbelief, but Jacques is serious.

'Weapons are to be forbidden. Their mattresses are to be made of wool, with sheets, blankets and a bolster. We must supply staff to cook and clean, and to wash their clothes.

In case of accident, doctors must be brought from Lyons to tend to the injured or ill. Workers are to be paid by the day and at a rate more than elsewhere.' There is a collective groan and sigh of resignation from his partners. By now they have learnt that Jacques Coeur is always right.

'My wife has helped me draw up this list because she hears what the miners' women have to say and complain about.' One of the lessons Jacques Coeur has learnt on his travels and by observation, is that if workers are content, they will produce well. As a result of these many conditions he imposes, when the work on his mines begins, his miners do indeed produce well.

As the merchant's businesses progress and expand, it is not long before he finds himself running a bank. His ability for swift calculation is well known, and he has always been willing to lend money for slightly less interest than others, to those he can trust to repay. In his new base he builds a large house he calls The Lodge, which becomes a kind of stock exchange for the many merchants taking advantage of Montpellier's tax advantages. As a result of his trading in metals – especially silver – Jacques begins to associate with alchemists, as well as gaining renown as a silversmith, someone who understands how to mix silver with baser metals. This he had learnt originally some years ago working for the Mint in Bourges, then at his own silver mines, he begins to experiment, inviting others skilled in alchemy to join him. Jacques is not a trained alchemist but is fascinated by the craft of those who are and with his sharp intelligence he picks up sufficient information to pass for one to the uninitiated.

It is understandable perhaps for the son of a simple furrier to wish to be thought of as an alchemist and accorded similar and considerable renown.

Through the success of Jacques Coeur's trading company in Montpellier among others elsewhere in the country, France is becoming a serious competitor to Barcelona and the great commercial republics of Italy. It is in this way that he comes into the orbit of the Knights of Rhodes and is able to offer them material assistance – and when asked, he even gives aid to La Serenissima, Venice herself. This is not merely philanthropy – Jacques Coeur is always first and foremost a merchant, and he believes they could become valuable allies in the future. Since his youth he has made a habit of creating connections, combining and keeping note of people who might be useful to one another and himself. 'That is the essence of being a successful trader,' he tells his sons, certainly his two elder ones seem set on higher ideals than trade. *Perhaps the younger ones*, he thinks idly …

Since the courtiers are among his principal customers for the luxury goods in his warehouse in Bourges, Jacques is always conscious of the court's activities. The king is often surrounded by his 'favourites', fine-looking young men who have shown courage or demonstrated their ability as soldiers. One of these is André de Villequier, a handsome young Norman knight, who is a steadily rising star in his monarch's employ and who, Jacques notices, enriches himself energetically. Another is Guillaume de Gouffier, an attractive equerry who is as greedy as

Villequier. There are a number of others whose only occupation seems to be involving themselves in intrigues, dressing in the most ostentatious way, and attending festivities and tournaments.

It does not take long for the courtiers to realize that Jacques Coeur has the ability and subtlety to give them and the king what they desire. Every sort of luxury arrives at his warehouses – a treasure trove of magical surprises located in Bourges, Lyons and Montpellier. From these three centres, consignments are moved to other smaller warehouses and then sent on to destinations within the country wherever they are required. His system of agents throughout France and the Levant provides him with merchandise delivered direct to his warehouses by his own ships avoiding the need for middlemen. And how does Jacques Coeur communicate with his many agents? Why, by use of the Arab invention of carrier pigeons!

The merchant of Bourges is known as Jacquet to his intimates, and in this way, people who owe him money feel he is their friend and even confide in him. The fact is that over time, everyone owes him money. The ladies buy on credit and the gentlemen of the court take out loans from him to pay for their wives' extravagance. Even Queen Marie and her daughter-in-law, the dauphine Margaret, buy furs and jewels from him in this way – should he refuse them? Most importantly, the king is able to finance his military exploits through the good offices and the enormous loans made to him indirectly by Jacques Coeur through his financial contacts in Italy, and elsewhere.

This makes Jacques popular and sought after, though for some, to be in his debt is difficult, causing resentment.

Being close to the King of France also has advantages and disadvantages, so Jacques does his best to temper his successes with generosity.

In 1435, the Treaty of Arras establishes the long sought peace between Charles VII and Philip of Burgundy who withdraws his support of the English as a result. The following year, the Constable of France, Arthur of Richemont, another of Queen Yolande's protégés, recovers Paris. It is at this time that Jacques Coeur finds himself once again brought into the presence of the all-seeing Yolande, Queen of Sicily and scrutinized by a master. What an extraordinary royal lady, he thinks; if only she were a man, this kingdom would be safe!

He is aware it is through Queen Yolande's efforts that good men replace the venal, greedy courtiers in the king's circle – and her influence on Charles VII cannot be overstated. As a result of a number of meetings with her, Yolande confides that she has worked long and hard to make peace between the king and the Duke of Burgundy. 'My good friend Jacques, I am sure you will agree that it is only through the reconciliation of the king and the duke and their respective followers that a united effort might succeed in banishing the English from French soil.'

'Madame and Majesty, I fully comprehend and indeed I do agree. I met one of the Duke of Burgundy's men recently in Damascus, a most able fellow, and discussed this very topic. It is clear that the combination of our forces is the only possible way forward.'

Then there is the problem of the number of French dukes who have been slowly shifting their loyalty from their rightful king to the English, in particular to benefit from the valuable trade with Flanders that the English control. Jacques has agents in every ducal household and is aware of the girls Queen Yolande places there to lure these faithless French dukes away from their allegiance to the English invader and back to France – carefully chosen young women from Anjou whom she inspires to do their duty to their king and country. Their role is to convince these sovereign lords with reasoning and arguments, and if necessary, with their nubile beauty into fulfilling their obligations as subjects of their king. And how well she succeeds! Each one of her ducal targets comes to realize through the persuasive logic she instils into her girls that the real commitment of a French ducal house must be to France, and not to conquering England. Jacques knows that René is not entirely in accord with these practices of his mother's, but there can be no doubt as to their positive results.The Queen of Sicily gazes into Jacques' eyes as if reading his mind – and he believes she can. 'My friend, I have heard tell much of you since our last meeting, and of your audacious travels. I can see from your presence that you are a man of sound judgement with a true heart. Will you allow me to make use of your remarkable talents?' she says charmingly.

'Madame,' and he bows low to give himself a moment to gather his thoughts, 'it is true that my travels to the Levant and the Near East have taught me much, although there is always more to learn. How can I be of service to your Majesty?'

The queen smiles her famous slightly crooked smile and observes him – *a strong man of medium height in his mid-thirties, and in his prime* she thinks, looking at his regular features. *Yes, he has worked hard and believes in himself and knows his path.* Then she says, 'I believe you can be of great service to both the king and the country, and that is our mutual goal, is it not?' He recalls he mumbled something in reply, but he must have passed her test, because he has no doubt it is through Queen Yolande's intervention that a year later, in 1436, he is summoned to Paris by the king.

Jacques has not met the king since his coronation although he has seen him often in Bourges and bowed to him in greeting, which Charles has always acknowledged. When he wants to buy something, or borrow money, the king sends courtiers to carry out the transaction. Even their business partnership is dealt with by minions. In fact, since the merchant's youthful disgrace at the Mint and despite his Letter of Pardon, Jacques Coeur has always considered himself outside the possible circle of the king's grace. Now here he is actually being summoned by him.

'Ah, Jacques Coeur!' he says in greeting. 'I have need of your fabled skills. I believe you have heard I wish to re-organize France's depleted monetary system?' Jacques bows in acquiescence. 'I have decided to hereby appoint you as Master of the Paris Mint.'

Jacques is taken completely by surprise, but he knows he cannot refuse. Once Charles VII has made up his mind, there is no turning back. He gulps and finds himself accepting a burdensome and time-consuming post that involves preparing all the ordinances concerning the coinage of France; essential work to re-establish the financial stability of the country. He also knows he can do it, and efficiently, which will help business – his goal after all.

Although Jacques knows the work is well within his ability, the long hours and frequent visits to Paris take a toll on his home life. He is aware that Marcée and the children do not see as much of him as they should and it concerns him. 'Marcée, my dear, you do understand why I have accepted these burdensome duties?' he ask her plaintively one evening. Her pursed lips say it all, but he holds her close nonetheless. His family is precious to him – they both know that – but his career perhaps more so.

Two years later, again, he believes, at the prompting of the Queen of Sicily, Jacques Coeur is installed as Charles VII's *'argentier'* – a sort of official bursar or purveyor of high-quality merchandise and luxuries to the king and his court. Inevitably the position is a double-edged sword. Princes and aristocrats are frequently in debt to such people – their credit ostensibly good, backed by their estates and capital – but actually paying those debts is another matter. It is up to him, subtly, to supply his clients with their desires – but only if he feels they can reimburse him – at some time. This new position also puts him in charge of the royal stables, filled with many horses in need of feeding, equipment, shoeing, and exercise yards – a myriad opportunities to make a handsome profit.

In addition, his various agents in Bourges have been negotiating with the king's representatives, and with good reports about him coming from the Queen of Sicily in Marseilles, the king enters into a number of open trading partnerships with Jacques Coeur. This is an unheard-of elevation, and it takes Jacques some time to come to terms with having the monarch as his business partner. Perhaps the glory of it even blurs the dangers somewhat, although Marcée's practical mind is sharper. 'My foolish Jacquet – don't you see you are being used, and to your disadvantage? How can you be an equal partner with the King of France? And in your natural humility, you will put yourself at a disadvantage all the time.'

'You undervalue me, my dearest, I am a merchant born even if not bred. No, the king will not outsmart me at my own trade.'

'Then he will over-rule you, mark my words,' – and she walks away fast to hide her stinging eyes. She has grown stouter following the birth of the children and firmer due to disciplining the younger ones herself in Jacques' constant absences, but she loves her dear, clever, blindly loyal husband as much as ever.

In fact, Jacques Coeur could not be on better official terms with the crown. He builds ships which sail in the name of France throughout the Mediterranean; he trades with the Ottoman Empire where contact with the *infidel* has been forbidden by Rome: gaining this permission was expensive, but he succeeds in obtaining a dispensation from the Pope. As a result, he establishes a number of trading posts for the joint profit of the king and himself.

Whenever Charles VII meets with Jacques Coeur, he treats him as a valued member of his staff – never over familiar, yet neither aloof nor too distant either. The merchant can see that he intrigues the king – a man from nowhere who is making a reputation as some sort of financial genius. Not only is there a great belief in the supernatural among the people at this time, but it is also common lore that persons who rise from obscurity to great wealth do so through the use of some kind of mystical knowledge. Jacques is a proud man, and since he does not have the education of his younger brother Nicholas who went into the Church, nor that of his two elder sons who will go the same way, he likes to be considered somewhat better educated than in fact he is. If people want to believe this, Jacques will not dissuade them, but nor will he pretend to knowledge he does not possess.

By 1445 the king is eager for the re-establishment of French trade in his southern ports which have been severely depleted due to plague and the aggressive practices of the Italian and Aragonese merchants, as well as the rise of Marseilles as a safe haven for French trade. For this reason, he encourages Jacques to bring his ships to Aigues-Mortes rather than Marseilles by allowing him to import spices tax free. This gives Jacques Coeur a valuable advantage over his competitors, as every other port charges ten per cent, and this advantage encourages him to focus on his trade in spices. Furthermore, the king gives him permission to forcibly conscript oarsmen for his galleys. This is not done anywhere else in the Mediterranean, but then, the king and Jacques are engaged in a commercial partnership, and they intend it to pay. Once Jacques succeeds in encouraging Charles to invest heavily in Aigues-Mortes himself he then moves the centre of his shipping trade there once the king agrees to Jacques' sole use of the port for their jointly owned trading ships. Naturally this sort of privilege does not endear Jacques to his competitors, but that, he believes, is the risk one runs in doing business.

Having tried and tested the first *galéasse* he built at his shipyard in Aigues-Mortes, with the help of the king's investment, Jacques builds a further seven such great trading ships there. The precious wood is floated down the Rhône, then into a canal leading to Aigues-Mortes. As for the names of his ships, at Marcée's urging Jacques links them to saints and symbols associated with the king and himself: *Nôtre-Dame-Saint-Denis* in honour of the burial place of French monarchs, *Nôtre-Dame-Sainte-Madeleine*, and *Nôtre-Dame-Saint-Jacques* for the association with his own patron saint.

Ever since Jacques Coeur learnt his lesson with the Mint in Bourges, the merchant has always sought to live within the law. For this reason it is important for his ships to sail out of Montpellier to the Levant making use of the town's special papal dispensation. Christians have long been forbidden by a succession of popes to trade with 'the infidel' and even if the Genoese and the Venetians ignore this edict, Jacques will not.

It is a great gift to be able to choose the right men to be of assistance in one's work, and Jacques Coeur has the good fortune to be most ably served by his nephew through marriage, Jean de Villages, who by now is a young man in his late twenties, tall, lean, strong like most sailors, and nimble both of foot and mind. He has taken charge of his uncle's shipping trade in the Mediterranean, as well as in Egypt and the Levant. Guillaume de Varye, a friend from Jacques' youth in Bourges, is put in charge of the company's finances within France, and becomes his agent in Geneva. It is Guillaume who helps with supplying the court and stocking his first warehouse in Bourges, for their perusal. He is also responsible for inventories, the registration of imports and the payment of taxes.

Another such reliable factor is Guillaume Grimart who married a relation of Jacques' mother, and received a most generous marriage portion from the merchant. Guillaume Grimart becomes the captain of the galley *'Nôtre Dame-Saint-Michel* – a great honour bestowed on him by his employer.

The third in command of Jacques' growing empire is Antoine Noir. His base is Montpellier, and together with his two brothers, his brief is to collect, gently and with tact, what is owed, though on occasion, he has been known to be a little over-zealous.

In all, at the peak of Jacques Coeur's success, he has in his employ some three hundred factors. It is an astonishing business, built on the knowledge of people: which clients can pay and will pay; how to extricate what is owed from those who prove more reluctant. Where necessary, he can wait – he is a patient man. And, he hopes, not a fool.

# Chapter Nine

$\mathcal{H}$aving met both René and Isabelle several times in Bourges, Jacques is always happy to have news of them. He is aware that when Isabelle of Lorraine's father died in 1431, his will stipulated that she and René were to inherit his duchy and rule it together. However, a Lorraine cousin refused to accept that a woman could inherit, and challenged the couple. On Yolande's advice, René fought his challenger and won several times, but then when his horse stumbled, he fell and was captured. Certain that he would be ransomed in the usual way, to his horror he found himself handed over to Philip of Burgundy. At last he could avenge the grave insult to his family of many years ago by the Anjous. Philip's sister had been betrothed to Louis III, the eldest son of Yolande and her husband, and had lived happily with them during four years of her childhood. It was when the Anjous realized that the little girl's father had ordered the murder of their beloved friend and Charles VI's brother, Louis d'Orléans, that they felt unable to join their family to this monster's and they cancelled the betrothal. Little Catherine of Burgundy had been living happily and adored by them all and it broke their hearts to send her back home, but they believed it was the right thing to do.

Perhaps it was the right thing to do, but it was also a terrible slight perpetrated by one branch of the royal family on another, and Philip of Burgundy would never forget or forgive. It was René, who was a small child at the time, who now had to pay the price of Catherine of Burgundy's shame. He was locked in Duke Philip's tower for almost three years following his capture and during this time, Louis d'Anjou died on the mainland of Sicily. It was a terrible blow to them all – Louis had been the family's golden boy, and now René, his brother's heir, is Burgundy's prisoner.

Just at this time, his enemy, Alfonso V, is obliged to return to Aragon from Naples where he had installed himself the previous year. The representatives of René's newly inherited kingdom would much prefer the crown to go to him, but they arrive from Naples to find their king-elect imprisoned. Determined to have an Anjou as their ruler, they crown his wife to represent René until his release.

Isabelle of Lorraine was well-chosen by Yolande for her second son. As well as being the heiress to her father's duchy, she has the same fire in her belly as her mother-in-law. Hearing that Alfonso has left Naples, she makes ready at once to claim her husband's throne on his behalf. Before leaving, she calls at Chinon with her court, including her children, pets and young *demoiselles*, to bid farewell and ask the blessing of the king and of her mother-in-law, henceforth to be known as the Old Queen of Sicily. Isabelle also needs to leave her five-year-old daughter Margaret, too young for the voyage, with Yolande, while her eldest son, ten-year-old Jean, will stay to represent his parents in Lorraine.

Jacques Coeur is at court at Chinon and observes the touching scene of the new young Queen of Sicily curtseying low to her mother-in-law, the Old Queen and the king while handing over her darling youngest and presenting her fledgling court. With his hawk eyes, Jacques is instantly aware of the reason for the frisson in the large room as the king leaves his throne to walk down the ranks of the *demoiselles* of Lorraine. Nor is he alone in noticing the seemingly casual attention the king pays to the last girl in the line, whose eyes are firmly fixed on the floor in natural modesty. No, he is not alone, but most importantly, Queen Yolande too notices not only the king's interest, but also the astonishing beauty of this very young and patently innocent *demoiselle*.

Jacques Coeur was greatly saddened by Louis III's death, even though he had predicted that the young man was too good to last long in this world. Now he is determined to help Isabelle as much as possible. He has been largely responsible for supplying her with whatever she will need in Naples, a court run for some time by a man and without any refinements. He resolves that he and his ships will pass by Naples whenever they make a voyage to the Near East and discover how he can assist this brave young queen.

During Isabelle's first year in Naples. Jacques hears from several of his sea captains who stop there of the warm welcome they receive at the new young court. When he himself visits, Queen Isabelle receives him most graciously, recalling their entertaining afternoon at his warehouse in Bourges. She does not know it was Jacques who provided her with the supplies for her residence, since he instructed his captains to say they were sent by Queen Yolande. In this way, neither queen thinks there is anything to pay.

The court of Naples is enchanting, full of charm and sophistication. All it lacks is the presence of its king. Queen Isabelle makes Jacques promise to call on her whenever he is in the vicinity and he does. Another promise he has made is to call on Queen Yolande in Marseilles whenever he is about to set sail on one of his galleys, and again on his return if she is in the port. If not, he meets with her representatives. In this way he is able to pass on news from the two queens to one another.

On his next voyage to his trading sources, Jacques stops in Naples. Once again Queen Isabelle is a gracious hostess, receiving him as if he were a trusted friend of long standing. Thereafter, Jacques makes a point of calling on her several times a year when he sails by Naples and it is always a pleasure.

One of his secret causes of satisfaction is the affection with which the half-grown cheetah he sent to Naples for King René is treated – Vitesse is as spoilt and as tame as a domestic cat! When he is invited to recount stories of his travels and adventures to the gathered company, it gives him an opportunity to meet Isabelle's *demoiselles* including the youngest his patroness mentioned once in passing

– the young girl with whom the king was so taken at Chinon. He learns from Isabelle that her name is Agnès Sorel and that she has the sole charge of Vitesse, the half-grown cheetah he sent to Naples for King René, since she is the only one who has never been afraid of the animal. Being the youngest at the court, Jacques surmises she has no close friend near her age and therefore befriended the cheetah. He is curious and asks Isabelle if he may speak with her, whereupon the queen puts her finger to her lips and leaves them.

'Mademoiselle Agnès, may I ask you about Vitesse?' The girl smiles shyly but with pleasure. 'Do you know how she came to be here?'

When she looks up at him, he thinks he will drown in the beauty of her eyes and that perfect oval face. 'Oh yes,' and this time a broad smile, 'she was a gift from you, Monsieur Coeur, to our Lord René all of us know that – but I am taking care of her until he comes.'

'I can see she is as fond of you as you are of her.'

'Oh yes, sir, Vitesse and I – well, we are inseparable. When we ride out in the countryside, she runs alongside my horse, and at night she sleeps on a rug by my bed. I leave a window open for her to go out, and with her by me, I am not afraid anyone will come in!' And she laughs, a sweet, unaffected peal of joy.

'And on what do you feed her, my child?'

'Well, she catches rabbits and small deer when we ride out, but most of the time our hunters bring in freshly killed game for her. It sounds unkind, I know, but I think it is good for her to catch her own food sometimes,' and she looks anxious.

'Of course it is,' he reassures her. 'She needs that for her health. I can see she has a good life with you looking after her.'

All the while they are chatting, Jacques is scrutinizing this breathtakingly lovely young girl: her every gesture, her voice, her modest gaze. There is something about her he cannot define, for despite her overwhelming beauty of which she must be aware, she behaves as if she is not. He can see that Yolande takes a special interest in Agnès Sorel, and he suspects the Old Queen has something particular in mind for her.

A further two years pass before Philip of Burgundy finally releases René to join his wife in Naples. Jacques Coeur continues to visit their court whenever he passes in one of his ships, and is sincerely impressed with the king's stewardship. The country is well run and the people show their gratitude to their ruler. During these visits, Jacques is able to form a genuine and lasting friendship with both René and Isabelle, entertaining them and the court with his stories of adventure, and enticing them with his merchandise.

How well René can understand the friendship between his mother and this clever trader, despite their difference in age. Jacques Coeur is not only a most engaging man, he has travelled widely, experienced many different cultures and it seems he understands the needs and desires of everyone. Although the merchant is a natural raconteur, René notes his readiness to listen; nor is he judgemental, even when someone is clearly in the wrong. He looks pensive, purses his lips, absorbs every detail and keeps his own counsel most of the time, unless asked.

The stories he tells enthral them all: René, his family and the *demoiselles* sitting around him wide-eyed as he begins:

'In Cairo,' he starts softly, 'at the slave market,' and there would follow an audible gasp from his mostly young and female audience, 'one day I saw twin blonde girls, about your age,' and he points to one of the *demoiselles* who utters a little shriek of feigned terror as the tale grows darker ...

Or he starts:

'When we were shipwrecked on a small island off the coast of Africa, we stood naked on the sand, drying our clothes by a fire we had made on the beach. After a while, we could feel eyes watching, but nothing stirred from the undergrowth around us. But then, as night fell ...' and they would sit so quietly no one seemed to breathe. His adventures as he tells them are extraordinary and neither René nor Isabelle is sure how many of them are true, until he admits that most are the adventures of others he has picked up just to entertain them.

Whatever Jacques Coeur brings back with him from his voyages to the Levant is sure to appeal to someone, and irresistibly! He always invites those at the court in Naples to visit his galleons; how small they seem for so many men to live and sleep in, as well as holding cargo and live animals for food.

The courtiers and ladies are constantly spellbound in the merchant's presence, and even come to recognize some of his men, who give them a cheery wave or call a greeting in passing. Sometimes he brings his captains to court, always treating senior employees as equals. These men know they have his trust, and he has their loyalty. He has such a clever way with people, from the king to the common man, and communicates with his employees in a way that everyone *wants* to work for him and with him. His enthusiasm is infectious and his hard work beyond doubt. 'That,' René tells Isabelle, 'is the secret of a great merchant prince.'

René, too, is a remarkable man. Queen Yolande is not alone in lauding his talents – people say that they are those of a great magnate, and Jacques agrees. From his grandfather, Louis I d'Anjou, René has inherited a deep love of history of art and its treasures. His parents have given him a wonderful library and a passion for architecture; and from his father-in-law, Duke Charles II of Lorraine, he has acquired a love of music and of Flemish paintings. During the years he spent in the Duke of Burgundy's tower, he learnt to paint with the guidance of a great Dutch artist in residence there. He is a writer of novels, a poet, a landscape gardener, and an organizer of spectacular tournaments for the king and his own numerous guests. Everyone Jacques meets agrees that this second son of Queen Yolande is intelligent, attractive, sensitive and tolerant, and he is pleased to be a resident in René's sovereign territory of Provence.

When Jacques Coeur meets with Queen Yolande again in Marseilles following a number of visits to her son's court at Naples, they walk along the busy quay watching ships unloading and nets being folded. She asks him several practical questions about ways in which she can help her son there, concerning the needs of the court and the children

– Isabelle has lost another recently, and Jacques brought her some Eastern medicine that seemed to help her. Just before leaving, she mentions Isabelle's *demoiselles*.

'Jacques, dear friend, I am curious to know how the youngest of the ladies with the court in Naples has settled into the life there. Can you tell me anything about the one called Agnès Sorel? I have a personal interest in her,' she says with her mysterious smile. Jacques is never really surprised by anything Queen Yolande asks – everything is ordained somehow.

'Majesty, she is quite the most natural beauty I have ever seen.'

'Yes, tell me more,' she urges him.

'Perhaps what makes her so unusual is her total lack of awareness of her own physical perfection, coupled with her astonishing sweetness of nature and expression.'

'Yes?' says the queen, moving on a little to examine a fisherman's catch, but clearly waiting to hear more.

'Madame, hers is an elusive beauty, rare, fragile, despite its overwhelming impact. Perfect features, light golden skin, flaxen hair. She colours easily when she feels she is being observed, which suits her. She is naturally modest, her eyes always cast down, her smile half nervous, half playful. It is almost as though she is unsure of herself, although she must have been praised often.'

'Thank you, dear friend. Tell me, do you find her intelligent? And what about the other *demoiselles*, and the court? Can you tell me how they react to Agnès? Do they resent her beauty? Is she conceited at all?'

'Oh no, Madame, quite the opposite. Everyone appears to adore her: the ladies, the gentlemen and the servants;

even the cheetah I brought for your son never leaves her side! And yes, she is both intuitive and intelligent. She thinks before she speaks.'

The Old Queen smiles to herself. 'Now tell me other news.' And Jacques Coeur discusses trade and the harbour and various points of business with his patroness while his mind circles around her earlier questions.

For the next few years, King René takes great pleasure in his new kingdom. Together with Isabelle he covers his territory and comes to know many of the landlords he visits, interesting himself in their crops and in farming in general. Having never been involved in the running of his family estates in Provence, he discovers a new inter-est in agriculture, and most of all in gardening. Since everything seems to grow on the peninsula, he is never short of new plants for the terraces around the palace, while the *demoiselles* spend part of each day arranging flowers in vases and in their hair. It is a charmed exist-ence for them all.

Then come the years of skirmishes with his cousin, Alfonso V, back from Aragon and seeking to take René's throne: some battles are won, others lost. Yolande hears regularly from the merchant and is in no doubt about the doomed outcome of her beloved son's dream, but she continues to send more money, more supplies.

Inevitably, the moment comes when René must face the future – which is bleak. Defeat by Alfonso's superior forces is inevitable, and the day arrives when René cannot allow the ladies of the court to remain near the fighting any longer.

Jacques has expected this decision for some time; two of his ships have been waiting in the port to carry the ladies and the non-fighting staff back to René's port of Marseilles. Paradise was too good to last.

# Chapter Ten

*E*arly in 1440, Queen Yolande had summoned Jacques Coeur to come to her dower château of Saumur in Anjou to bring a wardrobe for her granddaughter Marguerite, René and Isabelle's youngest. He saw she had blossomed into a dazzling twelve-year-old soon be presented to the young Holy Roman Emperor Frederick. He found the Old Queen looked well, and the Lady Marguerite was enchanting, but Jacques was aware that despite her warm welcome and light-hearted conversation, Yolande was only living for the homecoming of her son René. The merchant knew that she had done the calculations just as he had some six or more years ago. There were simply no more funds to send to Naples. The time was approaching for the dream to end and both knew then without saying that it was near.

They were right. Later that same year, Isabelle arrives from Naples with her entourage and Jacques Coeur is summoned once again to Saumur. He notes with pleasure from her requests that this young Queen of Sicily has the same refined taste as her mother-in-law, who knows there is much Isabelle will need from the good merchant to enhance her palaces in Lorraine and Anjou. During the past two years, while the fighting has been fierce on the Italian peninsula, Jacques has not been to visit the court of Naples, and he is curious, anxious in fact, to hear all that has happened in the meantime. As Isabelle tells the story, her voice fading as she relates how the sun slowly set on that enchanted period of their lives.

It is on this visit to Saumur that Jacques Coeur is struck by the vision of beauty the nineteen-year-old Agnès Sorel has grown to become in the past two years. Like the other ladies of Isabelle's suite, she wears her hairline plucked high, exposing her forehead; her eyebrows are shaped to a thin line in the current fashion, making her candid blue eyes appear even larger than they already are. Her profile is straight from the forehead to the tip of her very fine nose, without the usual dip between the eyes. Her mouth is small, with well-shaped lips, and he catches a glimpse of perfect little pearls of teeth whenever he manages to coax her to smile.

Withdrawing to the back of the room the merchant observes the *demoiselles* as they sit around the Old Queen discussing their favourite parts of Naples. They describe their rides out into the countryside, and recount how they climbed Vesuvius, with its thin trail of white smoke escaping from the top of the crater. They tell Yolande of the fruits and vegetables they did not know before, the various flowers climbing and tumbling everywhere, and the songs they learnt to sing. As the *demoiselles* continue with their storytelling, Agnès, who has her arm around the cheetah's neck, looks with fascination at a large blue pendant hanging from a long chain around the Old Queen's neck.

'Ah, Agnés – I see you are looking at this stone?' says Yolande, holding it between thumb and forefinger, and she smiles again as the other girls move closer to inspect it.

'I believe you all know our friend, the merchant Jacques Coeur,' and they nod in unison, unaware of his presence behind them. 'He found it in a city on the coast of Egypt called Alexandria. He was told that it had belonged to an Egyptian ruler in ancient times who had been given it by a Nubian potentate in exchange for his son's freedom.' She pauses, seeing their enraptured faces. 'It seems the prince had been captured in an ambush by Arabs as he rode in the desert, and was caught in a net. Still, it had taken a dozen of them to pin him down, and then they sold him as a slave. But due to his height, magnificent frame and handsome face, he was given to Pharaoh, Egypt's ruler.' Her voice is low and soft, like a caress – they could listen to her stories forever. 'Somehow this, the price of the young man's freedom, came to our friend, Jacques Coeur, and from him to me.' Then, with that winning and slightly crooked smile, she sends them off to see to their Lady Isabelle.

The Old Queen watches Jacques as he surveys the apparition that Agnès Sorel, has become. Quietly, when the others cannot hear, she asks the merchant to choose some quality fabric, enough for two dresses and a cloak for the *demoiselle*, since she has no warm clothes for the winter.

It is obvious to Jacques that Agnès is the most junior of Queen Isabelle's ladies, since she is always the last in line. So why is she being shown such favour? Later he discovers that the Old Queen plans for her to remain behind when Isabelle takes Marguerite home to Nancy. It seems Yolande will miss her granddaughter's joyful, youthful company, and Agnès is to replace her, yet he wonders ...

The Old Queen asks Jacques to show the girl his choices of fabrics for her winter wardrobe, and in doing so, try to gauge something of her character. Apart from talking to her alone about the cheetah years ago, he has not spent time in general conversation with Agnès. After a while, Jacques admits to his patroness that he has fallen under Agnès Sorel's honest, calm spell – where he suspects he will always remain.

# Chapter Eleven

Wherever the great merchant of Bourges has met with Queen Yolande, whether at court in Bourges, at Angers, Tours, her port of Marseilles or her château of Saumur, he has felt bewitched in some way. Each time she intrigues him more, and he takes every opportunity he can to converse with her. During his many years of travel within France and abroad, he has never met a character like hers anywhere. Despite her high-minded ideals and obvious morality, he is certain she will allow nothing to stand in the way of solving the problems of the kingdom.

Yolande is made of stern stuff and she is not prepared to give up on her quest to establish peace and a sound government in her husband's country. She continues guiding Charles VII, yet just when the country was in the young king's grasp, the crown on his head, the holy oil on his forehead, inexplicably he slipped back again, easily persuaded, towards his natural inclination for debauchery and self-defeat. She extricated him repeatedly from his own follies, but the pattern repeats itself time and again. Hard work; success; and when victory is within sight, reason gives way to dissipation. Why? Because the English are still on France's soil.

After many years of observing the Queen of Sicily, Jacques Coeur is at last beginning to understand her. He is aware that she wants to remain unobtrusively in the background, but with her hands firmly on the controls, forever passing any credit due over to her son-in-law, as dauphin and then as Charles VII. In fact, it is only now that Jacques, so sensitive and astute in other ways, realises it was Yolande who has been behind everything positive that has come the way of the king and other members of her family; advantages they think they themselves have earned. Yet she has never desired – never needed – credit; she just wants results. Jacques has observed it all, and then finally, after all she has done for Charles, the lacklustre boy she worked so hard to turn into a worthy king, and before her strength and indeed her life, fade completely, this astonishing queen produces her trump card: Agnès Sorel.

In November of the following year 1442, it grieves Jacques Coeur to hear of the death of this remarkable lady. She who has always been called 'the Four-Times-Queen' never actually ruled as queen in Sicily, or Naples, or Cyprus or Jerusalem, nor travelled to any of those places. And yet, with her naturally imperious aspect, this eldest daughter of the King of Aragon, granddaughter of France's great King Jean-le-Bon, could well have worn four crowns.

With considerable relief the merchant hears that one of his ships has brought King René safely back from Naples to Marseilles, though not in time to see his mother before she died at Saumur. When they meet at her funeral at Angers, René embraces the merchant, an unusual gesture from a king to a commoner, but this is the man who has saved the lives of his family and then his own. 'Jacques, my good friend, I thank you for all you have done for me and my family. Now, my failing to return before my mother's death distresses me even more than losing my throne.'

'Sire, at least she died knowing you had arrived safely in your land of Provence. Take comfort, I beseech you.'

The funeral is attended by her family, her many friends, the staff from her houses and estates, and those nobles who can be spared from the fight against the English; all witness the overwhelming sadness of King René. Jacques Coeur mixes freely with the courtiers, knowing them all, and feels the sincerity of their mourning for the great Queen of Sicily.

Isabelle of Lorraine arrives from Nancy, overjoyed to see her husband returned safely from Naples despite the sadness of the occasion, and they embrace for all the court to see. She has brought her *demoiselle* Agnès Sorel to attend to her. *A good choice*, thinks Jacques, *since she alone lived with Queen Yolande at Saumur during her last year*. As he catches the Lady Isabelle's eye and bows, he cannot help being curious about the plan the Old Queen was devising for this beautiful young *demoiselle*, keeping her by her side – teaching her – what? Certainly something important, for Queen Yolande always had a plan.

Charles VII cannot leave the army to attend the funeral

of his *'bonne mère'*, but it is well known that he revered her and mourns her sincerely. 'If he had only followed all her wise suggestions, and kept around him the men she sent him, his life would be much easier,' thinks Jacques – and he is probably not alone in that thought. The king's dramatic fluctuations of mood have always been a source of curiosity to the merchant, and he is certain the all-seeing queen noticed from his earliest years how Charles alternated between great energy and enthusiasm, only to fall into depressions so deep that he could barely stir himself out of his lethargy for days on end. Could the recurring madness of his father Charles VI have anything to do with it? Are these remarkable mood swings perhaps an inherited infirmity?

With time, the advisers installed at the suggestion of Queen Yolande *do* surround the king, his decisions improve accordingly, and the court becomes Angevin. Pierre de Brézé, is made the seneschal of Anjou, Yolande's home territory – it was in her gift and no doubt she suggested it to the king. Pierre has been a loyal member of the Anjou camp since he arrived a young page to serve her husband.

Queen Yolande's protégés have always been a source of interest to Jacques Coeur which is the reason he keeps an eye on the rapidly rising star of Pierre de Brézé. He finds the young man's character confusing. To some he is regarded as a paragon. The poet Jacques Milet of Orléans, a friend of the court, announced to René one day when they were discussing the Battle of Patay: 'That young Pierre de Brézé who is always by your side is really remarkable. He seems to have the courage of Hector, the wisdom of Nestor, and is a better military leader than Caesar!' René guffawed and when he repeated it to his cousin Jean de Dunois, was surprised when he just smiled and nodded. Jacques himself saw something of Pierre in action on the way to Rheims and was in no doubt then that he was a natural leader of men, a good soldier who took astonishing personal risks at the head of his troop.

Something else that struck the merchant during a conversation he had with Georges Chastellain from the court of Philip of Burgundy, a courtier who is not a friend of Pierre's – if anything, he is in the opposite camp – yet he declared: 'Pierre de Brézé is such a smooth talker: where his sword does not convince, his words will succeed.' Jacques has to agree; he too has always recognized Pierre as one of the most civilized knights of his time. As well as being incredibly brave, he is such a brilliant raconteur that no one could possibly fall asleep in his company! Pierre's ambition is obvious, but his true goals still elude the merchant's inquisitive mind – for the time being.

Charles de Dunois is another of the young men nurtured by Yolande with her children at Angers and in Provence. Jacques has observed Dunois, and admires him: the way he has always held back, loyal to the King and watching for those who want to entrap him. 'Clever, brave, a natural leader, born for military life,' is René's opinion. 'He has not changed since our childhood; always a credit to his father, Louis d'Orléans.' Much of what Jacques knows of the childhood of the royal cousins is due to Juana, Queen Yolande's Spanish governess, who she sent to Bourges to be with Marie, and who knew Charles Dunois since he came to live with them at Angers. Juana's friendship with Marcée grew steadily ever since she arrived in the city and in her loneliness, she would sit with the Coeurs in their home and tell them the stories of the Anjous' and their cousins' childhoods spent together in Angers and Provence. It was Juana who patched their wounds after fights and listened to them even more than Yolande.

Dunois is handsome, charming, tactful and inherently noble – a worthy product of the great queen's teaching in the nursery at Angers. Just looking at him, it is clear to Jacques that this young man would willingly die for his king – and for the Anjous to whom he recognizes he owes everything. *How proud he would have made his father.*

## Chapter Twelve

In 1441, Jacques Coeur, merchant of Bourges, son of a furrier, receives the king's letters of ennoblement for himself and his family. Marcée, thinks Jacques, is possibly even more overwhelmed than he is! She gives a dinner in their house in Bourges for their extended family and neighbours, as well as her husband's principle factors, all friends from his childhood: Jean de Villages, Guillaume Gimart, the three Noir brothers, and, of course, their ever-dependable Guillaume de Varye. These men are the backbone of Jacques Coeur's business empire, and he wants them to share in his good fortune.

But he has to laugh – *him*, a noble! If only my father could see me now, he thinks. How he would slap his thigh and guffaw! Jacques knows it is not for his talents or abilities that he is being honoured. It is much simpler than that: the king owes him money and this is one way he has of paying. However, it works both ways, since from this time onwards, Jacques is eligible to attend the court, where he can make important connections and woo future clients.

His elevation entitles him to a coat of arms, and the great man consults his family. 'Marcée my dear, you first: what do you think we should have as our emblem? A boat, representing the sailing merchant?' 'Well, you really made your first money from importing spices ...' 'Jean, you are my eldest – what do you think?' 'Papa, we don't really have a family animal do we? I think we should use our name of Coeur and use a heart for our name?' After more deliberation, Jacques asks: 'What do you feel about shells?' Blank looks. 'For coquilles Saint-Jacques,' and they all roar with laughter. 'Well why not?'

'But you aren't even involved in the fishing business,' laughs one of his boys.

'True, but I agree – a mixture of hearts for our family name, and shells for my given name. Not too grand and most appropriate?' And of course, no one wants to spoil this remarkable day, and they all agree.

'Now, the motto. On this one I have decided, because it is something in which I truly believe: "To a valiant heart, nothing is impossible". When he announces this, there is a chorus of 'Hurrah!' as well as 'Bravo!' And it is settled – at least within the family.

Although Jacques can see the advantages his ennoblement will bring to his business, he also knows that it pleases his dear Marcée, and that makes him happy. She is a good wife to him and a loving but firm mother to their children: sound, honest and hard-working. *Why shouldn't she enjoy having a title? I am truly fortunate to have her as my wife, my other half.*

*

One day, Pierre de Brézé says to Jacques: 'The Old Queen of Sicily, our great patroness, told me once that you were someone to watch, since men like you should sit on the King's Council.' Jacques is pleasantly surprised to hear this, and more so when, true to his word, Pierre puts forward his name and he is accepted – a position that gives him direct access to the monarch. This happened at a time, it is noticed – certainly by Jacques Coeur – that Pierre did not put forward the name of the dauphin.

During the next six years, the king makes use of Jacques Coeur's diplomatic skills, sending him on several ambassadorial missions to various parts of the country. As a member of the nobility, he takes his seat on the Council and reports on the tax situation within his area. The fact that he has also been appointed a judge and a lawyer due to his clever wording of contracts and years of methodically studying the legal aspects of his businesses enables him to be of great use to the king solving for him a variety of disputes within the country and abroad. In his slow, deliberate and sensible way, by reviewing past cases and consulting reference books, Jacques even manages to solve their disagreements with the Genoese – to the king's as well as their joint business advantage. The merchant is not a learned man like his younger brother Nicholas who went into the church. Jacques has no Latin, and his formal schooling did not go beyond the age of fourteen – but his intelligence and instinct has helped him acquire extensive knowledge through his travels and experiences in so many different parts of the known world.

*

Jacques Coeur's armed ships, with sixty rowers or more in each sail proudly under the colours of France, are carrying the king's commissions as well as his own. Since many of their enterprises are the same, sometimes it is difficult to know precisely where to divide their interests, but as long as they both make a profit, no reasons arise for them to disagree.

There are times when the anti-Christian sentiment of the Muslims makes trade in the Near East almost impossible. Jacques urges Charles VII to send an embassy to the Sultan of Egypt, and to this the king agrees. The delegation is led by Jean de Villages, his right-hand man in all his dealings, and captain of his new ship *La Madeleine*. Jacques chooses him because he is presentable, sensible, calm but quick-thinking; he is also blessed with a charming and convincing manner of persuasion, a rare gift of communication rather like Jacques' own. Jean de Villages has become the admiral of his uncle's fleet and has responsibility for his entire trade in the Levant. Placing his total confidence in this young man, Jacques Coeur regards him as his younger 'other self'.

Bearing letters from the King of France, as well as carefully chosen gifts, Jean de Villages does exactly as he has been briefed. As a result of his meeting with the Sultan, a guarantee with special privileges is granted to French merchant ships, which will henceforth be welcome throughout Egypt's ports. There could not be a better outcome: no more harassment of French ships or sailors; no more danger of piracy in Egyptian waters. And best of all, unrivalled access to the markets of Egypt's Sultan who recommends that France places consuls in the key cities of his country.

With such a solid assurance of non-aggression and even support for French merchants, Jacques Coeur begins to send the Egyptians French merchandise. One of their requests, which surprises him, is the demand for European-style dresses and coats, wigs and jewellery, all to be made in France especially for the Egyptians! Naturally, the French manufacturers oblige. As for furs and skins, he exports to Egypt every kind: lamb, karakul, sheep, deer, goat, rabbit – especially white – and squirrel. Nights, he knows, can be cold in the desert. The Egyptians also want leather – not only the tanned leather of cows, sheep and goats, but some unusual skins especially commissioned for his clients in Cairo: the delicately treated hides of dolphin, whale and tuna. Unsurprisingly, his main export is salt, plentiful in France and of vital importance in hot countries.

For those cold nights, he chooses wool cloth from Poitou, Normandy, Burgundy, Berry, Picardy and Flanders, from Rouen and other cities, all dyed in the most glorious colours. Lille and Bourges specialize in black dyes. Some of the wool is blanket weight, or medium weight for coats; then there are the fine weaves, which are prized by tribal sheikhs as they keep out the heat by day but warm them when the sun sets and the desert chill descends. The highly valued and costly camelot, a mixture of cashmere and mohair, is one of the more expensive textiles Jacques trades for export.

Fabrics in a multitude of colours woven from a mix of cotton and wool, or cotton mixed with linen, all sell well. Jacques fusses about in his warehouses, checking to see that the fabrics are carefully categorized for weight and quality, and marked accordingly. How he enjoys the organization – he has a tidy mind and everything in his world has its proper place. His beloved Marcée sometimes teases him about his absorption with minutiae, but that is the way he is. She visits him daily in the warehouse, bringing a basket of refreshments, but his two eldest sons never come. Since Jeanne d'Arc's stay in Bourges, these two boys have wanted to go into Holy Orders. Jacques' brother was a canon in the Sainte-Chapelle of Bourges, now appointed Bishop of Luçon, and the family consider it a great honour for one of their number to join a religious order. Much as he would have liked their companionship in trade especially in the Levant and the Near East, to share his varied experiences of on his travels, he joins in Marcée's pleasure at their, elder sons' decision.

Following the success of Jean de Villages' visit to the Sultan of Egypt, Jacques cannot resist making the next trip there himself as captain of his own little merchant fleet to see what else he can bring home from the Sultan's warehouses for the king and his many new customers. Arriving in Cairo, Jacques is welcomed warmly by the Sultan, and empties all his French merchandise. For the journey home, he is spoilt for choice and loads his ships in Alexandria as well as in Boulak on the Nile with extravagant offerings from the court in Cairo.

Among the gifts the sultan insists on presenting to Charles VII, and which Jacques is obliged to bring home, is a quantity of Chinese porcelain, and a fine young leopard. It seems the Sultan has heard how the court in Naples appreciated the cheetah Jacques brought them. Perhaps the Sultan imagines French kings like to be accompanied by spotted cats instead of hunting dogs? The merchant is not keen to bring back this dangerous gift, but he cannot refuse it either, especially once he has been assured that the beast has been carefully hand-reared with the King of France in mind.

The cheetah came as a docile cub and this is a fully grown and strong leopard, even if allegedly 'reared by gentle hands' (*and how many were bitten off – crosses his mind*). At first Jacques is anxious about what to feed the animal, but its presence on deck – on a chain – certainly makes the rowers pull harder! The four goats and three sheep brought on board for the crew will have to feed the leopard instead until they stop for water and get more. However, he knows the king will be pleased to receive the leopard, and in good health.

With his many purchases packed into the hold as well as the sixty rowers, there is not much extra space for live-stock – or the leopard, which Jacques decides to keep in his cabin at night, firmly tied in one corner. It was a relief to hear from the Sultan that he is relatively tame, but Jacques is taking no chances while he sleeps. His standing with the crew reaches new heights once they see him emerge smiling each morning with the leopard on its chain; in fact, he becomes quite fond of it. Every rower has a line hanging overboard to catch their own fish, and no one objects to their meat ration feeding the leopard.

As for his imports into France, each of his ships carries the contents of an Aladdin's cave. From the Baltic area come the best furs: ermine, mink, marten, lynx, fox – white and red – and, best of all, the prized sable. And the fabrics he brings home: damask embroidered with all the animals of the East; silk taffetas in every shade that crackle to the touch; the lightest, almost transparent woven silks from Baghdad and Bokhara; silk crêpe from Syria embroidered with thread of gold and dyed in a dozen hues of blue, turquoise, every red in the spectrum, and all the shades of yellow from the rising to the setting sun.

More silks come from India, in different exotic colours – shocking pinks, purples, deep greens and blues. Jacques collects the seeds that are sometimes used for making dyes, especially indigo from Bagdad. Packed carefully in his cases, he brings every tint of silk velvet, as soft to the touch as a baby rabbit's fur, sometimes embroidered with gold and silver thread.

Whole elephant tusks fit into the holds of his ships, and ivory carved ingeniously into myriad shapes: combs, the backs and handles of mirrors, the handles of knives, small figurines, little boxes, bibelots and dice. He even has sets of carved ivory teeth to replace those missing from a pretty face. There are exotic feathers from birds never seen in France, as well as from peacock, ostrich, golden and silver pheasant, emu: long feathers and short, in a thousand hues. How they will dance on the helmets of the knights and the head-bands of their prancing steeds!

As for spices and herbs, there are too many to count, and what delicious smells waft up from the ship's hold! Many of the herbs are medicinal – or some think them to be; others are used for dying cloth. He brings amber said to cure chest aches – to be worn in a small sachet hanging around the neck. There is powdered sugar from Cyprus, musk from China, and his customers' favourites: cinnamon, cloves and pepper. Some herbs and spices are employed as food preservatives, and because these are very expensive, it becomes a status symbol to use them as seasoning.

As for scents, there is an endless choice: bottles and bottles of different perfumes, heady enough to make a strong man weak with desire. And precious stones: there is no limit to quantity, quality or size, although rubies impress Jacques the most – red as blood – and of course, pearls. He has gold moulded or woven or beaten into jewellery such as has never been seen in France, nor could be imagined: bracelets set with precious stones; rings for fingers and toes; earrings and necklaces or torques; head ornaments and brooches of every shape and size, all glittering with coloured stones.

Not surprisingly, his imports always exceed the value of his exports, but he makes up the difference by paying his suppliers in silver ingots, a trade that is officially banned in France, though with the king as his partner, there is no difficulty. Since the Egyptians exchange it pound for pound with gold, Jacques makes a good profit for the king – and for himself. He is aware that there are spices to be had by way of the Atlantic Ocean, and naturally the gold trade from Africa is of interest to a merchant like him, but he decides not to deal beyond the Levant, and his business remains within the confines of the Mediterranean.

# Chapter Thirteen

𝒯he business interests of the king and those of Jacques Coeur are so interwoven that the merchant cannot but see the two as one and he continues to watch Queen Yolande's protégés. He is certain that the *demoiselle* Agnès Sorel is a part of that merging. When he saw her again at Saumur on her return with Isabelle from Naples, he realized at once that she will have a remarkable future. Yes, he had noticed her gentle beauty in Naples, but as one of the many lovely *demoiselles* around Queen Isabelle.

'Note her well,' she told him at Saumur, 'she will go far and have need of you.' And therefore he watches her, the graceful movements and her light laughter – a bubbling stream of sound, irresistible and intelligent. She is unassuming and knows her place, but Jacques can sense she is aware she has a mission of some kind. From his familiarity with women he can see that this maiden is pure, without guile or malice of any kind. Did the wise Old

Queen intend her for Good King René? Surely not! Pierre de Brézé, perhaps? He is a worthy protégé of Queen Yolande's – and rightly so, with his dedication, intelligence, charm, good looks, and voice of velvet. That voice alone can bring the birds out of the trees, just as it brings the pretty ladies of the court to surround him and hang on his every word. What a raconteur he is! And how gaily he greets the merchant:

'My dear Jacquet – what temptations are you dangling in front of the king and the court today? How can anyone resist your enticements? When I marry, I shall have to lock my wife away so she cannot ruin me buying the array of irresistible treasures you procure for us weak-willed courtiers and our ladies!'

For young and old Pierre's gallantries slip off his silver tongue. *One has to smile,* thinks Jacques. That young man has such a natural and easy appeal – but somehow the merchant has never been totally convinced. Pierre's charm is too practised, too smooth. Much of him *is* sincere, of that Jacques is sure – certainly his courage. But there is something that unnerves the cool merchant. Is it Pierre's shrewd showmanship? He always knows when to hold back, whereas most men with his looks, charm and obvious attraction would take more advantage of those gifts. Pierre waits – no matter how much he is tempted – his self-control is total. When Jacques offers him a remarkable stallion just arrived from the Barbary Coast, and at a price he knows Pierre can afford, he turns the animal down. This surprises him – he knows Pierre's love of horses, and this one is finer than any courtier's or even in the royal stables at Bourges.

So far, Jacques has not been able to put his finger on what it is that bothers him – just instinct. Like Charles de Maine – another handsome charmer without fortune; both he and Pierre are unashamedly ambitious, but Jacques still has to discover their true goals. As a son of Queen Yolande, Charles has the advantage of high birth, but possibly slightly less intelligence and courage than Pierre de Brézé. *It will be interesting to see what fate has in store for these two privileged young courtiers*, he muses to himself.

As the king's *argentier*, Jacques Coeur is in charge of the Civil List – the income paid to the royal family to cover their cost of living. The *argentier* is also appointed to provide the king and his court with their material desires, and more – to help them *have* those desires. Although the Coeur family has been ennobled, to his somewhat wry amusement Jacques notes that he is still stuck in the role of a merchant supplying an elite clientele – of which he is supposed to be a member!

No one would deny that he is a clever businessman, and tough. By offering better terms and more irresistible goods, it is not long before he eliminates the other court suppliers and creates a monopoly for himself. Not that the other merchants go quietly – there is much muttering in the inns and eating houses of how they have been ruined and must leave Bourges to seek markets elsewhere, since they cannot compete with that upstart Jacques Coeur. Not only does he seek out for his clientele the most beautiful, the most desirable products from all over the Near East; he enters into joint ventures with the bankers and merchants of Bruges and Geneva. The king realizes he can profit handsomely from his joint business ventures with his newly ennobled merchant, and agrees to finance the building of more vessels in Jacques' shipyards. Thereafter, even more of his trade is carried out for their mutual profit.

The merchant knows he is not loved by everyone and freely acknowledges it. To be a success, it is necessary to be tough with debtors, although he employs others to do this. He knows he is a hard man by any standards, and through his success, inevitably, jealousy and envy follow him. Many of his clients overspend, something he certainly does not attempt to prevent them doing. A number have even been ruined by their greed to possess what he has stored in his warehouses. Others claim that he charges the king too much for what he buys – *but that is always the way with trade*, Jacques reflects. *Those who cannot afford to buy accuse those who can of paying too much.* He chooses to ignore the complaints.

Nevertheless, there is a growing swell of discontent in the town. Marcée sees it in the wives of failed merchants as they gather in a huddle outside church bemoaning their lot and turning their backs to her. When she tells Jacques, he just hugs her and shrugs, 'Why don't they try and compete with me, and travel like I do and bring back more desirable goods than I do? Am I stopping anyone? Do I undercut the others? No, they should work harder.' But Marcée, who always has her ear to the ground, listens and does not like the increasing envy of women whom she counted formerly as being friendly acquaintances.

## Chapter Fourteen

𝓘n 1443, the two courts - that of the King of France and the court of Lorraine, whose duke and duchess are still called the King and Queen of Sicily – meet at Toulouse and join their vast entourages. Charles VII, a life-long lover of beauty, is forty years old and is observed to be instantly overwhelmed by the unparalleled loveliness of the twenty-year-old *demoiselle* from Lorraine, Agnès Sorel. His admiration of the virtuous Agnès is undisguised, and it does not take long for the rumours to begin. Jacques is not always with the court, but his agents keep him fully informed.

During the year that has passed since the Queen of Sicily asked him to bring warm clothes to Saumur for Agnès, it never crossed his mind for one instant that this girl was being carefully prepared and for such a long time for the delectation of the king *by his own mother-in-law*. At last Jacques realizes what she planned and yet he knows he has still not entirely appreciated the full measure of his late patroness. That queen was *steel* and now finally he realizes that nothing – *nothing* – mattered to Yolande as much as the well-being and the security of the king and the kingdom. After all, although she came to France a Spanish princess, Yolande of Aragon was born of a Valois mother. France was entrenched in her blood as well as in her heart. No price was too high to keep the king content, alert and inspired for the good of his kingdom.

Jacques did not expect her to die so soon – perhaps her strength of character gave him the impression she would live forever, and she was still strong and well by repute at her end. Now that he finally understands what she had been planning and for so long, he hopes the wise Old Queen had been able to spend enough time with Agnès to prepare her fully for the immense task ahead of her.

When the king begins to ask Jacques to provide small but exquisite trinkets, he knows for whom; then a quality Arabian mare; the softest cloth for court clothes and for a lady's riding apparel. Jacques says nothing but is prepared for every demand. When not at court himself, informers keep him abreast of every small development: the unusually long stay in Toulouse of both courts; the intimate dinners arranged by Lady Isabelle among friends with the king and always including Agnès, who is invited to sing or play the harp. Then her move away from the other *demoiselles'* apartment to one of her own – 'So that I can go to my Lady Isabelle and soothe her temples when her headaches come without disturbing the others,' is what he hears she tells them. Finally there is the shift from the Lady Isabelle's household to that of Queen Marie, and the whispers at court that inevitably follow.

Throughout all these small but significantly escalating changes in the position of this enchanting *demoiselle*, Jacques is frequently at court, and every time they meet, they exchange friendly words, followed soon by conversations. More and more often during the court's long stay in Toulouse, Jacques would pass by with business for the king and spontaneously bring him a trinket that perhaps he 'might wish to give a friend'. He comes to know her taste and more importantly, her heart, and it moves him to find one so pure amongst many quite the opposite.

Slowly, merchant and mistress begin to exchange ideas, he probing her likes and dislikes, gauging her taste and preferences. In this way he can better advise the king what to give her. More and more often she shares little queries or truths with him, treating him as if he is a benign older brother or uncle: 'Jacquet, for this is what I shall call you, what do you think I could give the king that would please him? Should I write a poem for him?'

'My lady, why not compose something on your harp – he says that your playing soothes him so.'

And they continue as well with small domestic exchanges – what colour silk she should wear, or his advice on her headdress. And her cheetah – since she is old now and hardly needs a lead at all, should Agnès not send her to Lorraine to live out her life in comfort there, rather than with the court?

'My lady, yes, she should be sent away, she still frightens the serving women, but without you, she would pine away. I think you will have to keep her by you, but perhaps more in your rooms, and fence off an area of garden for her since she hardly runs anymore.'

And in this tranquil manner, Jacques and Agnès build their friendship.

Although he finds her to be intelligent and sharp-witted, Jacques realizes at once that she has no ambition whatsoever for herself – all she cares about is the king, and discreetly sharing her good fortune. The merchant's greatest fear is the use that others could easily make of her goodness to their own advantage, and although he perceives Agnès as a potentially valuable customer, each time they come into contact, Jacques feels more protective towards her.

'Jacquet dear friend, I would like to give the dauphine a gift – can you suggest me something.' And he does. Their alliance is a joy to them both, and also the companionship of Marie de Belleville, another of the *demoiselles* of Lorraine moved to the service of Queen Marie. Jacques realizes this has been done solely for Agnès's comfort, since none of Queen Marie's ladies could afford to befriend the king's mistress. Nor does he want to think too much about Queen Marie and her feelings – he notes that she uses his services less since it is known he is Agnès's friend, but nonetheless, the queen is always courteous to him.

During the many months that the court spends in Toulouse, Jacques Coeur comes to understand the true character of Agnès Sorel. Surrounded often by the king's fawning courtiers, it is not surprising he has become a cynic, and so the quality that impresses him most is her genuine, total devotion to the *person of the king*, not just his position – even though they are one.

Wise as well as intuitive, the merchant can see that Agnès is most anxious not to cause envy – which she does by merely existing, let alone by virtue of the king's daily signs of devotion. Having observed the venal courtiers for many years, Jacques has almost lost sight of someone pure among them, and he really begins to appreciate Agnès for this unexpected quality.

'Oh, Jacquet, whenever you appear at the door of my suite, I know I am in trouble. Please put away whatever you have hidden in a secret pocket and do not show it to me,' she pleads. And he, knowing his victim is as susceptible as most women, says brightly: 'very well my lady, but may I just stay a little while and tell you a story?' Whereupon he sits and shares some rose sherbet with her or some delicious fruit juice and tells her a fable, just as he would sit down with the *demoiselles* at the court in Naples:

'Not long ago, when I was walking in the souk in Damascus – I am sure I have told you about it? No? Well, it is the longest covered market in the world, so long it seems there is no end to it, and just little points of light filter through the joins between the pieces of flat wood above forming its covering. Suddenly, I was approached by a very elegant gentleman, an Arab wearing a robe of the finest cream wool, covered by an even finer cloak in black – a woollen cloak woven so delicately it looked like chiffon and edged in the narrowest gold braid. He addresses me in French which surprises me: "Kind sir," he says, "I have heard you know much about beautiful things, might I beg you to give an opinion on this?" With that, he opens his hand and sitting in his palm there is an egg-shaped emerald the size of your small fist, completely covered with tiny, gold fleur-de-lys, laid into the stone so that its surface is completely smooth. Would you like to hold it?' And before she can refuse he opens his hand and puts it in hers. A small gold ring is attached at one end, and pulling a chain out of a pocket, he slips it in and hangs the jewel around her neck. Where, of course, it remains. She rushes to the looking glass and murmurs: 'Oh, Jacquet, sometimes I think you are an angel, but today you are surely the devil incarnate come to offer me the apple from the tree in the Garden of Eden!' It is the reason she sometimes refuses to allow Jacques to ask the king to give her gifts she visibly admires in his warehouse. Poor Agnès, torn in two by guilt and desire – whether on the merchant's account or the king's! She spends hours with her confessor, Father Denis, trying to reconcile her conscience. Jacques never doubts that her love for the king is total and pure – her first love, after all, and his – but she frets constantly that she is doing wrong. The merchant delights in her company and at the same time, knows he must protect her somehow. Agnès cannot see it, but he can. A wall of resentment is building around her, or is it a tidal wave that grows and grows and one day will crash down and drown her?

Nor is there any doubt in the merchant's mind that her high regard for Queen Marie is genuine; worse, he knows it hurts Agnès to be hurting the queen. What a paradox! Ever sceptical, Jacques thinks she overestimates that lady's feelings somewhat. He knows Queen Marie has been brought up in a hard school, like her mother – and *by* that mother. The king has enjoyed many infatuations with other women – and with men – and in his opinion, the queen is quite resigned and stalwart. She has her place and knows full well who she is, and the king sees to it that she receives the respect due to her. It is common knowledge at court that the Lady Agnès humbles herself at all times in Queen Marie's presence; and Jacques has no doubt she is sincere. Moreover, when the king wants to give Agnès something precious, she begs Jacques to have the king offer the queen a gift of similar value. It certainly lessens her guilt a little, and Jacques thinks her concern might even amuse the king in a strange, convoluted way.

In Agnès Sorel, Charles VII has found a happy, energetic, beautiful companion, a young woman who plainly adores him unselfishly and with all her heart. She is in love, loves life and wants those around her to do the same. Her infectious spirit and generous nature influence everyone who comes into contact with her: courtiers smile, laugh, dance, joke and find they cannot disapprove of someone who gives them so much of her own *joie de vivre*.

Her many years in tutelage to Queen Isabelle in Naples taught Agnès a great deal, and, in many ways, gave her a model to follow. At Isabelle's court she learnt to appreciate the arts, poetry, literature, and most of all, she shared King René's passion for music. No one would pretend that Agnès has reached the same level of culture as the king, but it is enough to delight him and keep him inspired. She adores playing chess and card games with the king and his companions, and she invents word games for their entertainment. Best of all, she is always good-humoured, smiling, and discreet. Jacques plainly admires her integrity, and therefore he can understand her dilemma – which, as a lady of the queen's household, is made worse by having been chosen by the same queen's mother – for the king. To his way of thinking, Queen Yolande was a wise and admirable lady, who put personal feelings aside for the good of the throne and the country, and expects her daughter, albeit the queen, to do the same. Agnès is a naturally caring young person, always looking out for the interest of others, and most of all, very anxious never to offend – especially Queen Marie. But what the queen herself feels or thinks about her young rival, no one knows. Nor could the merchant wish for a better model to exhibit his extravagant wares. Once the king has been inspired to help his citizens in the towns and the countryside, the courtiers do not then need to be comforted and distracted from the depression caused by the wasted landscape and general misery – they can be diverted to more joyful thoughts by his beautiful merchandise, trinkets and treasures – or so he tells Agnès. She is not entirely convinced by his reasoning and begs him instead to send cart-loads of provisions to this village or that – on her own charge – but in the king's name. This is something she learnt from Queen Yolande who always saw to it that the king received the credit for her ideas and measures which benefited his people. Of course, the merchant does as she bids him.

Jacques is aware that there are members of the court who admonish Charles VII, claiming he ruins himself buying luxuries for his mistress, but they cannot know how much of his largesse she gives to others. Besides, such decisions are for the king to make, not his merchant. Queen Marie indulges just as heavily, buying exquisite cloths of silk and gold thread, of wool and camelot; furs from Siberia and superb jewellery; but it is the mistress who is accused of extravagance, never the queen. *Human nature will ensure it will ever be thus,* Jacques muses. Sometimes he argues that extravagance creates work for many skilled hands and is essential for the economy; Agnès demurs, a little hesitantly, that his is just one point of view.

Domestic plotting with the merchant leads to charitable conniving. Often Jacques and Agnès plot and plan together how to present the king with an idea or a programme that will benefit his people in some practical way, and in this the merchant believes they are doing as Queen Yolande intended. He has travelled the length and breadth of France, and has seen how badly the country has been ravaged by the endless years of fighting, and when he tells Agnès of the dire state of much of the land, they often discuss ways of finding some clever scheme to alleviate suffering among the country people as well as those in the towns. Then, at an opportune moment, Agnès suggests the plan to the king, ideas she and Jacques have connived together. Time and again, he heeds her advice.

'Dear Jacquet – what a pleasure that you are at court today. Do you remember how we discussed the emptiness of some of the towns you passed through on your last trip to Marseilles, how plague and famine have left them deserted and what few inhabitants remain have taken shelter in the forests? Roofs that have fallen in, wells polluted, and livestock died of hunger or ran away? Well, I wrote down the names of those towns, and while we sat by the fire in the evening and talked, I told the king about them. He was moved, and promised me he would see about it in the morning. And do you know, this morning I heard him giving orders to one of his captains to go with a troop, take workmen and animals and put those towns to rights so that people may come out of the forests and have homes and work again.'

And with that, Agnès would beam her sunlit smile at Jacques. Yes, often the plans they discussed would lead to a positive result.

With the passing months of Agnès's occupation of the king's heart and by his side, Jacques watches as the king becomes a more confident ruler, a more conscientious man. His subjects' welfare begins to be important to him, something that never crossed his mind before Agnès came into his life. Slowly, their poor devastated country improves, and Charles VII becomes a better king. Perhaps, Jacques thinks, he might even become a great one.

The merchant often meets the king in Bourges, and, as a member of his Council, Charles asks him his opinion: 'Jacques, my good friend, give me your opinion on the matter raised this morning by the delegates from Orléans – I was not convinced by their reasoning.' And the king leads him to sit somewhere quiet at the palace for Jacques to tell him. 'But why did you not raise that point in the meeting this morning – only now does the matter in hand make perfect sense to me.'

'Sire, forgive me. I did not raise the point simply because it was not what the delegates from Orléans wanted to hear, especially from someone as unimportant as me.'

'I hear what you are saying, but know that if you were so unimportant, my dear Jacques, you would not *be* a member of my Council. You are there to give me your views, and if you feel it imprudent in the presence of others, I urge you, no, I command you, to tell me when we are alone afterwards – like we are now. If I am not properly made aware of the true situation in the country, I will not make the right decisions. I want all my advisers to do the same, but few have your sharp brain, I fear.' With that he smiled, patted the merchant's shoulder and left him.

*This king has such potential*, thinks Jacques. *I must pray he does not waste it in foolish pursuits.*

At home, he tells Marcée of the programmes he and Agnès arrange for the renovation of villages and towns, of the help for the young and the old, for improving the water supply and the roads and many other ideas that they dream up together. She looks at him in a strange, bemused way. 'Husband of my heart, you are behaving like a young man in love, when you really are an old fool. Agnès looks on you as a father figure although you are almost the age of our king, but while she is learning from you, *you* are falling into a great trap, my dearest.'

'Marcée, believe me, this is an innocent friendship. She has no one she can trust to whom she can talk but one other lady in the queen's court, and the dauphine.'

'Oh Jacquet, I know that, and I don't doubt you for an instant,' and she embraces him, 'but do not imagine that others who want to do you harm out of envy for your friendship will not insinuate otherwise. Be careful is all I am saying.'

Little by little, as Jacques comes to know him, he becomes conscious of the king's determination to succeed, to do his duty and lead his country back to independence from the English. And then, just as quickly, he would change into another person altogether. One moment he is kind, and then resentful, lazy; then eager to study and learn – which he does easily and well; full of energy and enthusiasm, then wasted and lethargic. He enjoys the company of clever, educated people, and yet appears to take pleasure in the vulgarity of others just as much. He can be miserly one day, and then extravagantly generous the next. There is no doubt he is pious, and yet he is also a libertine; a man of peace, but undeniably a brave and forceful soldier in battle.

'Do you think his tortured childhood resulted in these contradictions in his character?' Jacques asks his clever and discreet Marcée. Knowing him so well, she always allows him to voice his own thoughts. She just purses her lips and gets on with her sewing, a smile in her heart, an inscrutable look on her face.

Charles VII certainly confides in no one now that his *bonne mère* is gone. But Yolande d'Anjou had much too sharp a mind not to know this man thoroughly. She recognized his many weaknesses from boyhood and tried to counter them with wise advisers. But following her husband's death, she, too, had her duties to her sons and the kingdom of Naples, and could not always be by his side.

Jacques Coeur is not alone in believing that Agnès Sorel was the great queen's dying bequest to their king. More than anyone, Yolande understood that he needed an intelligent, honourable, beautiful young woman with whom he could really fall in love, and for the first time. With such a paragon by his side, there was a real chance for this king. She could nourish him, advise him, bring out his positive qualities, and more, make him happy. *If only Queen Marie, his capable, good and wise wife, had also been as beautiful as her mother Yolande, how different this king would have been,* Jacques muses. And he wonders whether the great Queen of Sicily ever considered the feelings of her daughter who he knew she loved dearly – just as Marie loves her husband the king – while she groomed her son-in-law's future mistress? 'King and country' Yolande had been instructed by her beloved husband and had taught her children the same, 'come even before our own flesh and blood.'

As the king matures, Jacques Coeur sees him change and become a man willing and ready to rule. *It has certainly taken him some time – longer than with most men.* Yet he hears that he often shuts himself up in his rooms alone, and he wonders what goes through his mind there. Does his shyness return to dominate his character; his childhood lack of confidence; his fear of the unknown? Jacques learns that the king consults alchemists. To what purpose? He cannot believe base metal can be turned to gold, surely? Rulers are different from mere mortals; theirs is a lonely position, always on their guard against enemies without and enemies – disguised as friends – within; constantly under pressure to make the right decision and to avoid dire consequences.

The king is forty years old, and since the arrival of Agnès Sorel in his life, there have been no more signs of his former decadence. *Thank heaven and the Queen of Sicily,* thinks Jacques.

# Chapter Fifteen

$\mathcal{I}$t seems impossible for everyone to be content, and there will always be those who carry grudges and show dissatisfaction, if not hostility. The merchant is not alone in thinking that Charles VII's son, the dauphin Louis, is one such malicious character. 'And yet,' he tells Marcée 'what good qualities he possesses if only he would allow them to emerge! He is intelligent, perhaps not so much as his father, but hates him to such a degree that spleen fair oozes out of him.' His wise Marcée just nods.

Since his birth in Bourges, and despite the unstinting efforts of his mother Queen Marie, and those of his grandmother, Queen Yolande, nothing was going to change him. Louis has always been a closed child, secretive; the sort, Jacques remembers thinking when he saw him on his arrival in Bourges, who tortures small animals – pulls the wings off flies, the tails off lizards – and when that palls, becomes more ambitious. Since most of his siblings died at birth or at an early age, he soon developed a morbid fascination with death, always wearing black like his poor mother who is constantly in mourning.

Nor is the dauphin an attractive young man. He has inherited his father's short legs and awkward walk. He has a slight speech impediment, which means he is not always understood, and it enrages him when he is not instantly obeyed. He will shout at his own staff in the street: 'Did you not hear me? Do I have to repeat all my orders?' And the local people would know they had simply not understood him, not disobeyed. Nor is he a refined man, preferring the company of the taverns. Rough and vulgar people amuse him, and he shares their uncouth table manners, eating and drinking coarsely and to excess, although at court he can be charm itself when he wants. Several tavern owners have told Jacques: 'When the dauphin Louis comes in, we send our wives and daughters away to the kitchens – he can be too rough with his hands for my liking!'

Louis talks too freely and often viciously, enjoying inflicting pain with his tongue, in particular on those not in a position to answer back. Who *is* in a position to answer back? Certainly not his poor wife, the delightful dauphine Margaret of Scotland, whom he openly despises for no better reason than that she was the choice of his father – and rightly so for political reasons.

It is clear to everyone that Louis hates his father – that is apparent when he is sober; let alone when he is drunk in the taverns. Jacques wants to ask Agnès why this should be, but then thinks better of it, as it could well be that she is one of the reasons. Perhaps also *because he realizes he is not as clever, nor as subtle as his father*; but certainly because he feels unappreciated and underfunded, and forced to marry without his consent. Nor was he given the means to afford such estate. In addition, he has been denied his rightful inheritance of the Dauphiné by his father. This independent territory is traditionally given to the heir to the throne when he reaches his majority. A number of the senior courtiers, Jean Dunois among others, agree that Louis is within his rights to complain.

The dislike between father and son is both instinctive and intense. No one at court can fathom why; they are like two dogs confined in a courtyard who snarl when they pass one another, almost as if they simply dislike the smell of one another. When they meet in public, the king is clearly welcoming, and yet, before he can place his hand on his son's shoulder, Louis will flinch away with a sneer. Everyone notices, but Charles merely shrugs and carries on talking to others.

Unlike the king, Louis takes no interest in his appearance or his clothes, and is often mistaken for a servant when away from home – with the inevitable reprisal inflicted on the unwary. One of his worst characteristics is one he shares with his father – cruelty. The unpleasant enjoyment he took in torturing small animals as a child has grown into gratuitous brutality towards vanquished or captured enemies.

There is no doubt that the dauphin Louis is the most troublesome aspect of everyone's lives at court. Jacques noticed the way he had watched Agnès Sorel at Queen Yolande's funeral in Angers, and later she told him, almost in tears, how Louis had insulted her. And yet, there are some at court who believe the dauphin is in love with her. Thereafter Agnès does all she can to stay out of his way.

'You know, Marcée,' Jacques tells his wife one day, 'the dauphin is an intelligent young man, but he does have quite an inflated opinion of himself, letting it be known that he feels overlooked and undervalued by his father.'

'Oh? And what do you think?' she replies, carrying on with her stitching.

'Well, to be truthful, I believe he may well have a point. Once he reached his majority at the age of fourteen, the whole court knew he ached to be given responsibilities in accordance with his rank and the custom.'

'And these rights are denied him?'

'Yes, and for no apparent reason. His father, I was told, had been a feeble, malleable young man, and yet look how *he* has grown into a power to be reckoned with.'

'Then perhaps he is of the opinion that his son is as feck-less as he was himself at that age?' Marcée says without looking up. She was told by Juana, Yolande's old nurse, that he was 'a bad one' as a child, just like his father was when he arrived to live with Marie's family in Anjou aged ten. But Charles grew out of it, so Juana prayed Louis would as well.

Jacques comes into contact with the dauphin quite often in Bourges and notes how Louis makes no effort to charm. 'Good morrow,' he will say, 'Jacques Coeur, isn't it?' He always greets Jacques the same way, despite having known him all his life. It is his way of making sure the merchant knows he does not count in his eyes. But Jacques pays him no mind, never forgetting that one day he will be king and command him. The merchant always replies pleasantly: 'Sire, good morrow, and how gracious of you to recall my name. Would it please you Sire, to visit my warehouse and see the new swords arrived from Damascus? Their steel is exceptionally finely worked.' Grudgingly he would reply: 'perhaps,' although Louis invariably sent someone from his household to take a look. They would leave with some blades for the dauphin to choose at the palace, but he himself never deigns to enter the place where both the king and queen and the Queen of Sicily were pleased to visit.

Jacques is not the only one aware of the dauphin's growing resentment of his father. In 1440, Louis makes the grave error of joining with a group of disaffected courtiers, including Queen Marie's brother, the king's favourite Charles of Maine and that honourable soldier, Jean de Dunois. Their grounds for discontent are not unreasonable, but through them, Louis attempts to unseat his father. The plot is discovered by Pierre de Brézé, whose swift action on the king's behalf crushes this minor insurrection. It is the making of Pierre, and the undoing of the dauphin. The king generously recognizes his own injustice and mistakes, and the plotters are forgiven. However, since then the king never really trusts his son again. He gives Louis permission to leave the court, yet his son chooses to remain, in deference to his father. However, he makes his displeasure known by cutting short the tails of his horses for it to be seen that their usefulness in swatting flies has been 'curtailed' like his own standing.

Thinking on this well-known issue of friction between the king and his heir, Jacques consults his soulmate: 'Marcée, my clever wife, advise me, do. Surely the time has come for our Charles VII to be instructing the dauphin in the business of ruling. I see the king is well enough but after the age of forty, he should begin to think about securing the succession. There is much to learn to become an effective monarch. Can you think of a way I can make them friends, or at least colleagues?' And Marcée promises to think on it.

Eventually the dauphin leaves the court to take part in several successful campaigns on behalf of his father. On his return, he expects – and with a certain justification – to be asked to join his father's Council. He is not invited, but finds that Agnès Sorel and Pierre de Brézé have been admitted. His successes on behalf of his father seem to have made no difference: the king shows no sign of trusting his son or even appreciating his efforts. Louis' resentment grows and festers.

One day in their comfortable palace at Nancy in Lorraine, René remarks to his wife Isabelle: 'Have you noticed there is never enough our friend Jacques Coeur can do for the king? He has made a number of trips as his ambassador to sort out the kind of regional problems only a man of great subtlety and understanding can succeed in solving.'

'Yes, dearest, I know,' she replies absent-mindedly, pre-occupied with arranging flowers.

'He is constantly on the lookout for ways to enhance the glory of his sovereign, who he lauds wherever he goes – have you noticed?'

'Hmmm …' is all he gets out of Isabelle.

'Remember when we heard in Naples that through his good services, the royal 'fleur-de-lys' of France appears once again in the great markets of the Orient when Alexandria and Cairo opened their doors to him.' And another 'hmm ...' from Isabelle while René muses on: 'Jacquet has such a clever and yet honest way about him that he is accepted everywhere and considered a worthy negotiator, tough but always fair ... You know,' René reminds her, 'my esteemed mother told me earnestly before I left to join you in Naples, and in her letters, that Jacques Coeur is a man to trust with any business interests I might have; someone on whom I can rely – and I have and always will.'

There would appear to be no reason for this statement but Isabelle has always been able to read René's mind. Something is troubling him, and it has to do with their friend.

'Charles has done the right thing, you know,' he continues, 'in my opinion at least: he has created a new class of noble – men of achievement, such as Jacques Coeur – to add to those who are noble by blood and heredity. The merchant class is gaining legitimacy and respectability, though it is still not yet socially acceptable in the eyes of some of the nobility,' and he sighs.

*So that is it*, thinks Isabelle. *He has heard the rumours circulating about Jacques.* There is so much envy directed at him, especially since he has put almost all the other merchants of Bourges out of business. And now these rumours concerning some kind of disloyalty on the merchant's part have reached them even in Nancy.

Nor is their friend's elevation to the nobility an exception – a good number of the urban bourgeoisie has progressed to the upper classes through sheer hard work and achievement. Isabelle has always been a sharp observer of the court, and at last she tells René:

'I have no doubt that it is Jacques' promotion to the King's Council that has caused the sharpest intakes of breath, not his ennoblement. This is what makes some of the more conventional aristocracy feel he has risen too high. You must have heard that Louis is outraged that both Agnès and Jacquet have been elected onto his father's Council while he has not been offered a place even after his military success?' And René nods. The entire court is aware of the dauphin's anger and sense of injustice and many of them believe he has every right to feel that way.

René d'Anjou is both liked and always welcomed by his cousin the king, but more in memory of his mother and of their shared childhood friendship, not because René is ever consulted, nor wishes to be. For the sake of his Anjou patrons, if not for the country, whenever he hears that René retires to his great fortress base at Angers, Jacques Coeur decides to keep his eye on the dauphin Louis, and charges those he trusts in his employ to do the same.

*Chapter Sixteen*

Under the patronage of Agnès Sorel, the mercantile career of Jacques Coeur flourishes. Inevitably there is not a damsel at court, or even in the country, who does not want to look and dress like the king's mistress. Jacques supplies her with lengths of cloth that caress her perfect body; delicate whispers of veils made of woven gold thread, veils as light as a breeze that fall from her headdress and circle the perfect oval of her face.

The Lady Agnès is not the first at court to love furs and jewels. Even before Jacques Coeur's father's time as furrier to the late Duke of Berry, sable, mink and marten was imported into France from Scandinavia, Germany and Russia. Clothes at this time are often edged around the neckline and wrists with subtly dyed fur trimmings, for comfort as well as fashion. Men love wearing fur as much as the ladies. Jacques Coeur will never forget Duke Jean buying from his father the pale golden stomach skins of ten thousand martens to line and trim his substantial wardrobe against the cold.

It is Queen Isabeu, mother of Charles VII, who is credited with inventing the *hennin*, that tall, conical headdress from the tip of which float delicate whispers of transparent silk veils. This is another quite ridiculous fashion, along with the headdresses made to resemble fat *horns* worn on either side of a lady's forehead. Clerics rail against these as they are frequently stuffed with hair from cadavers – who might have gone to hell, they say! But for Jacques – it is all simply business. Although Agnès does not invent any particular fashion, every style, no matter how extreme, looks perfect on her and is imitated. Nor is it true that she plucks her eyebrows until they are no longer there; they *are* there, merely very fine and blonde.

One of the strangest fashions ladies demand from Jacques Coeur is the small padded cushion that they like to wear tied around their waist under their clothes to sit over the stomach. Agnès always wears a small pad of goose-down feathers under her dress. This is to give a *delicate rounded look* to a lady, beneath a tiny, high waist which fits securely on a band just under the breasts. It is a most practical fashion for ladies who are with child, since they can still appear in public with their own 'rounded look' and no goose feather pad until they are near their delivery and must retire from the court.

Traditionally, clothes have always reflected the social status of the wearer. As a result of France's civil wars, however, members of all classes begin to wear what they like. This new behaviour even counted against Jeanne d'Arc who found it convenient to dress not only as a man, but as an *aristocratic* man, a knight, when, despite her ennoblement after the victory at Orléans, she was a peasant-born! On the other hand, she became accustomed to living the life of a soldier, where only a man's clothing was appropriate. But the Church's ruling was quite clear – women could not wear men's clothing. In Jeanne's case, it was a necessity. Had she been captured riding with the soldiers and recognised to be a woman, not even Burgundian soldiers, let alone English, would have respected her female status, but if she was thought to be a young French soldier, she had more of a chance.

There are sumptuary laws against such breaches of custom, but Charles VII defends the right of the middle classes – and anyone who can afford it – to buy exotic or extravagant clothes. It is good for trade, after all – his and Jacques Coeur's.

Although the sumptuary laws have been ignored during the wars, once peace is restored, the Lady Agnès symbolizes the way in which the court and society is returning to the excesses and extravagance of the old court – from the time before the English invasion in 1415. Ecclesiastics harangue their flock from their pulpits; the rich are spending on themselves instead of on what constitutes the public good, and, in particular, on the restoration and reconstruction of their country. Agnès is used as an example of all that illustrates. Charles VII loves luxury and joins in enthusiastically. He experienced enough poverty in his youth, knowing that he was entirely dependent on the generosity of the family of Anjou, in particular after the Treaty of Troyes deprived him of his status as dauphin and the income from his lands that accompanied his status as heir to his father's throne. With his naturally extravagant nature, now that he has his own money, he sees no reason to deny himself, or his lovely mistress, anything at all. He adores elegance in women, admires those who make an effort to please with their toilettes, and complains about those who do not. And Jacques Coeur is there to help the ladies please their monarch.

The king also enjoys spoiling his queen, Marie, to whom he has sent a wonderful dress from Jacques Coeur's warehouse following the birth of each child. On a whim, he orders four expensive dresses trimmed with fur as gifts for his daughter Jeanne. To the dauphine Margaret he gives a generous sum for her silken sheets, and a large number of stone marten skins to make a cloak. He is just as open-handed to his sister. The king's generosity is excellent for Jacques Coeur's business, but best of all, is peace. People work and earn once again, have money to spend, and enjoy doing so.

How much of the extravagant lifestyle among the courtiers of King Charles VII is due to Jacques Coeur? If one is honest, quite a lot. The fact is that Jacques is a real merchant adventurer. He loves to buy the treasures he discovers in parts of the world other merchants have not made the effort to explore. To justify this, he needs an affluent market, and that market consists predominantly of the rich courtiers of Charles VII, and of Burgundy in particular. Jacques is a persuasive man, and shrewd, and he recognizes the weaknesses of others. That is the true secret of his success – to give the buyer pleasure in possessing what he desires. After all, it is not a one-way relationship – both sides gain!

*Chapter Seventeen*

$\mathcal{P}$eace is what France needs and wants. It was the great aim of Queen Yolande to rid the country of the English, but if that is not yet possible, then at least peace gives everyone a chance to re-build their lives, restore their homes and their fields and resume their business. Traditionally, the greatest seal of peace between two warring factions has been a great dynastic marriage. The English king, Henry VI, son of the union of the victor of Agincourt and a sister of Charles VII, desires peace as much as the French, and once again, a marriage is proposed with a French princess to bring about a longed-for treaty between the two countries. But the negotiations will need to be handled very carefully – the King of England still claims to be King of France.

The bride chosen for Henry VI is Marguerite d'Anjou, youngest daughter of René and Isabelle, Duke and Duchess of Lorraine. The French king selects Pierre de Brézé as the ideal diplomat for this delicate mission: his intelligence, his skill with words and his charm are considered the perfect ingredients in the negotiation of such an important marriage. No one is surprised that Pierre achieves all that is asked of him with his usual skill, and both parties are satisfied.

During the Christmas season of 1443, René begins to organize a series of tournaments in honour of the marriage, which is to take place the following year. To supply his court with every kind of adornment required, he calls on the services of his good friend the merchant and their rescuer from Naples, Jacques Coeur.

That same year, Jacques carries out another service, this time to Agnès Sorel, providing her with every comfort she might need to give birth to her first child. This is arranged with the merchant's usual careful planning, and her absence from court goes virtually unnoticed. The king is with the army and cannot be present, but he sends her splendid gifts chosen and delivered by Jacques, as well as many loving letters with his couriers.

After the birth, Agnès arrives in Nancy with her cousin Antoinette de Maignelay, whom she has brought to court to keep her company. The baby, Marie, is left in the care of Antoinette's mother, a wet-nurse and other staff, as is the custom, and they are told to call on Jacques Coeur to send them anything they need.

The proxy wedding of Marguerite d'Anjou, which makes her England's queen in name, takes place in May 1444 at Nancy, and Jacques Coeur is engaged to make the occasion unforgettable. The city is flooded with cut-out marguerites, made of cloth of gold and silver, of silk, of gilded leather, of every imaginable substance. Balconies are draped with textiles covered in marguerites, and many children in the crowd even have daisies painted on their faces!

The bride herself, called by those welcoming this union between France and England 'the Peace Dove', wears white satin, and around her neck, her grandmother Yolande's necklace of blood-red rubies brought back by Jacques Coeur long ago from one of his journeys to the East. The rubies were René's gift to Isabelle, and now they dazzle around Marguerite's neck.

Jacques Coeur has arranged for food and drink to be distributed not only to the attendant royalty and nobility, but also to the common people of the town. This largesse expended in the celebration of Marguerite's betrothal is the first stage in constructing her queenly role as a generous patroness. But such munificence has René wondering anxiously how much the crown will contribute to his costs. Then he catches the merchant's eye, and as if he can read René's thoughts, he smiles and gives a slight nod. René knows that Jacques has organized the whole event, and that smile reassures him. His kingly brother-in-law will be constrained to acknowledge this marriage as an expense of state, rather than the impoverished King of Sicily's private obligation!

Moving between Nancy and Angers, though more often remaining in Provence, René keeps in touch with a number of friends through letters delivered by his own couriers, in particular with Jacques Coeur, since his ships come often into René's great trading port of Marseilles. Away from the court, René finds it easier to put its advantages and disadvantages into perspective. The success of

Jacques Coeur as a businessman and merchant troubles him, as he can see that his friend is rather *too* successful, incurring great envy among the courtiers, and he resolves to warn him.

It never fails to give René enormous satisfaction to receive Jacques Coeur at one of the Anjou palaces or mansions in Provence, and to hear his stories of adventures on his travels. No matter what fate has in store, of this he is certain: the merchant will always be the Anjous' friend. When Jacquet tells René and Isabelle about his new projects, his houses and properties, they can see the delight he takes in every detail, but it concerns his host.

'Jacques, my friend, and you know I am your friend, I ask you, hear my words. Never live better than your betters, because they will not be pleased for your success. No matter how much they praise you, or whatever they might say, believe me, *they will hate you for it.*'

Sitting with this wise and worldly man, only eight years his senior, and whom he has known all his adult life, it is easy for René to forget about the devious manoeuvrings of the courtiers, but still he tries again to caution Jacques not to become too ostentatious, and thus incur even more jealousy, though he fears his friend pays him no mind.

Both Jacques Coeur and Pierre de Brézé are fully aware that their friendship with the Lady Agnès brings them great advantages. The three of them often meet informally to discuss how they can help Charles VII – and one another. Pierre and Jacques are two of a kind: subtly anxious to gain both position and wealth in this world. Agnès is somewhat less so, although she does love beautiful things. Since she won her place without effort or ambition, she is not as aware as her two friends of the potential dangers from others who might want to move them aside.

Neither their friendship nor their ambition wins the trio friends at court; indeed, they have all gathered a number of enemies. It is natural that Agnès should ask the king to promote her family – namely her brothers and her uncle – and they benefit a great deal from church appointments and property. The nominees and family of Pierre de Brézé and Jacques Coeur do just as well. The three friends know and understand that they are victims of envy – how could they not be – but they accept this as the price of their success.

After the death of the Queen of Sicily, Jacques Coeur began to notice a change in Pierre de Brézé. Another development is that the king has come under the sway of Queen Yolande's youngest son, Charles of Maine, and both, Pierre and Jacques notice, his is not necessarily a good influence. Nor does Maine's constant close presence benefit Pierre de Brézé's ambition to make *himself* indispensable to the king, and become his First Minister. In view of his undeniable capabilities, Pierre's ambition is not at fault, and from the many conversations he shares with Jacques Coeur it is clear to the merchant that a number of his plans for the reform of the King's Council are both necessary and even ingenious.

Pierre is without doubt the most brilliant strategist the king possesses, and he realizes that the Angevin influence, in particular that of Charles of Maine, on the king needs diluting, something that is not lost on Jacques Coeur either.

Since his presence is required more and more at court, Jacques is able to observe Pierre's subtle moves towards forming a binding friendship with Agnès Sorel. He wants her to realize that he is the only man at court who is truly useful to the king, just as she is the only woman. At thirty-three, Pierre is irresistible to the ladies, but he is much too clever to even hint at a flirtation with Agnès. His plan is completely transparent – to help her to help the king. After all, were they not both trained to do just that by Yolande d'Anjou?

With this in mind, he takes the lead in reforming the government. To his clear thinking, the Angevins left at court are not sufficiently able, and are therefore expendable. He knows his own abilities and what can be achieved in the kingdom if only Charles VII would trust him as much as he trusted his *bonne-mère*, Yolande.

When the king's father, Charles VI, was young and still sane, he selected wise men from the bourgeoisie known as the Marmosets to help him rule, instead of his over-ambitious royal uncles. Once he lost his mind, however, his uncles rid the Council of the Marmosets, and how France suffered as a result. Charles VII and Pierre de Brézé, someone in whom the king places steadily more trust, both learned from that mistake. The universities of France are producing an impressive pool of talent from the bourgeoisie, trained in law, finance and trade. Some of these men of ability have been ennobled, just as Jacques Coeur has been. It is these talented men that Pierre wants to enlist to help govern the country.

As Grand Sénéschal of Anjou, Poitou, Comte d'Evreux, and chamberlain to the king since 1442, it is Pierre de Brézé, and not the Angevin clan, who holds the power from this time. He breaks with tradition and appoints men of accomplishment and quality to join the Council – lawyers, financiers, technicians; achievers renowned for their ability, not their rank. The only aristocrat he selects is Jean, Count de Dunois, illegitimate son of Prince Louis d'Orléans, a fine and subtle talker and another of Queen Yolande's protégés. There are some other appointments from the minor nobility, but essentially this is a Council that will run the country for its own good and not the good of its members.

Pierre de Brézé knows that no one hates the Angevins more than the dauphin. In Louis' eyes, King Réné and his brother Charles of Maine control everything in the kingdom. Actually, he is wrong. True, Charles is the king's favourite, but once Good King René, as he continues to be known, accepts that he has lost the battle for his kingdom of Naples and Sicily, he retires happily to Anjou and Provence, leaving his eldest son, Jean of Calabria, to rule in Lorraine with his mother.

In Anjou, René focuses on writing his works on chivalry and organizing dazzling tournaments for important state occasions. He is often assisted with these spectacles by Jacques Coeur, who supplies pieces of scenery, props, decorations, costumes and the like. It is clear to anyone who knows René d'Anjou that he has no political ambitions whatsoever.

# Chapter Eighteen

In the summer of 1444, the king decides that his beautiful Lady Agnès needs her own establishment and income. She is the first royal mistress for whom a complaisant husband has not been arranged in order to give the king's children a name. Charles will not share her and will take care of their children, which comes as a great relief to her. Then, to ease her anxiety about her financial dependence on him, he bestows on his beloved his first great gift – an enchanting royal domain: the Château de Beauté and its estates. In this way, not only does he provide Agnès with her first home and a considerable private income; he also grants her the title that comes with the estate. Henceforth she will be known as 'La Dame de Beauté', the Mistress of Beauty. Nothing could be more appropriate. The château is situated near Vincennes on the river Marne, surrounded by forests, streams, wonderful hunting, and 'good air' to avoid the permanent threat of plague.

Built by the king's grandfather, Charles V, Beauté was his favourite château and houses his remarkable library. The interiors are already very luxurious, but nonetheless, Jacques Coeur is summoned to ensure that Agnès has everything she might possibly want for her comfort. Jacques tells Marcée, 'If the king wishes to spoil his beloved Agnès and give her a great house, it needs to be filled with the most exquisite contents.' The new Mistress of Beauty never shows greed, just rapture at the sight of the glorious furnishings Jacques offers her. She has a natural eye for quality, combined with a dislike of anything over-elaborate or too ornate.

The jealousy of Agnès, particularly after she gives birth to the king's second daughter, continues to grow, as does that directed at Jacques Coeur's success. As she acquires properties from her royal lover, the merchant buys houses in almost every city in France, and landed estates as well. The country is growing prosperous again and the rich are buying what he has to sell. When they run up huge debts, he acquires their property as repayment. Both Jacques and Agnès are in the king's favour and grateful for it. Both pray it will last. The wily merchant has seen men fall from great heights before, and he does not wish such a future for himself, or for Agnès.

As well as the discord between the king and his ambitious son, there is another relationship at court that fascinates Jacques Coeur – namely, that between the dauphin and the king's rapidly ascending young mistress. In 1445, Louis returns to court the conquering hero, having reclaimed the port of Dieppe from the English. He comes bearing gifts for those in high positions, including Pierre de Brézé and Agnès Sorel. Pierre accepts the excellent wine given him by the dauphin with his usual grace. On Agnès he bestows a set of six magnificent biblical tapestries depicting the life of the chaste Suzanne. She has made her dislike of Louis plain from the first, no doubt influenced by the king, but also because of his cruel treatment of her friend the dauphine Margaret of Scotland. When the sad dauphine dies of pneumonia in August that year following a long struggle with ill health, Agnès is deeply affected by her loss as is the rest of the court. Two of Louis' tapestries Agnès keeps in a house she rarely visits; the rest she sends to the abbey of Loches. Her message to Louis is a clear rejection of his advances, and he becomes her implacable enemy.

Despite this, the numbers at court who are convinced of the dauphin's infatuation with the king's lady have grown considerably. That he may have fallen in love with Agnès is not difficult to believe – most of the courtiers are a little in love with her – but Pierre is of the opinion, and tells Jacques so, that not even Louis could have believed he could take Agnès from his father.

Charles VII is a mature man who knows himself and has achieved much. He has always been secretive, with a complex character, often changing his mind. Is he a good man? Jacques Coeur doubts it, but nor does he think him a bad one. When Pierre asks his opinion, Jacques replies:

'Who am I to judge? What I can see is a man in love, and in love with love. He is powerful and very rich; he can indulge his love however he wants. And he does. It would never occur to him that he could have a potential rival in his son; he is too sure of Agnès – and rightly so.'

'I think he wants to be a knight in shining armour fighting for his lady love,' says Pierre. 'Chivalry is what the king was all about when young and living with the Anjou family – and I believe that is still the case – at least on one side of his character.' *Yes*, thinks Jacques, *Queen Yolande recognized this need and supplied the remedy before she died.*

Charles VII never lets his guard down. Following the death of his *bonne mère*, he counts only on himself – no one else. And who can blame him after the misery of his childhood and haunted youth? Jacques recalls how René told him on one of their walks on the pier in Marseilles how much it had frightened the then dauphin when he had to leave the security of the Anjou family following the poisoning of his two elder brothers to go to Paris and take his place on the Council. 'Jacquet – you cannot know of the many humiliations visited on the king at that time, and the scorn of his subjects; the many treasonous acts he witnessed and continues to dread. Is it any wonder he fears crowds and unknown faces about him?'

But the man the courtiers see before them now is a conqueror, a man who has taken possession of the heart of the most beautiful young woman anyone has ever seen. He is a king – a man of stature, a man unconditionally in love. 'Long may it last,' Jacques and Pierre tell each other with feeling.

Kingship has taught Charles VII how to manage people, to use his position, his intelligence, enabling him to charm his way into any heart. The dauphin Louis, by contrast, lacks any semblance of charm and appears unwilling to acquire any. If he feels hurt by Agnès's lack of appreciation for his magnificent gift of the tapestries, he does not show it. Instead, he claims that his aversion to his father's mistress is due to his love for his scorned mother the queen, whom Agnès Sorel has usurped in his father's affections. Considering that Louis hardly ever saw his parents during his childhood, this explanation is not remotely convincing. Furthermore, Marie de Belleville, Agnès's only friend in Queen Marie's court, tells Pierre and Jacques how the Lady Agnès does everything she can to ease the queen's discomfort. She never stands by the king in the queen's company, or catches his eye, or acknowledges him in any but the most respectful way. A visitor to the court would not notice anything at all.

The marriage of the Constable of France, Arthur of Richemont to Catherine of Luxembourg, sister of the wife of Charles of Maine, increases the ascendancy of the Anjous at court, adding another powerful pillar to their support. Richemont has been Constable since 1425, and has a strong, positive influence on the king. He was chosen by Queen Yolande, and with time, Charles VII begins to appreciate the reasons behind her judgement. And yet there still lingers an insoluble difficulty.

Once Yolande is no longer there to remind the king of the Constable's outstanding qualities, Charles cannot help himself falling back into his life-long abhorrence of physical deformity. Not only does poor Arthur have to live with the gruesome scars caused by a wound to his face at the Battle of Agincourt in 1415, but he can tell that it visibly distresses the king to look at him. There are indeed some faces that *should* be removed from the court, but Arthur's is not one of them.

The Angevins' dominance causes Pierre de Brézé to react against them even more strongly than before, to the extent of joining forces with the dauphin to spread rumours about them at court. This really surprises Jacques. It is common knowledge that Louis hates Pierre for exposing his part in the insurrection of the disaffected nobles; is it possible that they are now somehow in league? Between them Pierre and Louis are eerily persuasive, and they manage to convince a powerful following of courtiers that the Angevins are planning another revolt.

The pressure becomes too much for the king, and he decides he has had enough of the Angevins saturating his court. René and Charles of Maine are told to leave with their followers and not return until recalled.

Although this edict comes as quite a shock, Jacques knows it does not bother Lord René at all. He has settled his debts and royally married his daughter to the King of England. His eldest son, the Duke of Calabria, is well installed governing the Lorraine, and the former King of Sicily is content at his great castle of Angers, working on his books of chivalry. Meanwhile, Charles of Maine quietly withdraws from the court until the king changes his mind – as he is prone to do. Charles amuses him, and he craves to be amused.

The only aristocrat from among the Anjou contingent remaining on the Council is Jean de Dunois. Through his own informants, Jacques Coeur knows that both Dunois and Brézé have been in clandestine contact for some time with the dauphin. Ever careful and circumspect, Jacques keeps silent, but he is curious about the covert alliance between Louis and Pierre de Brézé. He notices that the dauphin sends wine to the sénéschal at Chinon at Christmas, but surely Brézé's close alliance with the king's mistress will hinder any rapprochement with Louis? And yet … is the shrewd Pierre preparing the way for the future, for the next reign perhaps?

# Chapter Nineteen

In 1446, a small miracle occurs. Queen Marie gives birth at Tours to her fifth son, but this one is a healthy bouncing boy, who will live! The king is overjoyed, overwhelmed, and the dauphin is utterly dejected. He is no longer the only heir – there is another, and from the first, he hates him.

Since he cannot express his disappointment and rage to his baby brother or his father, instead Louis vents it on Agnès Sorel. A terrible scene takes place at court in full view of a large number of courtiers, including the king's *argentier*. Jacques tells Marcée about it afterwards.

'Dearest wife, you cannot imagine the scene that took place in Tours. The courtiers were all in attendance, spread throughout three or four reception rooms. The musicians were playing softly, elegant guests parading and talking; when there was a commotion and the throng parted. Agnès, her face as white as her dress, her hair covered but with one long blonde lock escaped from her headdress, rushed wide-eyed towards the king. Only then did I see the dauphin behind her, shouting, "Whore! Get out! How dare you take my mother the queen's place?" He was waving his drawn sword in front of him and the look on his face as he reached the throne room was something you cannot imagine. Almost as if he had become the very devil himself; the snarl of a rabid dog, foaming at the mouth! He stopped and sheathed his sword, and before the king could intervene, he hit Agnès so hard across the face that she fell.

'We were all in such shock that no one moved. Then, as her ladies rushed to help her, and the dauphin's followers caught up with him, the king turned towards his son. "Hear me," he said loudly, pointing at his son. "I banish you to your appanage of the Dauphiné. Do not leave this your territory, under pain of death!" And then he followed Agnès and her ladies from the hall. Most of the courtiers were still too stunned to speak, but we all saw the dauphin turn white and leave the reception rooms with his followers. Believe me, Marcée, my heart was pounding so hard I could almost hear it. In this strange way, Louis was finally granted his rightful territory of the Dauphiné, but under the most shocking of circumstances!'

Those present during this unpleasant confrontation are none the less astonished by the outcome. In spite of the dauphin's appalling behaviour, for the king to banish his son for rudeness to his mistress seems to all a punishment too harsh for the crime. No dauphin has ever acknowledged the existence of a mistress! It is generally considered natural and right for a son to support his mother. But since his efforts against the Lady Agnès have not succeeded, the dauphin does all he can to drive a wedge between the king and Pierre de Brézé, her friend.

The next day, the city talks of nothing else and that the dauphin left almost at once with his followers. *This time the king will not pardon him*, thinks Jacques. *He has been harbouring a serpent in his bosom for too long. And now he has another son …*

Following the king's order, Louis has no choice but to remain in the Dauphiné and to rule his province like a great feudal estate. It does not take long before Jacques Coeur hears that the territory has become a hotbed of plotters, conspirators, spies and malcontents. Some information that comes his way intrigues the merchant – that despite Louis' stated dislike for Pierre de Brézé, he hears that the king is daily more convinced the pair are in some sort of contact. Jacques himself is persuaded that there is something going on between them. It even enters the merchant's Minotaur-mind that perhaps the dauphin could be paying Pierre de Brézé? But if so, to what purpose?

Of one thing the merchant is sure: that in the majority of cases, loyalty among the courtiers depends upon who pays the most. However, he knows that this is not the case among the lower classes, certainly of Bourges, where family alliances are more important to their chances of survival. The cornerstone of any successful business operation in those social circles is trust. Any trader or merchant not considered trustworthy will never succeed. Nor is he alone in believing that is not the case among the aristocracy, where wives are bought, soldiers are bought, so why not loyalty?

While giving this some thought, Jacques meets Jean de Villages busy checking a new delivery of bales of cloth in his warehouse in Bourges. 'You know, Jean, I am becoming ever more distrustful as I grow older. Do you think everyone has a price? Can money buy loyalty, true loyalty?' and he mutters under his breath.

Jean puts down a heavy bale on an orderly pile and straightens his back, stretching after the exertion. 'Dear Uncle, I fear you are growing cynical from too much exposure to the court! Sell to them, but don't confuse your thoughts or feelings with theirs. And never trust any of them, I say.'

He may be right: Jacques has seen for himself how the king's favour can be a variable commodity. 'Jean, you know me, I am not blind about the aristocracy. And I do believe that those who have the king's support know they can just as quickly and easily find it has been withdrawn. I learnt that from Queen Yolande's experience with Jeanne d'Arc, when she tried to warn the Maid again and again not to trust the king.'

'Then I beg you Uncle, not to do so either,' says Jean, embracing him.

Throughout the 1440s Jacques Coeur acquires a great many properties – many of them estates which come to him as repossessions from nobles unable to pay their debts, or whose fortunes are lost due to the endless wars, or by having to pay their own or a son's ransom.

One day, the Coeur family is gathered for a birthday celebration at home. When they are sitting comfortably after an excellent meal, Jacques says to Marcée, 'Dear wife, look at us, sprawled all over this room, which is large enough, but we are grown into quite a big family, and since you,' he says, turning to his children, 'like to bring home your friends, I have been thinking about a bigger house – perhaps building one. What do you say?'

They all stop talking and look to their mother – she is the one who takes the major domestic decisions in their family. Jean de Villages and Jacques' niece Perrette are also among the family gathering when Marcée says:

'Dearest and most generous of husbands, how good of you to even ask our views when you have always made up your own mind about everything!' and laughs, and they all join in. It is true. Jacques puts big decisions to the family but he always has his way. 'So you want to build a bigger house, my dearest; and how shall it look?'

Jacques smiles and turns to a sideboard, where he has left a folder with papers. 'I have been gathering drawings for some years of any building or interior that has appealed to me on my travels in France and abroad. Now I am of an age when I feel I have seen enough and can incorporate my ideas into one large building for us all, where we can have our different sections and live together without getting in one another's way. What do you say?' He looks at the room filled with beaming faces. They are a close-knit family and prefer their own company to that of most others.

'And where is there space to build such a large building, dearest? As you all know, I could not live anywhere but here in Bourges, and the city has no vacant lots.'

'Then I shall make space,' says Jacques. 'I shall buy enough houses and pull them down to make room to build our own mansion!'

They all sigh and smile. Jacques Coeur has a new project, and like all his others, it will be a success – every detail, no matter how small, worked out in his head. Door handles, window embrasures, commodes and bathrooms, staircases, roof line, attics – there will be nothing that does not have his distinctive stamp.

Until this stage in his career, he has devoted his working life to establishing his business empire as well as that of the king. The time, he feels, has come to create an establishment for himself and his family to enjoy, one that will remain as a monument to his achievements.

It takes considerable effort and skilful negotiations until the merchant of Bourges has acquired the land he needs and in the centre of his city. Work is scheduled to continue for four years, and Jacques is passionately involved in every detail of the construction of his mansion. For the decoration both outside and within, he will use his symbols of a heart and a shell. The whole is to be a mixture of the flamboyant, soaring style of the cathedral at Bourges and the classical idiom of Greece and Rome, with columns, pediments and arches. Building has always been one of Jacques' passions, and he instructs his foreman that *there should be a small relief figure of him holding a mason's mallet on one of the walls.* At heart, he loves to buy and enjoys collecting furniture, tapestries, carpets and much else, but this time for himself – not to sell, but to furnish the house with the best carpets, tapestries and furniture he can find.

'Marcée, dearest, you must come to the warehouse today – I have a new shipment just arrived which contains much for our new house.' Such pronouncements are made each week and whoever is at home is taken off to his warehouse to examine crates and boxes being unpacked.

'I do believe you are like a child with a new game,' says his eldest son, Jean. 'There is a light in your eyes we have not seen for a long time!' It is true. The creating of his mansion has totally absorbed Jacques Coeur. It is to be his crowning glory, the summit of his many years of hard work: all the travelling, bargaining, searching, the finding and discovering of treasures no other trader has seen and which will delight the eye of the great collectors; the successes and the failures – because although he does not discuss them, there have been some trading disasters.

There was also that unfortunate business of the Muslim slave boy who stowed away on one of his ships and when discovered, claimed sanctuary as a Christian to avoid being returned to his owners. Yes, he had been beaten – the marks were all over his back – and would be beaten again for running away. But Jacques Coeur is wise and experienced in the ways of the Levant, and no Christian ship has the right to take on board a Muslim slave, no matter what he claims to be. Many of his sailors and the people of Montpellier thought him cruel to return the poor boy – and indeed it was. But why should he endanger his standing with the Sultan and risk losing the trade concessions he has earned – not only for himself but for every French ship? The freedom, even the life, of one slave is not worth that!

# Chapter Twenty

The king continues to use the services of his *argentier* in many and diverse ways. In 1447, he sends for him. 'My good and loyal friend, I need your subtle negotiating skills.' Jacques bows. 'As you know, Christendom has been disadvantaged for too long with the situation we have maintained nurturing *two* popes.

'For many years it has been the tradition that the French king supports the Pope in Avignon and the Holy Roman Emperor supports the Pope in Rome. There has been no Pope in Avignon for some years now, yet our loyalties are still divided – between Felix V, who was elected by the Council of Basel in 1439, and Nicholas V, who has now been installed in Rome as successor to Eugenius IV. 'By having two popes, both with a justifiably persuaded following, we are playing into the hands of the *infidels*, who are once again planning a massive advance to take Constantinople. Just as a divided France cannot defeat the

English, so too a divided leadership of Christendom cannot withstand the mighty Ottoman armies. It is Nicholas to whom I want to give my support.'

Jacques bows again, pursing his lips just as his wife often does when thinking. He knows exactly what that means – the Council of Basel's elected pope has to go. Charles VII prefers to accept Nicholas V because he has a greater following, which will be useful to the French king.

Even more surprising is that Pope Felix had eleven children before the death of his wife, and he became a reclusive monk. Some years ago, the Queen of Sicily's son and heir, Louis III d'Anjou, secretly married his daughter Margaret. It was her father, as Pope Felix V, who crowned Louis as King of Naples and Sicily and Jacques Coeur brokered the union. Why? He understood how helpful it would be to Louis when reigning as king in Naples to have the support of Pope Felix as his father-in-law. *And useful for the merchant's business as well.*

Jacques understands but does not relish his role. He decides it would be prudent to visit Pope Felix, a widower in his fifties with four surviving children, and whose official residence is his own castle of Ripaille in his county of Geneva. There he lived the life of a monk, until in 1439 he was elected Pope by the Council of Basel. He gave up his worldly role as Amadeo VIII, Duke of Savoy, and appointed his son as regent of his substantial territories. The king has given Jacques a delicate mission and in order to do his bidding successfully, he needs to meet Pope Felix and determine the true nature of the man, his ambitions if any, and whether he would accept an enforced retirement.

Although Amadeus VIII is a celebrated holy man, he has never been ordained. This did not present an obstacle to his election as Pope Felix V by the Council of Basel ten years ago and in his case, Jacques understands he will be negotiating with an honourable nobleman.

The journey by road from Bourges to Geneva takes Jacques a good eight days, but as a merchant, he is used to travelling long distances in the saddle. He arrives at the papal residence at dusk. Having sent a message the day before, he is expected, received graciously, and given an opportunity to wash and rest. Later, on entering the chamber, he immediately goes down on one knee to kiss the Pope's ring.

'Welcome, Jacques Coeur, from the court of King Charles VII. I have heard nothing other than in your favour, my friend. Come into my private parlour, where a fire will warm us and our voices will not echo, or the murals overwhelm.'

Jacques follows the white-robed Felix and they enter a charming chamber painted a delicate shade of pomegranate. With his professional eye, the merchant notices the glorious oriental carpets underfoot and comfortable deep-cushioned seating for guests. Felix sits in an upright chair with red velvet back and seat and gilded carved arms and legs. There is a low table in front of Jacques' chair, and a higher one next to the papal throne.

Refreshments are brought: sherbets, as well as tea from China, and small pastries. These are meant for the visitor; the Pope drinks only his pale tea, while observing Jacques with his shrewd eyes set in a finely moulded aristocratic face.

'My good Monsieur Coeur, I imagine you have come here with a special purpose in mind, and I am willing to listen to what you have to propose. I am an old man and I know many things about the world despite having been a recluse since the death of my wife long ago. Now, tell me why you have gone to such trouble to visit me here.'

Jacques sips his sherbet – deliciously spiced rose hip and cherry among other flavours he has yet to identify – and begins.

'Your Holiness, I have come here at my own instigation out of a combination of curiosity and as an appointee of the King of France's delegation destined for Rome. As I am sure you know, its purpose is to help heal the great schism that has divided Christendom for so long.' He hears the Pope suck in his breath through closed teeth, then sees him nod for Jacques to go on.

'I felt I could not be of use in the general discussion planned to take place soon in the Holy City if I did not know something of the character of the contenders. Monseigneur, as you are aware, it is quite clear that a divided France cannot defeat the English invader.' Felix nods. 'And I am not alone in the belief that a divided Christendom would be hard pressed to defeat the might of the Ottoman invading forces.'

'And that is why you are here? Yet you say you do not represent King Charles VII?'

'Your Holiness, that is correct. I do know that King Charles favours Pope Nicholas but that the English have a different choice for Pope in a new election in which you would also participate as a candidate. I have come on my own accord, and without the knowledge of my king, to try to find an acceptable compromise *before* the conclave in Rome – a way in which you would not suffer from the loss of your revenues from the Council of Basel's grant of the county of Geneva to your office; and at the same time, a way that will help preserve Christendom from being overwhelmed by the *infidel* hordes outside Constantinople and at our borders. Since no one is aware of my visit, there can be neither shame nor reprisal attached to my efforts if I fail.'

'My dear sir, now I understand. And tell me, what do you have in mind as a worthy compromise for me to consider in order to achieve this great purpose?' asks the Pope slowly, his eyes never leaving Jacques' own.

'Monseigneur, I am sure you are aware of my efforts to broker the marriage between your daughter Margaret of Savoy and the late Louis III d'Anjou, whom you yourself crowned King of Sicily?'

'Indeed, I am completely cognizant of your connection with that family and the late, remarkable Queen Yolande. Your representation was both fair and honest and is one of the reasons I have agreed to see you today. I also know you were a protégé of hers.' He says this last with a smile. 'She always chose well ...'

'Then, if you will allow, most esteemed Holy Father, I believe that in your heart you too are conscious of the advantage to Christendom of having but one head, one Pope, and at the seat of St Peter in Rome.' Jacques dreaded saying this, but he manages not to alter his voice or his pace.

Silence.

Felix rings a bell, and just as Jacques thinks he is about to be dismissed, their cups are refreshed. Some minutes pass. *Yes, this is the right moment*, he thinks. *I must make my offer now.*

'As a father myself, I know how difficult it is to be re-assured about the future of one's children. I am aware of the many advantages Your Holiness can put the way of your own children – clerical livings, prospective marriages with suitable partners. But it all costs money, does it not? I know our king is finding it difficult to finance his army against the English, let alone joining an alliance to repulse the growing Ottoman threat.'

'Yes,' muses Felix, sipping his tea, 'it does indeed cost.'

'Perhaps, Monseigneur, you might find it useful to consider how I could help your children, were you no longer able to support them as you would wish.'

'My good sir, are you saying that I should step down, and lose my revenues as a result?' There is a hard edge to his voice, and Jacques wonders whether he has gone too far. Then Felix rises and says: 'You will stay the night? We can continue tomorrow after early Mass.' Jacques bows and the Pope sweeps from the room.

The next day, following a Gregorian sung Mass by one of the most beautiful choirs Jacques has ever heard and at six a.m., Pope and merchant meet for a light repast.

'Holy Father, may I express my compliments on your choir? I felt transported to a celestial paradise with their singing.'

'Yes – music is surely one of God's greatest gifts to man.'

They eat in silence, and then Jacques says:

'Your Holiness, I must leave this morning on the king's

business elsewhere. Would you be willing to give my courier a list of your wishes for yourself and your family if I send him to you in, say, a week? Would that give you sufficient time to estimate your needs and theirs?'

The Pope thinks for a moment. 'And from where would this bounty come, Monsieur Coeur? Certainly not from France's king.'

Jacques purses his lips, looking at the bread on his plate.

'Ah, now I understand. This would be *your* doing and yours alone, hence the secrecy of your visit. Am I right?'

'Your Holiness, peace within France is one of my two great goals. Peace within the Church is the other. Both are worthy, noble ambitions, do you agree?'

'Yes, yes, my friend, I do. And now I understand that I cannot be a party to this conclave since I cannot win, and votes that come to me will only serve to weaken your candidate. Rest assured, I will be ready for your courier in a week's time. Give him this ring so that he may gain direct access to me and not be obliged to provide explanations to anyone.' With that he removes a small gold ring set with a carved cornelian from his little finger and hands it to Jacques.

Their meeting is over; the deal is done. Now it is only a question of numbers. Jacques is certain they will be reasonable – they must be in order to be acceptable to him. Now that Felix knows his compensation will come out of Jacques' own pocket, he will calculate carefully.

In April 1448, Charles VII sends to Rome an impressive body of officials, including Jacques Coeur, charged with the task of resolving the difficult state of affairs in the papacy. Both Felix and Nicholas V have agreed to step down in preparation for a new election for the one and only heir to St Peter. All parties recognize that this is the best possible solution. Then both popes change their minds and refuse to step down after all. *What a muddle – will there be three now?*

A large French delegation leaves Marseilles in a fleet of eleven of Jacques Coeur's merchant ships, heavily laden with supplies and gifts to ease their welcome into the Holy City, for they know their path will not be smooth. The English are determined to make an unforgettable impression on the citizens of Rome, and especially the Curia, the papal ruling body, in the hope that they will gain the necessary votes for their candidate – and in the opinion of most observers, they would seem to have succeeded.

The French delegation meets up with the rest of their embassy who travelled overland. They enter the Holy City in a parade of three hundred knights, superbly mounted, their horses caparisoned to the ground in light blue velvet sprinkled with gold-embroidered fleur-de-lys. The horses' bridles are just as ornate, and with each stride, tall white ostrich feathers bob on their brow bands. And this is just the beginning. The French entertain lavishly and return invitations, all the while spreading largesse and generous gifts. The cost, as is often the case, is borne by the *argentier*, but it is well worth it when the preferred French candidate, Nicholas V, is declared the legitimate and only pope.

Not one of Charles VII's entourage is aware that it is Jacques Coeur who induced Felix to step down, leaving the choice between the English and French candidates. The good merchant, who understands the needs of men, feels it prudent to provide more than sufficient compensation to Felix. Months later, when René enquires how he achieved the desired result of his mission, Jacques tells him with a rueful smile, 'Even an ex-pope has to live!'

After a stay of four weeks in Rome, the French delegation leaves – all but Jacques Coeur, who has fallen dangerously ill; so much so that Pope Nicholas has him brought to the Vatican. Entering his room, he is shocked by the merchant's appearance.

'My good friends Jacques – for indeed you have been a good friend to me. Now allow me to be a friend to you. I can see you are seriously ill, and with a high fever. Please put yourself in my care.' Too weak to decline, Jacques agrees. Soon his condition is so grave that Pope Nicholas insists his champion remain as his guest, to be treated constantly by the papal physician. Visiting him each day, the Pope sees Jacques slowly improving, until he can sit up and converse with his host.

'My dear Jacques, do I see a little colour in those wasted cheeks of yours today?'

The patient smiles

'Ah, that pleases me to see you smile.'

'Holy Father, if I am not in Heaven already, I feel as though I could well be with the kindness offered me by you and your staff here.'

'Dear and loyal Jacques, I have reason to know of the many efforts you make on behalf of your friends and therefore it is my wish to do the same for you. You have achieved a great deal for Christendom through your quiet and private intervention – no, don't stop me: much is revealed in the confessional. Your efforts to reunite a divided Church have succeeded, efforts that have been greater than those by anyone alive today. Whosoever is not aware of it will be made so by me!'

'Your Holiness, I am sure that what I did could have been done by others. It was not so much,' Jacques tries to demur.

'No, you are wrong, my friend. No one but you tried – and furthermore, you succeeded. Not only the Roman papacy but all Christendom is in your debt, a debt that can never be repaid in kind, though if ever there is a situation where it might be possible, I and my Curia will be ready to assist you, of that you can be sure.'

'Yes,' says Jacques with a small sigh, 'we do live in dangerous times.'

'My dear Jacques, I know the nature of your king. I have seen how he abandoned Jeanne d'Arc, someone to whom he owed his kingdom, his crown. Never imagine that he has developed a grateful soul now that the Queen of Sicily is no longer there to guide him.'

'Your Holiness, our king has changed, and all due to the influence of a pure young woman through whom he has known true love for the first time.'

'Yes, I have heard talk of the Lady of Beauty, Agnès Sorel. Tell me more.' And Jacques explains how Agnès has succeeded in guiding and comforting the king, helping to change many of his attitudes.

During his lengthy convalescence, the merchant continues

to have deep and serious discussions with Pope Nicholas about many subjects of interest to them both. As a result, they become committed friends. Nicholas V is a wise and worldly man, and feels strongly that such a blessed solution to a serious rift in Christendom is worthy of generous compensation.

'My dear Jacques, will you allow me to give you a token of my gratitude for all you have done to unite the Church?' he asks.

'Holy Father, you have saved my life! It is I who owe you!'

Before Jacques leaves Rome, His Holiness renews the dispensation granted him by his predecessor Eugenius IV in 1445. Not only are his galleys permitted to traffic with the *infidel* throughout his lifetime, but this great privilege enables Jacques to transport pilgrims to the Holy Land, a most blessed and profitable trade.

A clever man, the Pope understands Agnès Sorel's situation, and the honesty of her love for Charles VII. His gift to her is of a unique generosity: he grants her the right to a portable altar, which she may use to hear Mass wherever she is – a remarkable concession, and especially so for a king's mistress.

There is something else – something Jacques Coeur knows the Lady Agnès will treasure more than anything she possesses: a written papal dispensation of all her sins. This paper, in the Pope's own hand, guarantees that her sin of adultery with the king will be automatically absolved upon her death, something no other clergyman is in a position to grant. Obtaining this papal letter of absolution is the greatest reward Jacques Coeur can arrange for his dear friend Agnès in return for the support she has never failed to give him. In a way, he tells himself, he also does it for Queen Yolande, whose protégés both he and Agnès have been.

# Chapter Twenty-One

Since Jacques Cœur is the one man, other than her beloved king, whom Agnès Sorel totally trusts, it is her custom to ask his advice. Her question is a difficult one: can she allow her face to be used for that of the Madonna in a diptych for a church? For a sinner, an adulteress – such as she undoubtedly is – to be painted in the role of Christ's mother is surely the height of blasphemy? *Yet, dear Jacquet, it would be such an honour – and did not the same Christ give her that face?*

The diptych is to hang in a chapel her friend Étienne Chevalier has built for his beloved late wife in the church at his home town of Melun. Jacques knows the king's treasurer as a good, honest man who was devoted to his wife and regards Agnès as a dear sister. On reading her letter, he understands at once that she felt unable to hurt this gentle and sorrowing man with a refusal. In that case, there is no more to be said. He replies:

'By all means be painted for the diptych – if the king agrees.'

Reading between the lines of her letter, Jacques tells that Agnès is apprehensive, and once he sees the finished work, he understands why. Agnès is portrayed as Christ's mother Mary, Queen of Heaven. She wears a great crown and sits on a throne, a blue mantle lined in ermine over her shoulders with one breast exposed and her baby, her third with the king, representing the Christ Child. It is not the pose that is inappropriate: the Madonna of the Milk is a popular and familiar subject for painters and sculptors at this time. It is the role reversal that shocks both the court and society in general. For the king's mistress to be painted as Mary Magdalene perhaps … but never as the Virgin Mary!

Beautiful though it is, the diptych causes a tremendous scandal. All Bourges is talking about it, and criticizing Agnès. When asked at home by Marcée, Jacques admits that with time, the fashions worn by the king's lady have become somewhat exaggerated. 'Yes,' agrees Marcée, 'I hear that her trains are now a third longer than anyone else's; her hennins are taller; but most of all, it is said that sometimes when at the court, she leaves her front lacings undone exposing one of her breasts.'

'Well, I for one have never seen her so undressed, at court or in her houses.' And Marcée gives her husband what their children call *one of her looks*.

No one is surprised when the following year, 1449, war with the English begins again. Although the young King of England, Henry VI, himself half French, disapproves of his country's antagonism towards France, his French-born queen, Marguerite d'Anjou, and to the understandable resentment of the English people, openly supports her homeland. Furthermore, the French, in particular the Anjou family, are outraged that the English still refuse to return René d'Anjou's territory of Maine in accordance with the wedding treaty of his daughter to Henry VI.

The confrontational incidences accelerate on the Norman–French border, but still Charles VII hesitates before calling for Jacques Coeur. Only the merchant can help him to take a decision based on supplies and cost. Five years of peace have been extremely beneficial for the country; why return to the horror of war, despite the deliberate provocation of the English? Finally, and largely due to the urging of the queen and with the support of Agnès, the king summons Jacques to discuss the financing of yet another campaign against their old enemy.

Since he knows her so well, it surprises Jacques Coeur that the Lady Agnès is in favour of war. But aware of the queen's enthusiasm and the king's disinclination, she wants to please them both. In order to achieve this, she announces: 'Why don't the ladies of the court go to the Front to give their support to our brave knights; and then entertain them between battles?' And her suggestion is greeted with loud hurrahs by the company!

From the merchant's point of view, war is good business. For several years Charles VII has urged him to stock up on weapons and armour as well as horses, in case they might be needed. Now Jacques is ready and able to equip the king's professional forces *and* lend him the funds needed to finance victory. He has remained in contact with the great banking merchants of Italy and Spain for just such an eventuality. He knows he is in a position to help and agrees unequivocally to support a new, great effort to rid France once and for all of the hated English.

There is no doubt in Jacques Coeur's wily mind that the English army will be led by the redoubtable Earl of Shrewsbury, an eighty-year-old legend in this never-ending conflict between their two countries. But the French have good generals as well, and both the king and Jacques have confidence in their new professional army. Urged on by the queen, Agnès, and the courtiers, reluctantly the king agrees, and the country begins to prepare once again for war.

But instead of joining the ladies at the Front, to her anguish, Agnès has no choice but to stay behind at Bellevue, her tranquil manor at Loches, unwell, as never before, with her fourth pregnancy. It is at this time that Jacques Coeur becomes aware that her flighty cousin Antoinette de Maignelay who Agnès brought to court out of kindness, is spending time alone with the king in the absence of his mistress. There are many people in debt to Jacques Coeur, and he is often told secrets in some sort of part-payment. Out of loyalty to the Lady of Beauty, he feels obliged to establish if these rumours are true.

When he discovers his fears are correct – that this wretched cousin is taking advantage of Agnès's pregnancy to betray her benefactress – he cannot decide what to do. *Surely when the baby is born all will revert to normal again? The king is only using Antoinette, as men might do while they are away from their homes.* Antoinette is thought by some to be as beautiful as Agnès; but unlike her generous cousin, she is clearly ambitious and using Agnès for her own advancement. Something about her troubles Jacques more than he likes to admit, even to himself. From the first day of her arrival at court, he has seen Antoinette de Maignelay for what she is, and he hopes he is right in his assumption that her relationship with the king is no more than a passing fancy.

Then another little piece of interesting information comes his way. While his treasured Agnès is absent at Loches, the king has given Antoinette the lands of Maignelais, which her family lost at some time in the past. Is this more-than-generous gift merely a gesture for the sake of his Lady Agnès, to give her pleasure – Jacques is sure it will be presented as such – or is it some kind of payment for services rendered? He wonders, and none too positively ...

While Agnès remains in her villa at Loches, Jacques joins the king on his triumphal tour of victories. As they advance into Normandy, town after town previously con-quered by the enemy falls to them, until they reach the capital, the walled city of Rouen. To the surprise of the king and the army, the gates are opened to them from within by the populace, who welcome the return of their French sovereign with undisguised enthusiasm.

And what a king he looks. Jacques Coeur has outfitted Charles VII as a true conquering hero. He wears a hat of grey beaver trimmed with deep red satin overlaid with gold lace and sporting a huge diamond on the brim. He sits on his white charger caparisoned to the ground in sky-blue velvet covered in fleur-de-lys stitched with gold thread. Escorted by his band of Scottish archers, his pages in short ruby satin tunics worn over ruby hose, their sleeves laced with semi-precious stones, Charles VII appears in every way the victorious king.

A rider-less white horse led by a footman carries on its back a casket of precious jewels. On either side of the white steed process the king's cousins, the two Anjou princes René and Charles, each riding a black stallion, as if the appointed guardians of the royal regalia. Behind them follow Pierre de Brézé, Jean de Dunois and Jacques Coeur. Charles VII has taken great care with the details of the parade and arranged for these last three to be dressed identically. Their jackets are of ruby-red velvet trimmed with marten fur, their hats are of black velvet, and each wears a sword with a golden hilt bejewelled with rubies and diamonds.

Being an honest man, Jacques frankly intimates to Jean de Dunois that he feels somewhat out of place in such distinguished company, but both Jean and Pierre assure him that the king wishes it known how much the merchant has contributed financially to the happy outcome. Moreover, it is made deliberately clear to the people that without Jacques Coeur's loans to finance the army, the French could not have attained victory. The three men – as well as the king himself – all began as Queen Yolande's protégés, and Jacques admits to his neighbours on either side that he feels a glow of pride and satisfaction to be among them on this unremarkable day.

While they are still in Rouen, Jacques hears disturbing news concerning the Lady Agnès. It seems that she is on her way to join the king and intends to reach him at Jumièges in Normandy. This sudden decision to travel north by litter in the worst of the winter weather puzzles him, but he is informed by one of his agents that she has received important information that only she can pass on to the king. This is unlikely, and does not convince him.

They call Jacques Coeur 'the eyes and ears of the king' – and it is true he has seen into the hearts of many of his sovereign's subjects. For the sake of the Lady Agnès, for some time the merchant has been watching the sly looks Antoinette de Maignelay has given the king when his mistress was not in the room. Then again, he has also heard that Antoinette has been very much in the company of André de Villequier, a handsome former chamberlain of the king's, who was dismissed but seems to be back at court, once again in favour. Agnès must surely know about Villequier's relationship with Antoinette, but since he was sent by the king to accompany her escort to the north, she must feel even more uncomfortable knowing that her cousin is with the court without either her there or Antoinette's lover to prevent her giving the king seductive glances and lacing her conversation with innuendo.

Jacques knows that Agnès wanted to keep Antoinette with her at Loches, but could not prevent her leaving with the court once Queen Marie requested she join her suite. What a strange request from the queen, who never tolerates voluptuous women in her entourage! What could have entered her mind to ask for Antoinette, for whom her ladies do not think she has much affection? Surely it is not possible that Queen Marie wants to punish Agnès with a rival? No – that really is not possible …

Something else unusual strikes Jacques: the queen has sent her own doctor, the famous Robert Poitevin – he who was at the deathbed of the poor dauphine Margaret – to stay with the Lady Agnès – her husband's mistress – and help with her difficult pregnancy. The doctor's loyalty to the queen is beyond any doubt, and Jacques is certain he will take good care of his charge. But is he able, at his advanced age, to accompany Agnès on this folly of a journey in such remarkably cold weather?

What could have persuaded her to go on this perilous expedition in her condition? All the court knows she is having a troublesome pregnancy. Could she perhaps have heard of a reason to fear for the king's life? Or to doubt the king's love? Jacques' informers in her household write that Dr Poitevin brought her letters. Could they have contained information about Antoinette? Or about a genuine plot against the king? Even so, it does not seem likely that Agnès felt unable to confide in someone near her to save her going to meet the king herself– unless that danger comes from someone so close that her warning would never reach the king?

The court is at Jumièges, and all there hear of her slow progress, and of the king's pleasure at the thought of her arrival as well as his concern for her health, but the war effort takes much of his attention – as it should. Jacques is not yet privy to what or who occupies his attention during the night, but he is determined to find out.

And then, although he is not there to greet her himself, he hears that after a long and painful journey, Agnès and her party have arrived. They are quickly installed at the comfortable manor of Mesnil-sous-Jumièges, which belongs to the abbey nearby.

It is a happy time for the lovers. The king has success to

glory in, and he can rejoice in the presence of his beloved Agnès by his side, admiration for him glowing from her eyes. Jacques has a good man in the king's domestic service, and he hears at once that the king totally disregards his beloved's fears of a plot against his life. Most probably he imagines fondly that she missed him, and simply had to join him despite the ferocious elements. When Jacques arrives at the manor house, he sees the king full of good humour due to the combination of victory and the love of his lady, and everyone there rejoices for him. Privately, Jacques is grievously concerned for Agnès's health. Her smile and her eyes might hide her condition from the king, but not from him, and he tries to warn his sovereign.

He cannot stay, but hears that they spend two weeks in a glow of love, with company by day and alone at night, and even by day they manage to slip away.

In the short time Jacques spends at Jumièges after Agnès's arrival, his sharply observant eyes notice quite a change in the manner of Antoinette de Maignelay towards her cousin. Nothing he can put his finger on, but as he hastily tells Marie de Belleville, who has accompanied Agnès from Loches, he has a nose for this sort of thing, and in his absence, can she please take good care of her mistress? The king avoids Antoinette's eyes, but Jacques sees something different in the way this false friend of his lady's looks at them both: a new confidence, almost arrogance – also in the way she moves – and no significant diffidence towards either of them. Then he must start for Rouen on the king's business, and he leaves Jumièges greatly troubled.

At last the time comes when the king must return to the army. Following an exchange of many tender farewells with his beloved, he mounts his white charger, and as he rides away, he is heard calling out his promise to her: 'I will be back in time for the birth – count on me!'

## Chapter Twenty-Two

Soon after the king's departure for the Front, Agnès goes into labour. It is a slow, painful, difficult birth, and the sad result is a stillborn girl foetus of not much more than seven months. There is no time for sorrow – the mother is their greatest concern. The Lady of Beauty, no longer true to her name, is surrounded by helpful hands – the queen's doctor, Robert Poitevin; the king's doctor, too: both good men. They say that Agnès is suffering from parasites in her intestines, and treat her with mercury, as is customary. A messenger is sent to the king, who hurries back to comfort her as best he can, but his visit is brief and then he must return to the Front.

Marie de Belleville is with Agnès, and her new favourite, Jeanne, the wife of Pierre de Brézé, has returned from her home in Rouen to be with her too, passing Jacques Coeur on the way. Antoinette and her other ladies are also in attendance, assisting the doctors or trying to offer relief.

Jacques hears that her friend Etienne de Chevalier, whom he trusts, is ready to send for anything that might ease her suffering. And of course, good Father Denis, her chaplain, always on his knees nearby, is praying for her.

During the time Jacques Coeur spends in Rouen, he receives news regularly of Agnès's condition, but there is something that keeps bothering him. While he was still in Jumièges, Marie de Belleville came to him especially to thank him on her lady's behalf for the medicines he had arranged to be sent to Loches with Dr Poitevin. Now the merchant casts his mind back to occasions when he could have recommended something to her, or to the doctors, perhaps. It is possible, but strange. He is a careful man, especially where medications are concerned, and in particular if intended for his most important customer and friend.

In the ten days since the birth, the doctors have been administering many different herbal remedies and unguents, which are taken into Agnès's room, past where her ladies and faithful Etienne sit and wait. They hear from one of the maids that she has even agreed to swallow a whole bowl of some thick white tincture containing mercury that they see carried in by her cousin Antoinette. This, she assures them as she passes, is liberally laced with honey to make it bearable, and the queen's doctor says it will rid her stomach of the painful flux. All they can do is pray and hope.

Then Jacques receives news that instead of improving, the beloved patient is visibly disintegrating. Whenever her friends hear her cry out in pain, it is as if a knife is thrust into their hearts, and they gaze at one another, their eyes draining of hope. The days go by unbearably slowly and with no sign of improvement, *but at least she is able to rest and sleep*, he reads in Jeanne de Brézé's letter.

The nightmare continues for three more days before Jacques arrives back at Mesnil. When she hears he is there, Agnès sends one of her women to fetch him and Etienne. Both are shocked to see the shadow of the adorable paragon of beauty. She asks them to witness her testament, and with their hearts heavy, they willingly oblige. 'I have no regrets,' she tells them. 'I have loved one man, my king, with all my heart,' and she likens herself to her patron saint, Mary Magdalene, calling for her intercession before God and the Virgin. Together with the good doctor they sign, and withdraw in sorrow to the next room to pray with Marie de Belleville, and Jeanne de Brézé. Now and again Antoinette joins them.

When they hear that Agnès has asked for her *Book of Hours*, they know the end is near. The portable altar Jacques arranged for her with Pope Nicholas V is carried into her room for her to hear Mass. She asks for the Pope's other great gift – the indulgence absolving her sins on her deathbed. After a frantic search, they learn that the original document is at her home in Loches. How it troubles her not to have it with her, but it is too late to send for it. Father Denis, good soul that he is, accepts her word and grants her absolution before she takes Communion.

Etienne and Jacques remain outside her room with the ladies. When Father Denis appears again, he whispers: 'Her spirit departed her decaying body at six o'clock this evening, Monday the ninth of February, in the Year of Our Lord 1450,' and he kneels with them to pray.

Messengers are sent at once to the king, and when he arrives, he gives Etienne Chevalier – dear, true friend to Agnès – responsibility for the arrangements for a most sumptuous funeral. She is to receive the full honours normally reserved for a royal princess. The king created her a duchess before leaving for the Front – a title Agnès had been fearful of accepting previously; she may have been right in feeling that there was a limit to the queen's tolerance – and that of others.

Following her death, there is no restraint on the monarch in either his grief or his desire to honour his only true love. He orders her heart to be placed in a magnificent urn in the church at Jumièges. Her wasted body is to be embalmed by Dr Poitevin and then transported in state to the cathedral of Our Lady of Loches. Etienne Chevalier is charged by the king to lead the cortège there, and he willingly obeys his sovereign. Jacques Coeur journeys to Loches on Charles VII's orders as a witness to the splendid funeral. Further, the king commands that a magnificent tomb be built of alabaster with her effigy lying on top. Around her head she is to have the circlet of a duchess, a dukedom being the most noble title for a king to bestow, and rarely given directly to a woman. Pierre de Brézé asks the young poet Jacques Milet to compose a verse to be engraved at the base of her memorial, extolling her beauty, gentleness and generosity.

The magnificence of the monuments the king plans to raise to his beloved Mistress of Beauty constitutes a total break with tradition – never before has a private lady, let alone a mere mistress or concubine, been elevated to such a height, and officially. During her lifetime, the king has honoured her and paraded her publicly, but the extent of his devotion comes as a revelation to the court. *And, no doubt, to the queen,* thinks Jacques.

As to the dispositions in her testament, which Jacques witnessed with the doctor and Etienne, all she had, she wrote, came from the king, and was to be carefully distributed to the Church and to the poor. Her will makes no mention of her family, or of her three daughters. Illegitimate at birth, by law the three girls belong to their father, and will be dependent upon his bounty.

The cause of her death, both royal doctors agree, was probably puerperal fever, so common following childbirth – and what a dreadful labour hers was. All who were in attendance on her were aware of her torment both during and after the confinement – and worse, of her decomposition. How this fastidious lady must have been distressed, not only due to pain, but also by disgust at her own decaying body.

Whenever an important person dies suddenly and unexpectedly, talk of poison is inevitable. After all, poison is the most common cause of a quick death in court circles. But once the facts become known – the difficult pregnancy, the terrible journey she undertook to join the king in the north during the worst winter in living memory, the painful premature birth and the dead child – such talk soon ceases.

It is true Agnès Sorel had a number of enemies, not so much of her person, but on account of her position by the king's side, and in his bed. Most thought her influence on the sovereign was much stronger than in fact it was; according to those closest to him, Charles VII did not really listen to anyone. There is a faction at court who deeply resented her interference – even her presence – at the meetings of the King's Council. Jacques Coeur discussed this with Pierre de Brézé and both agreed that in truth the king they have both observed over a number of years is really two persons in one – the seeker of pleasure and the Head of State – and these two rarely combined their thinking or their actions.

Within three months of the death of the Lady Agnès, Antoinette de Maignelay is established as the king's new mistress. But there is a difference. Whereas Charles VII could not bear for Agnès to follow the custom of having an official husband complaisant enough to give his name to her children, he quickly arranges a marriage for Antoinette, choosing for her André de Villequier, formerly his chamberlain and a royal favourite.

At the time of the scandal of the dauphine Margaret's death, Villequier had struck Jacques Coeur as a most avaricious character – which would make him a good match for Antoinette. If rumour is to be believed, Villequier has been her lover for some time – perhaps she even suggested him herself to the king as a suitable husband.

The marriage, which takes place seven months after the death of Agnès Sorel, is a most splendid affair, with the bridegroom receiving surprising largesse from the king in properties and position. He is made a member of the Council and becomes governor of La Rochelle – a good distance from the court. Jean de Dunois is obliged to renounce the properties he was given for his many services rendered, and they are conferred instead on Antoinette.

Villequier is granted the Norman Saint-Sauveur-le-Vicomte, while Antoinette receives a number of islands. The king gives her a marriage portion of two thousand *livres* a year for life – although Jacques tells Marie de Belleville with sly pleasure that it is only half the amount he gave annually to the Lady Agnès.

Jacques Coeur did not like Antoinette de Maignelais from the day she arrived at court, and he could see that Pierre de Brézé, charged with him by the king to take care of his beloved, felt the same, but more tactfully! She was always patently out for what she could get from everyone, and neither of these, Agnès's guardians, detected any real affection towards the king's lady, only envy. As one would expect from a scrupulous opportunist, Antoinette has played her part to perfection. It could be that, at times, she *was* good company for Agnès, who had initially invited Antoinette to Loches to take care of her children – not a post that would satisfy her ambitious cousin at all.

The king's bequests to his new mistress continue. He bestows upon her Agnès's château and town of Issoudun, an enormously generous gift, since Jacques Coeur filled the house with wonderful treasures chosen together with the Lady Agnès from his warehouses. How he hates the idea of Antoinette stepping into her shoes in this way.

The speed with which this duplicitous couple have risen to prominence following the death of Agnès preys on the merchant's mind. Had they perhaps some inkling of it in advance? Did Antoinette conceive the idea of the letters threatening the king's life that persuaded her to make that terrible journey, a journey on which she might well have miscarried and died? It was Antoinette who remained with Agnès once she arrived at Jumièges, and who did not leave her side until her death.

Then again, if she was already in the king's bed, she may well have had the same future whether or not his beloved had lived. Jacques is not alone in sensing that the king had already 'tasted' the fair Antoinette. After all, Agnès was pregnant four times in six years, occasions when she withdrew from the court for months at a time. It was only with this last, painful confinement that Jacques perceived her beauty fading, though no one near had any sense of the king's devotion to her fading as well. Charles VII was wise enough to have recognized her genuine love for him. Yes, she enjoyed his spoiling of her, but she never asked for anything – and her love could be said to have been truly disinterested.

What really distresses Agnès's friends about the king's new mistress is that Antoinette has none of the fine qualities of her predecessor. She possesses neither purity of heart nor that of spirit, and it is becoming clear that she is capable of tempting the king to indulge again in his weakness for dissipation and debauchery, and in this way holding him fast. What a sad legacy for Queen Yolande, after spending a lifetime of effort on the king, and for the honesty of the Lady Agnès's love for him; and what misfortune her death brings now on the quality of the court and the country – but Jacques only shares these thoughts with his wife Marcée.

*

Guillaume Gouffier is another who Jacques thinks brings the court into disrepute. He was one of Agnès's guardians at Bellevue and on the journey to Jumièges and is one of the many young gentlemen of the court who comes regularly to Jacques Coeur's warehouses to treat himself to the luxuries on offer there. Gouffier loves opulence and indulges enthusiastically; but the merchant wonders from where does he have so much money to spend, especially on beautiful fabrics, furs and horses? How he loves horses – a passion the king allows him to indulge. Why? Is Gouffier some sort of spy for the king? Jacques has never trusted him and nothing would surprise him either – not even such a crime as he hardly dares to imagine.

Once the two magnificent internments of the Lady Agnès are over, one at Jumièges, and the other at Loches, war has kept Charles VII too occupied to show his sorrow for his lost love in public. And then he has Antoinette. The devoted friends of Agnès grieve silently as well, but the needs of life and business continue.

# Chapter Twenty-Three

During the previous twenty years, through his hard work and astuteness, Jacques Coeur has amassed enormous commercial power. His three hundred agents are spread throughout the ports of Europe and the East and his fleet of merchant ships flying the flag of France are respected. In fact, his international renown could be equated to that of his friend Cosimo de' Medici, who also began as a simple merchant and became a mighty ruler. There is a saying in Bourges: 'As rich as Jacques Coeur', which is as much as people there can imagine. Another myth attributed to the extent of his wealth is that his horses are shod in silver from his mines!

The great house he has had built in his hometown for his family and himself is intended to be a monument to live on after him and in his honour. It reveals many different aspects of Jacques Coeur the merchant: his travels; his cultural delights; his discoveries; his love of flora and fauna; his interest in alchemy; his passion for games and secrets. In fact, it is a house full of secrets both in the detail and the decoration.

The manor has a large central courtyard, and turrets over three of the staircases – there are a total of eight, giving independence to each part of the house. The hub of the building is a prominent central tower. Jacques loves to build, and his house in Bourges becomes a satisfying exercise, something he thoroughly enjoys creating. Throughout the four years of its construction, he collects furniture, tapestries, carpets and many other things that he feels will suitably enhance his mansion, but his greatest pleasure is contained in the decoration.

When Jean de Villages comes to Bourges with his wife Perette, her uncle cannot resist taking them through every detail. 'Jean, my good nephew, and Perette, beloved niece, I will explain my idea: can you see how the plan of the building is irregular in shape?' He does not give them time to reply; his enthusiasm runs on: 'That is because it is restricted by its surrounding Roman wall on one side and walls of other houses on the other. Don't you think that despite the building's two facades being erected in different styles, the whole effect is somehow harmonious?'

And they have to agree, strange as it seems. On the rampart side of the mansion there are three towers, one with a balustrade, at unequal distances from one another and of varying shapes and heights. On the other side, the facade facing the street has two towers and carvings in the flamboyant style.

'Now look here, both of you, see between the towers? There is a balcony with an elaborate open balustrade adorned with my motto: "To a valiant heart, nothing is impossible". What do you think of that?' Both Jean and Perette cannot help smiling, watching their uncle's delight.

When the young couple see Marcée, Jean tells her: 'Dearest Aunt, I have been away from Bourges for so long on Uncle Jacques' business elsewhere, I had not realized how advanced the new manor has become.'

'And what is your opinion, my Jean?'

'I must say, I find the whole extremely pleasing to the eye and quite deliciously mysterious in much of the decoration.'

Then Perette adds, 'I could not help noticing that on each side of the elegant balcony facing the street, there are two false window embrasures cut into the stone as if the windows are half open, and there is a figure leaning out of each – one a man, the other a woman, posed as if keeping a lookout; a most unusual form of decoration for the outside of a house.' Jean gives his wife a hard look.

'It's all right,' laughs Marcée. 'I know what people say, that they are portraits of you two! I honestly do not know if that is what either your uncle or the sculptor intended, but I think it is a charming conceit, since you both keep a sharp lookout on your uncle's business interests and my extensive domestic life.' And they all smile, Jean and Perette with a certain relief.

Throughout the large building, with its odd heights and widths of the unevenly shaped windows and doors, high on the walls of the rooms there are friezes with sayings and mottoes, some clearer than others. Jean de Village is too wise a trusted employee and since he married into the Coeur family, he will certainly not cause any friction by showing untoward curiosity, but he cannot help asking his wife: 'Perrette dearest, why does your uncle decorate his house with so many secret words and pictures – or try to have his guests believe that he does? I mean, someone with *real* secrets would hardly expose them to discovery – like in a game?' Perrette loves her husband and is also as shrewd as he, or even perhaps as her uncle. 'I must confess that I have always thought Uncle Jacques to be involved in some sort of secret society sect – or even more than one – there are enough conspiracies in our town and you have told me of others you have noticed on your travels. I really do not know the answer, but I have to agree – there is something binding in his life that not even Aunt Marcée is prepared to talk about, but I honestly believe whatever it is that he is involved with is in a good cause.' Jean de Village gives his wife a long look. 'Yes, I think you are right and I too believe he is involved in something we are not to know about or he will tell us.' And with that they leave the subject alone. In addition to the strange words and carvings, hearts and shells and the family's new coat of arms proliferate – on surfaces and ceilings, painted, carved, sculpted; on the capitals of columns; on window frames and the surrounds of chimney pieces. Then there is the merchant's motto: 'To a valiant heart, nothing is impossible' – a charming play on his own name – which is repeated again and again, carved in stone and wood, even on furniture. Both niece and nephew know it is something he resolutely believes, somewhat in the manner of the knights of chivalry. As they discuss this, Marcée adds: 'You are right – *that* is the secret of this husband of mine. Since his youthful visits to our city's Duke Jean with his father, he has always sworn by the virtues of chivalry: honesty, duty and courage.'

And yet, he is also a merchant, a very successful one, and that in itself belies these great and noble aspirations, for to make money in this way usually means through the greed or foolishness of others.

As well as Jacques' own motto, there are three words repeated several times throughout the house: 'faire, dire, taire'; sometimes 'taire' alone. These refer to the alchemists' famous saying: 'De ma joie du grand oeuvre; dire peu; faire beaucoup; taire toujours'.

'The great work (alchemy) brings me joy; but say little; do much; and keep quiet about it'.

The alchemists' fraternity of Bourges do not consider Jacques Coeur to be one of their number; rather, he owns mines and exploits them for trade. If, with his decorations and word games on the walls of his mansion, he wants to appear mysterious and more knowledgeable than perhaps he is – why not? However, he has become rich from trading silver, gold and other metals, and how better to flatter the town's real alchemists than by using their symbols within his glorious mansion? Jean de Villages mulls over this puzzle as his uncle continues to show his nephew and niece around: 'See there – the carvings in connection with my travels – galleons in full sail; palm trees with dates representing my Mediterranean trade, which you care for so well, dear Jean. Over there, another depicts the acacia trees of Constantinople; and there, the orange trees that I introduced with success to Provence as well as the palm trees with dates.'

Perette notices that certain flowers have been carved beneath the orange trees. 'Uncle Jacques, these flowers, did you bring them to Provence from the Near East, or even from your stops in Naples? I know they would not survive a winter here in Bourges, so they must come from abroad.'

'Clever girl,' Jacques exclaims with delight. 'Yes, I often traded plants and trees from Provence with the local people in Naples and also with the court for the royal garden. You are right, they would not survive in Bourges, but in Provence they quickly became established.'

'I have also noticed that several times there is a carving of a feather standing upright. Does this represent the fabulous bird you used to tell us about as children? The one that was written about in the stories of the poets of Persia and Arabia?'

'No, my observant niece – it is a reference to the pigeons I learnt from the Arabs how to train and then use to carry messages. Come and I will show you the pigeon house built up inside against the roof with more carvings of vertical feathers.'

A number of figures are cut into the stone walls in high relief. 'Jean, look, this must be Uncle Jacques!' calls Perrett, and there he is, wearing a furred gown and a chain, a dagger by his side and a turban headdress with toggles hanging down over his ears. 'How clever – you are holding a mason's mallet.'

'Well, I am the builder after all – and see, in my other hand there is a bouquet of flowers I am presenting to Marcée!'

In this carving he is surrounded by ten other figures, equally elegantly dressed. Nearby another saying has been carved high on the wall and which appears several times: 'A fly cannot enter a shut mouth' – a reference to keeping secrets, which he is known to do, like a priest in the confessional. Then there is a carving of a lady resting on the ground, wearing a crown, with a hand raised as if to remove it; another crowned head peeps through the foliage looking concerned, and a third figure, that of a fool, with bauble, cap and bells, is grinning.

Jean and Perette exchange looks. 'Uncle Jacques, what does all this mean?' And their uncle just smiles his enigmatic smile.

*'Secrets, my dears, just secrets. For me to know and for you to fathom!'*

In another tower, they find a strong room so well constructed that should the heavy metal door with concealed hinges close by chance with the key left inside, the wall would have to be taken down to enter again!

'Is it true, dear Uncle, that you have built extensive underground vaults and a series of tunnels by which chests and barrels can be moved to Bourges all the way from Sancerre, where you have your vineyards?'

'Yes, my dear, and why not? Rolling barrels is a much simpler way of transport than by donkey cart! Now come with me to the roof – there is much still to see.'

Up they climb, and wonder at the exquisitely ornamented chimneys. 'Oh! Uncle, more alternating shells and hearts – yet only the pigeons can admire them up here.'

The merchant smiles with pleasure at her appreciation. 'Then come and look at the gargoyles beneath the balconies – there is one of a monkey carrying away a small child on its back, which people claim actually happened.'

'Did it?' asks Perette anxiously.

'I doubt it very much,' says Jacques. 'Where would we find a monkey here?'

Their tour continues, and both Jean and his wife are in awe seeing the decoration inside the house. Walls are covered with tapestries; carpets lie on the floors; silver and gold vessels and ornaments stand on the sideboards; and painted leather close covers the lids of coffers. Perette tries the carved chairs and benches for comfort, as well as the top of the clothes coffers, made comfortable with cushions of velvet.

'See the high galleries in the great rooms for the musicians to play for the pleasure of the guests during meals,' Jacques tells them, 'while I want attendants to stand holding great flaming torches to light the company.' He says all this with such pride and pleasure that they cannot but share in his joy.

Just as the windows are not aligned or of similar sizes and shapes, so too are the doors made of different shapes and sizes, some huge and others so small only one person can enter at a time. 'Uncle, I am as slim as a lady can be and I can hardly fit through one of these doors' laughs Perette. 'Jean, do look at the studs on the nails of the doors – their heads are in the shapes of hearts!' Such are the charming amusements of architect and client.

But Jean de Villages is fascinated by the astrological instruments depicted in stone, and others for astronomy. Jacques is the commander of his merchant fleet, and Jean is aware how he has listened and learnt from his sea captains until he knows as much about the skies as they do sharing their interest in both astrology and astronomy.

But *could there be more to his interest* is the thought that keeps turning around in Jean's mind…

Bourges possesses an extraordinary astronomical clock, installed in 1424, when Jacques was twenty-four. Being a young man with a dazzling talent for mathematics, this clock has always held him spellbound. 'Jean, do you recall my telling you about the first time I saw the astronomical clock here in Bourges? I came almost daily for years to study it. As my career progressed and my good fortune followed, my conversations with learned men on these subjects are what gave rise to the myth that I possess the Philosopher's Stone and can turn base metal into gold! It has never ceased to amuse me.' And both men laugh.

Their next stop is a tiny chapel with perfect proportions and a delicate twisted staircase leading to it. Frescoes of beautiful angels in floating white robes are painted on a lapis-blue ceiling covered in golden stars. Perette is entranced gazing at the angels, who each hold a banderol showing quotations from the scriptures. 'How thoughtful of you, dear Uncle,' she says, pointing to the corner of the chapel, seeing a small fireplace for the comfort of those at prayer in the colder months. The windows above are of beautifully painted glass, and a side door leads to Jacques and Marcée's private apartments.

By now they are exhausted with the wonder of their uncle's house, and tell him so. 'Just a little more,' he says leading them out into the courtyard. There stand two equestrian statues: one of the king, Charles VII, on a fine charger, fully armed; the other of the merchant mounted on a mule with its shod feet pointing backwards. 'Is this another of your little mysteries?' asks Perette, and Jacques laughs.

'Well, it might be to some; however, among miners, there is a well-known story of a man who found a seam of gold. To avoid giving away its location, he shod the shoes of his mule the wrong way round so that no one could follow his tracks back to the mine!'

One of the truly innovative additions to the mansion is the garden. Jacques has made use of land next to his house where the town's defences used to stand, filled the ditches with soil, and planted flowers and shrubs he has brought back from his travels throughout France, Provence and the East. Whenever he stopped in Naples, the palace gardeners would give him plants from the area on the instruction of Queen Isabelle. When his ships arrived at Marseilles he would have his factors there ready with plants and trees from Provence to take home with him to Bourges. There was no shortage of variety for his garden which was unique and flourished, although some of the more delicate varieties did not survive winter. No one else in the city has a garden attached to their house, and the flowers blooming right on the street are a rare and pleasing sight.

It has taken time and much effort, but finally, after four years' toil and careful supervision, the king's *argentier* has completed his magnificent town house – surely the most impressive anyone has ever seen. Although it is not yet ready for full occupation, Jacques is satisfied – and secretly delighted – with the result. Marcée, his family and friends are full of admiration.

# Chapter Twenty-Four

Since Jacques is frequently in his home town over-seeing the building of his house, he decides to add a sacristy to the cathedral of Bourges, and a chapel where he and his family will be buried. In 1441, his brother Nicholas was appointed the Bishop of Luçon and gave up his position as canon of the Sainte-Chappelle in Bourges in favour of their half-brother. Jacques has great hopes of further ecclesiastical promotions within his family, which can only place him even higher with the king and the court.

His optimism was well placed. Five years later, Jean Coeur, the eldest of Marcée and Jacques' sons, is appointed Archbishop of Bourges at the age of just twenty-five. The family members are overwhelmed, but never forget that their roots are among the people. Jean's elevation to such a high-ranking ecclesiastical position is an incredible tribute for someone from a family as simple as theirs, despite his father's achievements, and they feel sincerely honoured and humbled.

The appointment is not immediately confirmed by the Holy See, but when it is finally ratified in September 1450, Jacques decides to hold a splendid reception in honour of the new Archbishop of Bourges. He is understandably proud to have a house fit to receive important guests and to represent what the family has achieved.

Jean's official entry into Bourges that year, with the foremost of the king's counsellors riding by his side, is a triumphant moment for his parents. There stands Jacques Coeur, the son of an unimportant local furrier, watching with his wife and children as the great barons of Berry carry his son on his dais. For once this display has not been arranged by the merchant but by the clergy of his son's new office. Then the feast Jacques gives in the new archbishop's honour is the most sumptuous ever seen in the city.

Despite his euphoria at his son's elevation and the pleasure derived from his new mansion, the shrewd merchant's instincts tell him that something strange is happening. A few weeks have passed since the inauguration of his town house in Bourges, when, to his disbelief, he hears that one of his close friends, a lawyer working for the king and a member of his Council, has been arrested for irregularities in his bookkeeping. He is accused of merging his business with that of the king – *to the Crown's disadvantage*.

This news greatly perturbs Marcée, but why should it reflect on Jacques? He does his best to reassure her that he has never been in a more trusted position, or in better standing with the king, than at this time.

'No, my dear, be assured that such an accusation will never be levelled at me. Did the king not publicly honour me recently, during his entry into Rouen, hailing me as the man without whom victory over the English could not have been possible?'

It is July 1451. A year and a half has passed since the death of Jacques' dear friend the Lady Agnès, and he misses her still. Seeing her was always a pleasure: her innocent delight in his stories; her unfeigned glee in the surprising treasures that he would produce from invisible pockets as if by magic. How she would laugh – like a child! And with what enthusiasm she entered into the spirit of any scheme to help the king and the people that Jacques might suggest. Naturally every such scheme was to his benefit as well, but the main point for her was a benevolent one. What fun they had plotting!

On 31 July, Charles VII and the court are at the Château de Taillebourg, where the king is visiting his four daughters. Jacques Coeur is staying with friends nearby. Suddenly, without any warning, the king's men arrive at his friends' manor house, and to the merchant's astonishment and disbelief, they arrest him, charging him with the murder of Agnès Sorel!

This absurd accusation has been filed by Jeanne de Vendôme, wife of one of Jacques' debtors. Another of his debtors, an Italian, Jacques Colonna, has added his name to the charge. Both have signed sworn statements that the Lady Agnès was poisoned by one of the witnesses of her testament. Nor does anyone tell Jacques Coeur what proof exists for such a bizarre allegation.

He calls for a lawyer, for the king's representatives, for anyone to listen to him. Instead, with his mouth bound to silence his protests, and his hands tied behind him, he is mounted on his horse and led at a fast pace away for trial.

# Chapter Twenty-Five

*Is this some kind of nightmare? These two accusers are minor members of the court and I have no argument with them. What is happening?*

*Where are they taking me? Why have they bound my mouth and tied my hands like a criminal? What is going on?*

*We ride at a fast pace for what seems like hours. I hear Poitiers mentioned. I know this country well, and if we are heading for Poitiers, it will be a hard two days' journey. What is waiting for me there? I am untied and fed, but no one speaks to me. I sleep by the side of the road, and in the morning we ride on.*

*A day later, at night, I hear my captors saying that we have arrived. They have put a hood over my head, as well as tied a cloth tightly across my mouth so I cannot shout, or even see them. I am hauled off my horse and forced to walk over rough ground, then down stone stairs. Their spurs are clinking; there is a creaking as a door is opened and I am thrust inside. Only then is the hood taken off my head and the cloth untied from my* mouth. I recognize my captors: members of the king's guard. No point in talking to them – they have their orders. My door is shut hard and I sit in the dark on a dirt floor.

My mind is spinning, but despite these indignities, I must keep my head and think. Marcée's anxieties about my lawyer friend were right. Women have an instinct about these things.

I am accused as being one of the three witnesses to the Lady Agnès's testament and that I am the one who poisoned her. Have the other two been arrested? Étienne Chevalier and Dr Poitevin? Étienne was always the one nearest to Agnès, her devoted companion and protector. With nothing to gain and everything lost with her death, he must be innocent. The doctor is a man of the Church as well as the queen's own trusted physician. If Agnès was poisoned, he would have had opportunity enough to do it at her bedside in Loches, without needing to undergo the dreadful journey to Jumièges with her. All her own staff knew he was treating her for various internal ailments, but why would he poison her? And if he had, at whose bidding? He certainly had nothing personally to gain.

I am the third witness to her testament, but to accuse me is pure folly! The Lady Agnès was my friend, my best customer; she brought me countless clients. What motive could I possibly have? Why would anyone listen to these two courtiers anyway? How would they know what went on in the king's inner circle, or in the quarters of the Lady Agnès at Jumièges?

Of course! I am such a fool. It is to everyone's advantage to remove me. Is there anyone who does not owe me money, apart from the dauphin? And yet, of all those who stand to benefit from the death of Agnès Sorel, he is the one who hated her the most. Perhaps he did feel distress for his mother's shame – never before has a monarch paraded his mistress so openly. But Louis *is far away in the Dauphiné, and it is hard to believe he was involved in Agnès's death. Or am I wrong? Who else would have dared risk the king's anger and retribution? Could Louis have ordered someone close to Agnès to give her poison when she was weak after the birth?*

*When the dauphin left the court three years ago, he threatened Agnès's life. No one can forget that horrible scene. After all, the Lady of Beauty was the cause of his banishment; it was she who usurped his position next to the throne. The dauphin is thoroughly disliked by the people and in love with power, nor can he wait for his turn to rule. And yet – kill Agnès? Why? Yet, who has a motive better than the dauphin Louis, known to hate his father's mistress enough to wish her dead – and return to court himself – something Agnès begged the king not to allow, certain that Louis would kill her... Could I be considered his accomplice in order to secure my position with the future ruler?*

*Does the king know of my secret dealings with the dauphin? But if he wanted Agnès dead, he could have accomplished it in a much simpler way than by using me! Louis is the only man of high stature in the country who does not owe me money or favour, so where is his motive in accusing me? Would I not be of greater use to him alive – as I have been to his father throughout his reign?*

*Assassination is not uncommon in royal circles – it has happened on several occasions during the king's lifetime: the murder of his two uncles, the handsome Louis d'Orléans and 'Jean-sans-Peur' of Burgundy; and then there was the almost certain poisoning of the two dauphins before their younger brother Charles, our king, came to the throne – both of them killed for their place in the line of succession.*

*Who else stands to gain from Agnès's death? Well, there is*

*Antoine de Chabannes, Count of Dammartin and the courtier closest to the king. It would not be difficult for Chabannes to imply to Charles that Louis used me – Jacques Coeur, purveyor of everything to everyone – to poison Agnès. No, I cannot, in reason, suspect the dauphin, or Chabannes.*

*I must put aside these thoughts and trust in Dr Poitevin who told us all in the room next to hers that, horrifying as it was, the death of the Lady Agnès Sorel was due to the weakness of her body following her journey to Jumiège from Loches. This and her suffering due to the most complicated birth of a still-born girl foetus, and the presence of the flux in her stomach. On her arrival in Jumièges, it seemed clear to me that she was so weak she would not survive the birth. Why did anyone imagine they needed to poison her? Nature would have taken its course.*

*Whoever may have wanted to lessen Agnès Sorel's positive influence on the king must have known of his attraction to Antoinette and the possible outcome of Agnès' death. Who would profit from this other than that lady herself and her lover, now her husband? I should ask Marcée's opinion – she understands women's hold on men better than I do. But will they even let me see her? I find it so hard to believe that Agnès was poisoned.*

*Time passes. I hear a creak; a small hatch in the wall opens and a bowl of some sort of soup is pushed through. It is warm and tastes of nothing with a few lumps floating. Vegetables? Meat? Impossible to say.*

*I doze on the floor, and when the hatch opens again, I shout: 'What is happening? Where am I? Where is my lawyer?' But it shuts again and I am left with my bowl and its contents. I have found another metal pot in the corner of my dark room, and I know what that is for. How long will this go on before someone comes?*

*I cast my mind back to those who were always around Agnès in her last weeks and days. There are many whose careers benefited comprehensively from the departure of the king's mistress. I did notice at the time that Guillaume Gouffier, her trusted young valet, who was always by her side and who accompanied her on the journey to Jumièges, was ever present and whispering to the king. He did not appear unduly moved by her death. The king is deeply attached to him and perhaps even used him to keep an eye on her. After her death, and on the recent occasion of Gouffier's marriage, the king presented him with one of Agnès's most beloved properties, the mighty fortress and estate of Roquecezière. Did he ask for it? Was it for some service rendered?*

*My mind is beginning to clear, and I realize how unwise I have been to underestimate the envy of the courtiers. Have I been overbearing? Imprudent? Have I overstepped my place? Probably all those things. I have rejoiced in the success of others when justly earned – what a fool I am to imagine everyone feels the same.*

*When did the desire begin among members of the court to be rid of me? When I was made Master of the Mint in Paris? When I became 'argentier'? Or when the king ennobled me and my family? Did they put pressure on the king to unseat me? Were the two minor courtiers who lodged the accusation of murder against me put up to it by others?*

*Alone for days, weeks, in a darkened cell, I have time to think, but can I think clearly? I am fed a little better now, and even given a candle and writing materials. And a mattress of sorts has been pushed into my room. I measure my space – twelve paces one way and seven the other. There is a high window, barred and shuttered, but some air does come in and it is quite cold at night. Yesterday I received a blanket.*

*Yes, I believe my reasoning is clear despite my circumstances. I am making notes, but I cannot tell when it is day or night. I sleep when I am tired, and I can hear a tower clock strike the hours.*

*Now and again someone comes to my cell door and brings me food instead of pushing it through the hatch. I try to address them, but no one will speak to me during these first weeks. Then I begin to find messages under my food bowl. My friends outside are finding ways of opening closed doors. Everyone has a price. I am confident that someone will be sent to speak with me. I must hold my nerve and wait patiently. And exercise. I must exercise several times a day or my muscles will weaken. I must stretch, swing my arms and march on the spot. Every few days I am brought another candle, and also a bowl of warm water and towel to wash. Today I received a change of clothing – thank God. Does that mean I will be brought in front of a judge?*

*When my son was appointed Archbishop of Bourges, I was understandably proud and wanted to entertain in a house worthy of my family and all we have achieved. His official entry into Bourges was a triumphant moment for me and my dear Marcée, but it was not my doing  it was arranged by his church. The feast I gave in his honour was a tribute to his achievement. Was that not my right as his proud father?*

*Was it so wrong to build my magnificent manor house in my home town? I created it as an amalgam of the many palaces I have studied on my travels, and its like has never before been seen in France. How the courtiers must have burned inside with envy at its magnificence.*

*How wrong I was to give that great feast for the raising of our son. Archbishop of Bourges in his home town! Did Marcée and I not have reason to be proud? And yet how foolish to parade my family's new finery in the city where I started – the son of a furrier ... a seller of animal skins ...*

*What an honour the king paid me on his entry to Rouen, only a few months ago. How could I ever forget being a part of that moment, riding just behind my sovereign with those two great soldiers, Pierre de Brézé and Jean de Dunois on either side, the three of us most extravagantly attired at the king's pleasure? I was understandably overcome with emotion that the king wanted me to be acknowledged alongside his two most successful and courageous captains. He wanted it known that part of his military triumph was also due to me, the merchant of Bourges; that I provided the funding for his army.*

*What has changed that recognition of me? My reasoning is going around in circles. I have given much to the poor, carried out innumerable acts of charity. Did it appear as though I was trying to cleanse my image or repay my own sins of greed?*

*They come now and then to look at me through the tiny hatch in my cell. Yes, I am still alive and sitting in the dark. My beard has grown and also my hair. My fingernails I try to bite. There is a little daylight now from the single window at the top of my cell. They must have lifted the cover slightly. It is enough for me to write these notes.*

*Has King Charles been planning my disgrace for some time? Since the death of the Lady Agnès? Or even before? Did he imagine that I disapprove of her replacement? Throughout my life I have been scrupulously careful to keep my feelings to myself. It is commonly said that no one can read my eyes. What business is it of mine to disapprove of anyone the king chooses* as his companion? Antoinette de Maignelay would no doubt have become as regular a visitor to my warehouse as her predecessor.

I have made my money, not inherited or been given it like the rest of the court. I have worked with my hands and my head to create my fortune and I have used it often for the good of the king and the country. I have houses in most of the principal cities of the kingdom, including Paris. I have countless estates – some forty, I think – but I have five children to endow, and a large extended family I care for. I own mines in the south of the country and a fleet of ships to carry my produce all over the world. But I have never exercised my financial power with threats of extortion against a single soul. For what reason am I to be the king's and the court's scapegoat?

When will someone talk to me?

I ask each person who brings me food and removes my pot, but no one replies. My cell is dark but dry, my bed is bearable. It is not cold.

But why does no one come?

This much is true: I have steadily become the richest man in France partly through the debts of the nobility. I have acquired most of my land holdings through their unpaid bills, their losses in war, the money paid for their own or their children's ransoms and often borrowed from me. How they must hate me! Why did I not see this coming? I have sinned in tempting the court, even the king, with my glorious wares shipped from distant corners of the world. I thought their indebtedness to me was my security, but without the protection of the Lady Agnès, their obligations have become the noose around my neck.

When I look into my heart, I can see my faults and great misjudgement. The king must know I have been dealing in secret with the dauphin – but never against his father, solely for his own needs. This I did to secure the future of my house, my descendants. Louis will be king in a few years, and I and my family will need him as a benefactor.

Have I been denounced to the king for my connection with his heir? Perhaps he has learned that I was the one who helped negotiate the dauphin's second marriage, to Charlotte of Savoy, aged six at the time and a granddaughter of the former Pope Felix V, a marriage the king energetically contested. Did Louis himself inform his father of my involvement? Frankly, the king would have opposed any marriage of his heir to a woman he had not himself chosen. Why did I help the dauphin in this instance? Business, of course! I wanted him as a client, and I thought there was no need for his father to know. Louis was banished at the time, after all.

It surprised me to discover that Charles VII had warned the dauphin at the beginning of 1451 not to get involved with me. This was exactly the time when Louis was seeking his father's permission to marry Charlotte of Savoy. It was also not long after I had to 'induce' Pope Felix V to step down to allow there to be but one pope, and that Charles VII's choice was Nicholas V.

Pope Felix is Charlotte of Savoy's grandfather. Perhaps he did not want this girl's progeny on the throne of France? A Queen of France whose grandfather had been removed as pope? In February, the king refused to approve the union, but the dauphin went ahead with the ceremony before Charles's herald could arrive to prevent it. Does the king believe I was instrumental in his son's disobedience? If he does, then I am guilty of the worst crime short of regicide: that of lèse majesté. It was my lawyer who negotiated the bride's dowry, just three months before my arrest. No sooner was I charged than I heard he fled to the

*Dauphiné for protection. Yes, my arrest could well be due to this matter.*

*Worse, I financed Duke Louis of Savoy's expedition against France's ally, the powerful Visconti family of Milan. Why did I do this? My considerations have always been purely financial, neither political nor personal. No, that is not true. I have also been concerned with the well-being of my country, and that becomes political. But I have never sought political power or position. Business is what I am engaged in. Negotiations of any kind bring in profits. And helping my country will also bring profits eventually. Emotion does not enter into my business affairs.*

# Chapter Twenty-Six

*H*ow long have I been here? They have moved me to different prisons twice now, always blindfolded and without a word. I receive almost daily notes with my food. My agents outside are bribing well. I hear that the king has made it known he will forgive me all my other transgressions if I am found innocent of poisoning Agnès Sorel. To have made such an offer, he must know I am innocent, or he would arrange somehow to have me found guilty. How could I be found guilty?

This absurd and shameful accusation has affected my family, my business associates, my entire world. My houses, my wealth, my goods are all confiscated. My extended family and many childhood friends are all in my employ. What will become of them? What will become of me? As yet, no information has been passed to me in my cell about a trial.

A letter comes that brings me the saddest news. My dearly beloved wife Marcée has died. I know she asked often for permission to visit me and was refused. How I suffered for her having to endure my shame, being evicted from her own houses, even those she inherited from her parents. Immediately after my arrest I received word that she had moved to one of our rural estates. She had done all she could to salvage silver and linen from the Bourges house, all part of her dowry, and had hidden it at Menetou-Salon, another of my great houses outside the city. I grieve for my Marcée. Alone in my dark cell, I mourn my dear love, mother of my children, comfort of us all. She was a good and loyal wife, always supportive, never questioning, and brought up our children according to my wishes. Her death makes me desolate.

She was my greatest reason to come out of this hole in which I find myself. Now she is gone. My twin heart beats no longer.

My son Jean, the Archbishop of Bourges, has good and loyal connections. I even gave him the sapphire ring Queen Yolande left me so I might have access to the king should I need it. It will not do me any good now. I doubt the king will agree to see Jean even with that ring.

These endless days of confinement dig the pain of betrayal deeper into my soul. I have been a faithful subject of my king and country, and it has taken my incarceration to make me realize how inconvenient I have become. The king owes me more money than he can repay. Did he expect me to cancel his debt in return for that public acknowledgement during our splendid entry into Rouen? How could I when I was obliged to borrow heavily from the world's great merchant banks to fund the loan? Did he really expect me to cancel a loan that would bankrupt me? He has more than bankrupted me – in diverse and even more painful ways. It was shame that killed my beloved wife.

*And why have I received no message from the queen, the daughter of my patroness Yolande d'Anjou? I hoped for a word of support from her. Yet ever since the arrival of Agnès Sorel at court, our relationship has been a delicate one. I felt sure she understood her mother's reasoning in producing Agnès for her husband – a good, sound companion to take him away from the slatterns with whom he consorted. I realize she has never had any other option but to remain silent – as she has always done whatever the circumstances. Why did the queen ask for Antoinette to stay with her? Why did she send her own doctor to Agnès at Loches? I must think on these actions of the queen's who I have always considered a true follower of her mother's teaching. Perhaps she has developed her own mind with time and her mother's death ...*

*I have made many friends among ecclesiastics, and the clergy have done all they can to assist me. Not only is my brother Nicholas, the Bishop of Luçon, well regarded, but my son Jean is respected as the Archbishop of Bourges. A note tells me that the Archbishop of Paris, Jacques Juvénal des Ursins, has tried to have the king turn me over to the clergy for judgement as a 'lapsed churchman' on the basis of my education at the hands of the fathers of the Sainte-Chapelle in Bourges, and my childhood committed to wearing the tonsure as would an apprentice monk. If he is successful in this, it would entitle me to a far lighter sentence.*

*Why did I trust in the king's apparent friendship – I, who have always believed I know and understand the hearts of men? Was my head turned by his great position, as with many others in the presence of royalty? Did Charles VII not prove false to Jeanne d'Arc, the girl from Lorraine through whose dedication he was consecrated King of France and regained his kingdom?*

*How quickly he forgot her great achievement. He turned against the Angevins despite owing everything to his 'bonne mére', Yolande. And Agnès – the king's first true love – even she was unknowingly betrayed by him. I receive word that my properties have been divided among the king's new favourites, most notably the dauphin's enemy and former comrade, Antoine de Chabannes; and that Antoinette de Maignelay has been given Menetou-Salon, that great palace outside Bourges where Marcée hid her linen and silver – I hope carefully! Even Agnès's beloved Aunt Marie and her son have some of my properties bestowed on them. Does she believe I am responsible for her niece's death? Have the king's people convinced even my Lady's family of my guilt?*

*If the Lady Agnès really was poisoned, then why, following her autopsy, did the queen's own doctor declare that she had died of natural causes? He could not be mistaken – he is the best in the country. Could Agnès have been poisoned by Dr Poitevin himself? By accident? Of his own volition? Or that of the queen? But neither had any reason to want my death. Since he was the one to open the body, only he would know if there was poison. If he had poisoned her, he would deny the presence of poison in her body. If he had not poisoned her and there was poison in her body, he would have said so.*

*The king has promised publicly that he will drop all other charges against me if I am innocent of the death of Agnès. Even if the queen and the doctor were involved, given the doctor's evidence, I will be cleared. Everyone knows that Queen Marie sent her own physician to tend to the Lady Agnès in her concern for the difficulties she was having during her pregnancy. What an extraordinary gesture for a wife to her husband's mistress carrying his child.*

*Have I been lulled into a false sense of the queen's compliance with the position of Agnès in her household? Just because Queen Marie was always in childbed or burying one of her children, did she really tolerate the presence of her husband's strikingly lovely mistress silently despite her upbringing to put king and country before herself, even her children? She, the older and far less attractive woman, faced each day with a beautiful young lady with whom her husband was deeply in love? Would she have confided her unhappiness at her public betrayal and humiliation to her son? Could the dauphin have orchestrated such a terrible murder? Or might the good doctor, who cared so much for the queen and her suffering, he who had brought the dauphin and all the other of the queen's children, both dead and living, into the world, could he have suggested he go to Agnès at Loches and 'help' with her illness?*

*It was Dr Poitevin who brought Agnès the anonymous letters – did he know what they contained? Did he have them written? Was it he who urged her to go to the king under those terrible wintry conditions? The journey could easily have been the death of them both. Would he have done that of his own volition, or at the queen's behest? Was our gentle Queen Marie not bred with the same steel as her mother, Yolande d'Aragon? Surely she must have inherited something of her invincible Spanish spirit. Yolande did not hesitate to order the death of several of the king's favourites who interfered with the good of the kingdom. In the reasoning of the queen her daughter, or of her loyal physician, was Agnès Sorel interfering with the good of the kingdom?*

*If the Lady of Beauty was poisoned, here is my list of suspects who had a motive and the means:*

*Antoinette de Maignelay:*

*The king might have encouraged her to believe she could take* the place of her cousin, or she imagined she could do so. With the help of André de Villequier, a most ambitious courtier and her lover, she could have acquired the poison and sent it with Dr Poitevin as if from me to give to Agnès at Loches. I have sent the doctor medicines I have brought with me from the East before – and with success. If he believed it came from me, and why not, since Antoinette was with the Queen's suite and the loving cousin of Agnès, he would have administered it to her throughout the long journey to Jumièges. If she did not die on that tortuous journey due to a miscarriage, Antoinette would continue to give Agnès the poison at Jumièges. Villequier and Antoinette could have hatched the plot between them for her to replace Agnès; Antoinette could have persuaded the king to allow her to marry Villequier; as a result, they would become both powerful and rich. Antoinette understood the king's leanings towards debauchery and could provide the means of fulfilling his tastes. With Agnès out of the way, there would be no one at court to stop them.

Dr Poitevin:

He could have felt deeply sorry for Queen Marie and her shame. It might have been his idea to write the letters; his idea to persuade the queen that he should go to Loches and try to help the Lady Agnès. In her kindness, the queen agreed. At Loches, he began to give Agnès the poison, a little to ease her genuine discomfort due to her flux of the stomach. Then he gave her more on the journey and at Jumièges, and the rest after the birth. Perhaps he acted on his own, and the queen simply wanted to help Agnès. Since Queen Marie was travelling with the court, she would have access to the king's doctor and therefore had little need of her own. And yet – much as he was loyal to the queen, surely Poitevin would not feel so aggrieved for her as to murder her rival – a crime far worse than adultery?

239

*Or perhaps it was the queen who urged Dr Poitevin to go to Loches. Her fear was that Agnès might give birth to a healthy boy this time, and such a birth would take some of the lustre away from her own baby son. She might have hoped the journey would make Agnès miscarry and possibly even die as a result. This could have been a plot conceived by Dr Poitevin in his adoration of the queen, or a plot planned by the queen in her love for her husband.*

*Another thought occurs to me. Dr Poitevin knew that the dauphin Louis hated his wife, Margaret of Scotland, and that she could not or would not give him an heir. Perhaps he agreed with the dauphin that Margaret was not a suitable future queen. Dr Poitevin had delivered the dauphin to his mother's joy. Was he close to the dauphin? Might he have disposed of his wife in the interests of France? Agnès and Marguerite loved one another; both were hated by the dauphin; both women died in the care of the same doctor; both were treated with the same medication before they died. Dr Poitevin carried out the autopsy on the dauphine, and also on Agnès Sorel, both times alone – meaning there were no other witnesses if there was poison in their bodies.*

*Guillaume Gouffier:*

*He was always in the king's favour and was one of the few of his gentlemen of the court invited to share his bed, a most singular privilege. It was to Gouffier alone that the king confided the secret told to him by Jeanne d'Arc at Chinon. Everyone at court knew that the Maid had shared a great secret with the king, but no matter how I tried, I could not discover what it was. Nor could Queen Yolande – she told me so. To the best of my information – and mine is the best – Gouffier has never been known to tell anyone else; or was he paid to keep silent? The king*

QUICKSILVER

allowed him unlimited credit with me. In other words, this was a man on whose discretion his master could rely, but who did not show loyalty to his mistress. But why should Gouffier poison Agnès Sorel? Is he not the king's man, and I believe the king really loved Agnès. Was Gouffier also in the pay of the dauphin, perhaps, or in league with Antoinette? He was with us at Jumièges and could have added more mercury to the medicine.

If Agnès Sorel was poisoned, then these are my main suspects, although both Etienne Chevalier and Antoine de Chabannes had a lot to gain by my being convicted, since they owe me so much money. On the other hand, they have not accused me of killing Agnès Sorel. Nor has Guillaume Gouffier. The fact is, most of the court has a motive to have me removed, but none has a real motive to have Agnès poisoned. Perhaps she did die of natural causes and the whole poisoning issue was invented to have me arrested. But the accusation will never stand when the doctor gives his evidence that he has found no poison, which the court knows, and therefore it is pointless to charge me.

Time passes – days become weeks, weeks turn into months – and I am moved again. It makes no difference where they take me; the horrors are the same, though my friends find ways to alleviate my suffering with small comforts – more blankets, better food, and writing materials. My mind continues to go around in circles.

The one with the most to gain from my conviction is the king. But I believe he sincerely loved the Lady Agnès, even if he dallied with her cousin when his beloved was away from the court. In my wildest, most disparaging thoughts, I cannot believe he would have wanted the Lady Agnès dead. He would always

241

*have loved her, even if her looks faded and he no longer desired her, as I truly believe their bond went much deeper than the physical. Queen Yolande had trained her well. But once she was dead, an accusation against me would suit him very well. After all, he owes me more than he can repay.*

*I read in a note that Guillaume Gouffier is to be one of my judges. I was more than generous to him on his marriage, supplying goods for his house, but like my other debtors, he has turned against me. Perhaps they all believe I did have something to do with the death of my Lady Agnès? No, no one could be so blind or stupid. I am the only one with no motive at all.*

*But I am not being tried for the murder of the king's mistress. I do not believe for an instant that the king thinks me culpable. I am on trial for my success, my arrogance, my presumption – and for the greatest of my crimes, that of being richer and even better housed than the king.*

# Chapter Twenty-Seven

*I* am not permitted to give evidence at my trial, or even to
*I* be present, but thanks to my outside contacts, who have discovered which of the guards are amenable to gold coins, I am kept
well informed of its progress. It seems that one foolish witness
after another is called. Finally it is the turn of Dr Poitevin, and
all my anxieties are pushed aside. He declares himself the doctor
to Queen Marie; that he was sent by her to Loches due to her
concern for the Lady Agnès, who, it seems, was having a difficult
pregnancy. He arrived at the Lady Agnès's house, Beaulieu-lès-
Loches, treated her and remained with her there. When the Lady
Agnès insisted, he says he felt obliged to accompany her on that
terrible journey to Jumièges. He describes the conditions in the
depth of winter: horses sliding on the ice, wind whistling through
the leather curtains of the litters, horses and riders covered in wolf
skin capes. He never left her side, and treated her daily.

The doctor gives his evidence plainly; how he was present
when the Lady Agnès went into premature labour, and describes

*the horror of the confinement. He tells the court that she gave birth to a seven-month stillborn girl and then he details the state of Agnès's health after the birth and until her death two weeks later. Hers was a slow deterioration, and when he himself performed the autopsy, there was no sign of poison in her body. His testimony leaves no room for error.*

*When I receive these notes of the doctor's evidence, how my spirits soar! I am exonerated at last. The nightmare is over. Even if nothing can bring back my dearest Marcée, I am proven innocent of that ludicrous charge. I will return to royal favour, my goods restored, my family again in the ascendant.*

*Again, I have completely misjudged the situation. I, who have always been considered the shrewdest man in the kingdom – why can I not be more perceptive regarding myself? It seems there is no limit to the poison aimed in my direction. Although it does not take the court long to reach their verdict that due to lack of any motive or evidence, I did not poison Agnès Sorel, they do not determine the cause of her death. The king promised to overlook any other offences I may have committed if I am acquitted of poisoning his lady love. But I am not acquitted – the verdict has been left open! My trial will continue, this time I am charged with financial misdemeanours against the crown.*

*My only small consolation, and one in which I am able to take some satisfaction, is that my two accusers are condemned for bearing false witness and severely punished. Whoever put them up to it cannot or will not save them from their just retribution. Nor does either of them blame anyone else, which I find strange. Since their sentence is a harsh imprisonment, perhaps they have been privately assured they will be freed and recompensed handsomely. They should not count on it!*

*My trial for alleged financial offences begins. The list of transgressions of which I am accused is endless, but essentially they amount to my merging my own business interests with those of the Crown to the king's disadvantage. Yet if anything, he reaped greater profits from our joint business interests than I did.*

*My gaolers are becoming rich on passing me messages, but I am grateful to know details of my trial. According to the notes from my faithful employees, the proceedings are becoming a total farce. To save face, the king decides the matter will no longer be heard in open court, but in secret and by a tribunal. My three judges are Commissioners Extraordinary, the declared enemies of merchants. The moment I read their names, I know they will make sure I am found guilty – all three are heavily in my debt. I hear they have already cast greedy eyes upon my possessions, and expect their own debts to be cancelled once I am convicted. I know these men well: Guillaume Gouffier, Antoine de Chabannes, and the king's own treasurer, Otto Castelani, who will take my place at court as argentier. There is no doubt in my mind hereafter that I have any chance of an acquittal. Again I have misjudged my position. How could I have imagined the king would allow me a fair trial and let me go free?*

*For twenty-two months I have been incarcerated in great discomfort in five different prisons, always dark, always cold and damp. There must be some plan to this endless moving about. Could it be that they do it to avoid my being rescued? Yet the delivery of small comforts after each move must be proof that my friends outside know where I am. This, my last jail before my trial, is in the dungeon of the château of Lusignan near Poitou*

*– I recall seeing a picture of it in the Duke of Berry's* Très Riches Heures *... how strange that I should think of that now.*

*The catalogue of my crimes is growing. I am accused of transacting payment for goods in French silver – for which I have the king's written permission; of receiving gold – to our mutual profit – in exchange; of coining light money – in my youth, and long ago forgiven by a royal letter of pardon; of abducting oarsmen for my galleys – again with the king's written authorization; of sending back a Christian slave who had taken sanctuary on board one of my ships – the slave was no Christian, and it would have harmed my relations with my Muslim trading partners if I had kept him; of committing financial fraud in the Languedoc 'to the king's prejudice' – possibly slightly true!*

*Many other charges of a similar nature are brought forward, the most serious of which is for trading with the infidel, true, but something for which I received both the Pope's and the king's written permission; and, in particular, trading arms – again, with the necessary written permissions.*

*Once I hear that my trial is to proceed in secret and I may attend, I am permitted to wash and change, though my beard must stay. My hair is also long and my vision is poor after existing for so long in near-darkness. I am given a list of the accusations against me. Perhaps I may even defend myself!*

*My three judges face me dressed in formal red gowns and flat black hats. Do I detect smirks on their faces, or is that my imagination? Here are three men for whom I have done considerable services, who all professed friendship for me over a number of years. Now they are pleased to be in this unattractive room with white-washed walls and small, high windows to sit in judgement over me. I have not been given any opportunity to produce evidence in my favour; no chance to retrieve my papers* to prove my innocence. But that is not the point. I am to be found GUILTY, not innocent, so there is no need for me to produce evidence to the contrary.

I defend myself with all the intelligence and energy I can muster, and even without the written proof, it is patently clear I am innocent.

The verdict is a foregone conclusion.

On 29 May 1453, at the château belonging to my first patron, the late Jean, Duke of Berry, my sentence is passed. I am found guilty and condemned to death.

# Chapter Twenty-Eight

*Just as I think He has almost forgotten me, God comes to my aid. Or is the Maid watching over me, I wonder? Or my royal patroness Queen Yolande? When the news of my sentence reaches Rome, Pope Nicholas V sends the king an urgent request: my life must be spared.*

*I am blessed with some good and grateful friends after all. It seems the Pope's intervention is due to the Holy See's gratitude for the good work I did to heal the Great Schism that almost split Christendom. He wrote to tell the King of France that it was my 'personal persuasive gesture' that finally convinced Felix V to relinquish his position and accept a cardinal's hat instead.*

*The Pope's intervention saves my life, but I am doomed to spend the rest of my days in solitary confinement. I could not have been sent to a more miserable or inaccessible place – the medieval castle of Poitiers, that dank and horrible prison where this nightmare began. This time I have a real window; it is small, high, barred but open, allowing in an angry cold wind* and a little daylight. I have writing materials again to continue this account of my tribulations. I have been brought some warmer clothes. My faithful friends have been particularly thoughtful.

The latest news is that all my worldly goods have been confiscated in perpetuity by the Crown. My foolish debtors believe they have been released from their responsibility. To me, yes, but in taking my property, the king now owns my debtors. If they thought to get rid of their loans this way, then they underestimated the greed of the monarch. I know the king better than that – his plan was always to condemn me and then force my debtors to pay him what they owe me. Yet if it was his sorrow at the loss of his beloved Agnès that brought out a fierce rage in him to punish someone, how could that explain, even in part, his desire to maltreat me? He can be in no doubt that I, of all people, had no reason to harm his lady.

I have always believed myself able to read the character of Charles VII. My great patroness, Queen Yolande, warned me repeatedly to be careful of his fluctuating moods and loyalties. His is a lonely position, and one that he needs to exploit in order to be successful. And I always thought I knew better, and trusted him. I hoped he saw me at least as a loyal subject.

I have been very successful in my trade as a merchant. To arrive at my position, I have had to be able to read the minds and hearts of men and women. I thought I would always be a step ahead of the king's schemes or the plots of the dauphin. I was not. My mistake has been to believe in honour – at least, that honour is inherent in those born above my station in life. To my cost I have discovered that in the world I know, there is more honour among the lower classes than the aristocracy. I am considered wise, and now I see that I am in reality a fool.

*Information reaches me that the king's court, under the leadership of Antoinette de Maignelay, has returned to its old licentious ways; that the king's new mistress procures young girls for him for his pleasure. It seems he spoils them with extravagant clothes and gifts, especially jewellery. He travels with them from one château to another, seeking distraction. He himself dresses in extraordinary luxury and wears hats covered in precious stones. Occasionally he removes one to hand to a favoured young lady, sometimes before or after their assignation. Queen Marie follows him and does not complain. When did she ever complain? According to my informers, it seems the king has returned to type, and all the hard work of his 'bonne mère' and the honest love shown him by Agnès Sorel was for nothing. Both ladies groomed and trained a feckless man of little character into becoming a remarkable king, a king victorious! Now it would seem he has reverted to the dissipated mediocrity of his earlier years.*

*My cell is small and my hopes few, though money from outside still buys information, and sealed messages arrive even in this hellhole in which I am imprisoned. I hear there is talk of using torture to discover where I might have hidden more of my wealth … Damp covers parts of my walls and floor, despite the rushes my friends have paid to have laid on the ground. I am coughing, a deep pain in my chest – or is that the ache of a broken heart? Time is passing, and I am deteriorating.*

*I have been in this miserable prison for more than a year. Today, at last, I have received some glimmer of hope. A message from Jean de Villages, written in our code, tells me that he has a plan for my rescue. Please, dear Lord God, let it be true! I can receive messages but I cannot send any; I am unable to reply. I pray that my friends will come for me before I am tortured. No one can withstand the king's torturer – that much I do know.*

*My friends have paid for my chains to be removed, and a divan bed with a bearable mattress has been placed in my cell. Washing facilities are non-existent. My pot is emptied once a day, and it leaves by the same hand as pushes my daily meal through the hatch in my wall. That is the only time I see anyone here – not even a face, as in my other prisons, just a dirty arm and a hand with one finger, the smallest, missing. I pass my day in writing and thinking, and singing to myself a little. It cheers me. I sing Gregorian Masses rather than pray. It is my way. Now that I have a chance of being rescued, I have a real reason to sing, but softly, so as not to alert attention. My gaolers probably think I am going mad. Perhaps I am ...*

*I know the king cannot reach my network outside France – a complex set of connections I have built up over many years: loyal friends, relations, employees. They will come for me. I know it. I must be patient. I must not let my mind dwell on the torturer. I have time to think, but not about that. I must pass my hours imagining the routes my friends will have mapped out. I must prepare myself for the shock of daylight and movement. I must exercise – stretch, walk on the spot – or I will not be able to go far should I ever get out of here. Escape plans fill my head and are a welcome distraction. I pray earnestly that they will come to pass.*

# Chapter Twenty-Nine

*I*t is the end of October 1454. I have not been dreaming. It is here – the day for which I have been praying and waiting has arrived! My heart leaps – but will my feet move? My loyal men have paid the gaolers well. I hear voices, the rattle of the key in the lock. The voices are kind, soft, not the usual rough, barking orders. My arm is taken gently and I am led outside.

'It is Jean, Jean de Villages, dear Uncle,' *says a voice.* 'You are blinded from the darkness and will not be able to bear the unaccustomed daylight. Allow me to cover your eyes with a scarf. I will lead you. We are leaving the prison. I am helping you to escape. Can you hear me?'

*I must appear dazed; Jean is talking to me as he would to a child.*

'I am leading you down the passageway … now some steps – five.' *As he counts them for me, I obey.* 'Now we are going outside. You will feel the wind. I will help you onto your horse; trust me. Just breathe deeply, dearest Uncle.'

*He embraces me. How good it is to feel his arms around my shoulders. I must not cry. I am not yet safe, but how reassuring to have the warm greeting of a friend.*

'We must ride a long way – across France to Provence and your good friend King René, who is waiting. No, do not try to speak. I will tell you more at our first stop to rest.'

*With his help, I feel my way into the saddle and breathe in deeply as Jean tells me to do. How different the world outside smells – of wet autumn leaves, and grass.*

'I will tie you onto your saddle, dear Uncle, as I doubt you have muscles for riding anymore.'

*They tie me firmly onto a high-backed saddle and lead me at a fast pace. Yes, Jean is right. We need to escape to Provence, sovereign territory of Good King René, son of my excellent Queen Yolande. I know I have his support, and sense the kind hand of his mother, my patroness, reaching down from heaven to help me.*

*We halt after several hours. Again Jean is beside me; he unties me and helps me gently to the ground. I cannot stand, and he sets me down on a covering placed on the grass.*

'Dear Uncle, drink and eat,' *he says as he gives me a leather goblet with a little wine added to the water.*

*I eat some bread and take a piece of meat from his hands. I lift the scarf from my eyes; I can see a little, but Jean suggests I wear the cloth for a while longer so they have more time to adjust. He knows my muscles will hurt and offers to rub my legs with an ointment he has brought for the purpose. I let him do it.*

'Uncle, dear Uncle, forgive me not coming sooner. There was so much to arrange. We will have to avoid the king's men, as your escape will be noticed all too soon. No amount of money could keep that quiet, and the king will send his best men after you. With the help of your sons in the Church and your many friends in ecclesiastic circles, I have arranged a long line of safe houses – monasteries, priories and abbeys, where you are entitled by law to receive sanctuary. It has taken time. I needed to be sure of the people I entrusted with this task. Even a man of God would betray you for the right amount,' *he admits wryly.*

'Good nephew, my dear Jean, do not imagine I am ignorant of the effort you have expended for my rescue,' *I reassure him.* 'Since I became aware of your plans some weeks ago, I have been exercising in my cell to try to prepare my body for this ordeal. I am not as fragile as I might appear, and my eyes are slowly beginning to see again. Knowing I am no longer in that hellhole of a prison is enough to give me strength beyond even my fertile imagination!' *And I laugh for the first time since my arrest.*

*Jean is touching in his concern.* 'If only I could take you more slowly, dear Uncle, but we cannot risk the king's men catching up with us.' *It is indeed going to be a long journey, and hard, but freedom is worth every painful, difficult moment.*

*That first night we stop with the good monks in the cold granite abbey of Saint-Savin, south of Poitou. They await our arrival and welcome us with warm soup. We are given hot water to wash in – my first since my arrest so long ago – and Jean helps me to wipe my wasted body with a warm wet towel. To my relief, they have lotions prepared to soothe my aching limbs. I am asleep before the monks finish their ministrations. In the morning, with fond farewells and new rations, we are away again before dawn. Our party is a group of twelve – Jean and*

*two others of my loyal former employees, plus eight strong sol-
diers to guard us, chosen carefully by King René from his army
in Anjou.*

'If we had more, we would arouse too much attention,'
Jean explains.

*Our route takes us from one religious establishment to the
next, the way prepared by my faithful friends. As we ride, I
silently pray that they have been careful. Our journey to
Provence is long, and potentially treacherous.*

*Our next goal is the Benedictine monastery of Saint-Martial
near Limoges. My second son is a canon of the cathedral, and I
have other contacts there too. When we arrive, I see my boy
Henri and embrace him joyfully. Our eyes say everything; there
is no need for words. Over a good meal, the abbot tells us of their
difficulties during our endless war, but I hardly hear, and with a
beaker of their excellent liqueur inside me, I sleep like one dead.
Again we rise at dawn and leave our worthy hosts, fortunately
on fresh mounts, arranged in advance.*

*I am becoming stronger – I feel it, despite my aching muscles
and fatigue. I am a marionette – I move like a puppet, one foot in
front of the other. Our next destination is Cahors, to rest with a
local bishop recommended by my son Jean, who has been stripped
of his post as Archbishop of Bourges. The next day we ride for
Toulouse. At last I can see; my eyes have cleared and I can make
out the great bell tower of the abbey glowing ahead of us for kilometres as we ride into the sunset. We arrive as night falls. More
good monks, more encouragement, more kindness. Our scouts
catch up with anxious messages urging us to make more haste
– the king's men have been gaining on us daily.*

*From Toulouse we make our way to the outskirts of
Carcassonne, and the ancient Jacobin monastery there. We enter*

to wonderful singing from the chapel by the monks, famed for their music. 'Am I in heaven? Is this celestial music?' I ask the abbot – who smiles and leads me to my surprisingly comfortable bed. In the morning, we slip in to Carcassonne's walled city to meet one of my faithful contacts, who will provide me with more funds. We will surely need money to bribe someone soon.

It is in Carcassonne that we are almost caught: word has reached the city that the king's men are looking for a group of horsemen, and somehow we are recognized as those they seek. They discover us in a church. My heart races and my contact pushes us out through a door, which is firmly jammed behind us with wooden pews. As we leave, we hear the king's soldiers shouting as they try to gain entry. But for the quick thinking of the monks, who are moving more heavy benches against an outer door, we would not have escaped. I thank God I am blessed with a network that has permitted me to flee again, but I know they will be punished by the king.

With great relief, we are given asylum in a Dominican house nearby. We regroup, and ride on swiftly to Narbonne where my people await me. We receive more reports from our agents about the advance of the soldiers and try to throw them off the scent by changing our route, riding first to the east and then to the west to confuse, but it does not take them long to track us again. I watch the anxious faces of my friends leading me, and sense that the enemy is closing in.

I claim sanctuary in the famous Cistercian abbey of Fontfroide, the largest abbey in France, some kilometres inland from Narbonne. The abbot is a man I was able to help once in the past. 'My friend,' he tells me, 'I will never forget your goodness to me and my family when we were in dire need some twenty years ago. I have never stopped praying for you and the hope that I might return your generosity,' *he says embracing me. How good of him to remember. I have almost lost faith in kindness being rewarded. The abbot gives us fresh horses and food, saying:* 'I owe you much more than this, but I pray it is of some help.' *Then he blesses me.*

*There is nowhere we dare stay now and risk a delay. The soldiers are close. I am so tired I no longer have any idea of day or time; all I know is I cannot afford to stop.* 'Tie me to my saddle again, as when we started. We must press on and ride through the night,' *I shout to the others.*

*That the king is determined to catch me and bring me back in chains has become very clear. All our informants testify to the amount of bribes passing hands. At least we have reached territory where I know I have dependable connections, but the pressure has not lessened.*

*We are in the Languedoc region, and how happy I am at last to find myself not far from Montpellier. When I am untied from my horse, I fall into the arms of my helpers – my legs won't move any more. I am carried into the Abbey of Saint-Felix for the night. The monks handle me tenderly, wash me and feed me a little broth. My heart has not stopped pounding since our near-capture at Carcassonne, and I tremble at every shadow. How silently the monks move in their sandals, and yet I jump at the slightest sound, even the tiniest rattle of rosary beads. Again we are warned that the soldiers are closing in, but I cannot ride any further tonight.*

*I am almost on home territory and know the area well. But I cannot go to my great house in Montpellier, since I assume it has been confiscated. The most dangerous terrain still lies ahead.*

*From our scouts we learn that a large reward has been posted in every village of the Languedoc area for my capture. I begin to feel like a stag which, when chased by hounds, makes for the middle of a lake, hoping it is safe. But the hounds swim out and hold him fast for the hunters to dispatch. Will that be my fate too? I wonder as I fall asleep.*

*I have remained in contact with my former staff in Montpellier and again we are saved through their efforts, and just in time. I am beginning to believe I must have been a good employer to find past members of my workforce willing to risk the king's fury for helping me to escape. We follow the coast, arriving exhausted outside Beaucaire, a planned halt for the night at the fifth-century Abbey of Saint-Roman. As we enter the abbey, I smell lavender, the welcome of Provence. Jean de Villages left earlier, riding ahead to make sure our boats are ready and everything is prepared. We must leave at dawn from the bank of the great river Rhône – our last obstacle to freedom.*

*Just when I am preparing to collapse into my bed, I hear shouting, running feet, metal on stone. What is happening? I call for Jean; I call for help; I cannot move. Is this the end? After all I have been through, and the long journey? To be captured so close to freedom? Suddenly, Jean is by my side and hurrying me out, whistling for his best men to come to him. I know that whistle. It was always a panic call down at the quays and on the ships ... It seems Jean received word of the enemy's presence in Beaucaire and hastened back. I hear a great commotion as our soldiers breach the outer wall of the monastery, and reach us before the king's men do. There is fighting, sword on sword, as I am spirited away.*

*I confess I felt sheer terror at the sound of my enemies so close. If caught, I would have faced certain death; word would have been put about that I died attempting to escape from justice. Yet my pursuers know – as we do – that Beaucaire is their last chance of catching me. Once across the Rhône, I will have left the France of Charles VII and be in René d'Anjou's sovereign land of Provence – and beyond the reach of the king's soldiers.*

*This is the most difficult part of the plan. A safe house has been arranged where I can rest until an hour before dawn. On the other side of the river Rhône sits the mighty château of Tarascon, pale and forbidding, though not to me, not this night. Tarascon is safety; Tarascon, built by Louis II d'Anjou at the time of his marriage to Yolande d'Aragon to be their new capital of Provence. It was always a haven for them, and after his death, for her, my royal patroness. Now the property of her son, my friend King René, Tarascon represents freedom. I must get there tomorrow.*

*It is still dark as I am woken, and I feel as if I have slept one hour, not five. I hear there are many more of the king's men out to stop me crossing the river. Jean de Villages has chosen a little-known inlet on the outskirts of Beaucaire for our boats to wait for us at the widest crossing point. He reasons that our enemies will be looking for us at the narrowest places. I pray he is right. I kneel quickly and take a handful of soil. It is my farewell to France – I know I can never return. Dawn is near, but the sky is still dark. Two boats are waiting to row us across. I climb into the one in front with my party; the Angevin archers, our guardians sent by King René, are in the boat behind to cover us.*

*No enemy appears at this early hour – Jean has chosen well. Our paddles slip silently into the water; soon we are out of bowshot, and the wind in our faces from the east is no help to arrows anyway. Dawn is just breaking as our ghostly shadows reach the steps leading up to the château. As my feet touch the first step, I see the sun turning the high white stone turrets to a warm, glowing pink. The sure knowledge that I am safe overwhelms me. I have escaped from France … from imprisonment … from death.*

*But for the sight of King René himself walking towards me, I know I would have collapsed. His arms are open wide to fold me into his welcoming embrace.* 'My dear Jacquet!' *His voice is loud and bold.* 'I welcome you with sincere friendship to my land of Provence, where we have always been pleased to receive you.'

*What a true and loyal friend he has been to me! It was King René who refused to let Charles VII's agents extradite Jean de Villages from Marseilles; who allowed my ships safe harbour in his port to continue to sail on my behalf; who arranged for my goods and possessions to be shipped to Marseilles from my base in Montpellier claiming they were his own. I feel my benefactress, his excellent mother, smiling down on me.*

'After breakfast, we will begin our journey to Marseilles. I suggest we go by boat down the Rhône to Arles, our ancient capital, where we will be well received. My soldiers are guarding all the crossing points of the Rhône; not even King Charles's men would dare to enter my sovereign territory. Fresh horses will await us, and we will ride from Arles to spend the night in Aix.'

*Hearing his confident words, I can feel the tension beginning to ease out of my battered body.*

'Unlike the mad dash you have undertaken thus far, this will be a pleasant journey, and you can relax on the boat,' *he continues.* 'Once we reach Marseilles, I will feel safer having you under my roof there. We are a little too close to France here at Tarascon, and I do not want to tempt fate with a potential abduction by the king's men!'

*Dawn has broken, and before we leave, I climb to the top of one of Tarascon's towers and glance out of a window. In the glow of the early-morning sun, I take my last look at France.*

## Chapter Thirty

*T*he boat journey to Arles is as uneventful as King René promised, and I sleep most of the way. After a night in René's beautiful mansion, he asks me with concern:

'Shall we stay and have you rest more?' *I must look exhausted.*

'No, no my Lord and dear friend, we should move on to Aix.'

*The horses are fresh and we have no need to ride fast. Another relaxing night spent in Aix, and I will feel sufficiently revived to join in the dinner King René has organized. With what joy I will meet again a number of old friends gathered to greet me, and music – there is always music wherever this king goes!*

*The next day we rise in a leisurely fashion and the party rides at a comfortable pace towards Marseilles. We talk little on the way, but René's smile tells me that he is less anxious about me.*

*

Close to the city, they stop on a rise. There below them, the great harbour of Marseilles sparkles in the sunlight. The merchant dismounts, and as he catches sight of his flag flying proudly on the tall mast of one of his ships, he kneels to cross himself and thank God.

'Jacquet, my good friend,' says dear King René as he turns to him with a joyful face, and his hands on Jacques' shoulders, 'It is over. You are safe and yet still within your sphere of influence in my country. I want you to stay a while here in the comfort of my palace, for we have much to discuss!'

Jacques feels tears coming – he cannot help it. Then, with a start, he remembers that Isabelle of Lorraine, King René's beloved wife, died at her home in Nancy at the time of his arrest more than three years ago – how shaming not to have thought about her during all his own troubles. She was a remarkable lady, and how tenaciously she held the throne in Naples until her husband's arrival. He learns that the king has married again and his new wife awaits them.

On the gentle ride down into the city, René tells Jacques of his shock at the king's behaviour once he lost the restraining hand of his 'bonne mère' and the good influence of Agnès, leaving him rudderless and susceptible to the encouragement of Antoinette, and how quickly he has succumbed into his former state of degeneracy. His disgust at his cousin's behaviour was what finally decided the good King of Sicily to leave France. With his new wife to invigorate him, he took the decision to retire from the court of Charles VII to live and rule in his own sovereign territory of Provence.

When they reach his great portal, Jeanne de Laval is waiting. Jacques is surprised at how young she is – some twenty years René's junior, and attractive. 'Welcome, dear friend Jacquet,' she says with a warm smile that reaches her eyes. 'I have heard much of you and we are pleased to have you here with us.' With that she leads Jacques to his room.

On his first evening, they dine, hear music; mutual friends join them and they rejoice. Jacques sleeps as one who has never slept before, aware at last of a true sense of freedom. It does him good to spend this time resting in King René's wonderful house, enjoying the sight of ships in the harbour, visiting several of his own vessels. His host's doctor tends to the merchant's various small ailments, mostly deep fatigue, muscle cramp and saddle sores. His eyes seem completely recovered and his vision as sharp as ever.

René's wife Jeanne visits him in his quarters several times, bringing refreshments, and always stops briefly to exchange some pleasantries. She is intelligent and clearly shares her husband's literary and musical pursuits; she tells him about her stays in Anjou and Saumur, her love of Provence and the many plans they have for literary events at the court. Her enthusiasm is infectious and her love and admiration for her husband shines out of her eyes. She speaks of her joy in her stepchildren, and her sadness that she and René have not yet had any of their own. Jacques comes to know and admire Jeanne de Laval, and understands René's need for someone to share his life after Isabelle's death. He even wonders if he himself will feel the same one day …

During his stay, Jacques has learnt a great deal from René about developments at court, and about Charles VII's vendetta against him personally. It would appear the king feels that Jacques' escape belittles him, and doubly so since many of the French people have made it clear they take the merchant's side. No one believes he had anything to do with the death of Agnès Sorel, despite the indictments against him on posters in every village and town; and these are secretly removed at night, to the fury of the king's men. Jacques' life-long generosity to the poor and his enormous loans to the king and the court are well known and recognized.

Marseilles has always welcomed Jacques Coeur and his ships, and he has many friends and colleagues in the port. One afternoon during his second week, he has finally relaxed and René judges the time is right to suggest they sit down to talk. The time has come to exchange their thoughts on everything that has happened since the death of Agnès Sorel.

'Jacquet, my old friend, now that you have been able to rest and renew your strength, may I say how different you look from the fugitive I met at Tarascon, and I am glad of it!' René laughs, with a mighty slap on his ample thigh. 'With your beard and hair cut, you are a different man! Now, let us begin – so much is unexplained between us.'

They settle with comfortable cushions on divans on his terrace, the afternoon sun warming them despite the late season.

'First of all, how did this absurd charge of murder come about? Everyone in France knows of your good relations with Agnès, how she helped you make your name, and in part, your fortune, just as you dressed her in all the finery the king could buy. Tell me everything you know and then I will tell you what I think.'

And so Jacques does – from the time of their last meeting in Marseilles, when René asked him how his house in Bourges was progressing. He recalls how his host suggested gently that perhaps his new mansion, his palace, was becoming a little too splendid for 'the pleasure' of the king and the courtiers. 'Do you remember that conversation?' he asks. 'I do. And in honesty, I thought you were being overcautious, my Lord, and I was carried away with the satisfaction the creation of my house gave me.'

'Ah yes,' René says, a little sadly, 'the joy of creation. I experienced that in Naples. But I have learnt to let go of what you cannot hold. It is easier on the sentiment, easier on the heart. Now let us imagine that we have no heart – it will make our search for the truth much smoother.'

There is a tray of fruit juices on the table between them, and always a plate of sweetmeats for René. From somewhere in the distance, perhaps in the grounds, Jacques can hear sweet music, wind instruments and some strings.

René continues: 'With time and misfortune, I have learnt to go back to a simple philosophy, and it is this: do not imagine that others have the same instincts for good or evil that you do. They may have both, but to different degrees, or none at all. I have heard from you the saga of your arrest and imprisonment, and what and who you think might have brought all that about. Now it is my turn to tell you what I think.'

He gets up at this and comes back with a goblet of wine mixed with water.

'I have known our King Charles since early childhood, and must be honest when I say I have never had any real illusions about his character, even when I hero-worshipped him as a boy, six years his junior. He was always unfathomable and held dark secrets close. I remember witnessing his terror of thunder, yet just a few years later, he ordered our cousin Jean de Dunois to storm the château of Azay-le-Rideau and hang and decapitate the two hundred soldiers there – French soldiers – because their commander had insulted him!

'Yes, it is true – in that short time, his character underwent a great change. He was seventeen, a man, when the dishonourable Treaty of Troyes denied him his rights as dauphin, and thereafter he became two people: one a promising king; the other a wastrel who saw no future – and therefore no reason to adhere to my mother's teachings.

'It was when he abandoned Jeanne d'Arc to her fate without a thought that I realized – as did my brother Louis and a number of our close friends – that he could turn against *any* of us if need be; anyone other than perhaps my mother. He accepted no recriminations except from her; no one else would dare reproach him. I corresponded from Lorraine with my mother and sister about him and we three were in agreement. Once Louis was occupied with regaining Naples, my sister and I decided not to trouble him with the activities of the king at home, while our younger brother, Charles of Maine, was in awe and envisioned possible advantages for himself at court. He was in need after all – the land of Maine I gave him is still in English hands despite the terms of my daughter's marriage contract to King Henry VI. But with time, military success improved the character of our king somewhat, made him prouder, and with my mother's help, he was surrounded by sound advisers. Sadly, my wise sister Marie had little influence; he never hearkened to her, and she remained occupied with her endless pregnancies, births and deaths.'

While René continues in a tranquil manner, Jacques listens carefully.

'When King Charles met Agnès at the joining of our two courts in Toulouse in 1443, he was older and wiser and recognized in her what he had idealized all his life – beauty, truth, intelligence, loyalty, honesty and the ability to give and receive joy: a young version of my mother, if you like, the only woman he had ever admired. Just as she had carefully planned and foreseen, he fell deeply in love with Agnès and she with him. But as we men know, passion for one woman does not last forever, although love certainly can.'

Jacques says nothing, he listens. 'Fidelity is not a male concept – look at nature. How many animals mate for life? True. A few – swans, eagles, wolves? If one dies, the other does not pine away, it takes another partner, just as we do when widowed; as I have done,' he says with a smile, 'but that does not mean I did not cherish my darling Isabelle, as you know all too well. Back to what I want to tell you.

'Once my mother died, no one criticized our king, or refused him anything again. Then he saw Agnès and inadvertently, she presented him with a challenge – no one else did. She was a maid and an honest one, and in her eyes, he was less the king than a man married. For her to return his love, he could see he would have to win her, become her knight in shining armour. He took his time, a careful predator; the wooing was half the pleasure.

Then, when he won her love, treasure her he did, his first true love. Ultimately, he betrayed her with her own cousin, although he did take great care that Agnès did not know. I suspect that you allayed any fears she might have had? Yes, I thought so. She trusted you more than anyone and knew you would know the truth. So if you denied it, then her doubts were unfounded. I have a feeling he also made that quite clear to Antoinette or their relationship would be over. He never wanted to hurt Agnès, of that I am sure.'

At this point Jacques sits up as he had not reckoned with the turn this monologue was taking. For the king to have dallied with another during Agnès's absences while pregnant was almost to be expected, hardly a *betrayal*, especially if she was unaware. But now he sees it was a betrayal – of her pure love and trust which he had from no one else except his wife Marie, and he betrayed her all the time.

'And when she was no more, there was no one left to fight for, to make proud of him; no one for whom it was worth donning that shining armour again, to enjoy *genuine*, *disinterested* admiration. Yes, others gave him admiration, but he wanted hers, because it was honest and for him alone, although she was so beautiful that everyone wanted her. Even the war with England had ceased to be a challenge – he kept winning. So what, or who, stood between him and what he wanted? Why, only you, dear Jacques!'

'What do you mean, my Lord?' asks the merchant, puzzled. 'I laid myself and my fortune at his feet to command. Everyone heard me say so.'

'Ah yes, my dear friend, and he took you at your word! He borrowed and owed you money, a great deal of money. And it brought him success against England, which pleased him. But what he really wanted was *revenge*; revenge to assuage the death of Agnès, his one and only true, unselfish lover, who was no longer there to share his success with him, to admire him with all her heart. Someone had to pay for his loss, to suffer, because he recognized that her absence left a hole, a vast emptiness in his life. No amount of dissipation and debauchery satisfied him. And he hated himself for it. He had reformed, but without her to help him, he fell back easily into his old obsessions. Had she lived, he would never have sunk to such depths again – and he knew it. Some small, unimportant dalliances perhaps, yes, but never such vulgarity again. My mother had seen to that and Agnès could never have borne it.'

He pauses. Drinks are poured. More delicious little pastries offered.

'But to accuse *me* of her death?' Jacques asks incredulously.

'The king did not accuse you. It was two of his minor courtiers who were put up to it, perhaps believing it was his wish and they would be rewarded.' René takes a chicken leg from the spread on the table. He gestures with the chewed limb.

'The king's sorrow and pain at Agnès's death transformed slowly into a burning anger. And in his misery, he decided that someone had to pay. I do not believe it was his idea that you should be accused, but someone may have suggested it, perhaps not even to him, but to another, and slowly the king became aware of your name as a possible scapegoat, and perhaps he found it appropriate. Yes, why *not* Jacques Coeur, to whom he was heavily indebted? I believe the suggestion grew in the king's mind with the help of subtle encouragement from the inventor of the lie, and maybe that person's cohorts.'

Another walk to the table spread with food – King René's girth has become that of a champion wrestler!

'Remember,' he continues, 'we do not know that Agnès was poisoned. The queen's doctor, the excellent Poitevin who performed the autopsy, stated clearly and positively at your trial that he found no poison, despite the fact that everyone around her knew she was being treated with mercury.

'"But,"' testified the good doctor, '"not enough to cause anything but a beneficial result."'

When René said it, Jacques remembered that Dr Poitivin had been alone when he performed the autopsy on Agnès. He was surprised when one of his agents at court had told him and he recalled thinking it unusual – a doctor usually has one or two assistants for this difficult undertaking. 'Yes,' René continues, 'once I heard about his solitary performance on the body of Agnès, I went to the trouble of finding out if he had carried out the autopsy on the dauphine – and also alone. And the answer was yes. Why do you think he did that? Did *he poison them both???* Or perhaps he was covering for someone who might have done? I have thought a great deal about the answer.'

Jacques sits silent, hardly daring to breathe.

'You have told me who you suspect if Agnès *had* been poisoned. Personally, I think she was, but I think you are quite wrong about your possible suspects.'

With that he gets up to pour himself some more wine. Jacques thinks René has ended the conversation – at least for the moment. He is in shock and needs a respite to think clearly. Despite the doctor's statement at his trial, King René believes Agnès *had* been poisoned. If so, the doctor must have found evidence of poison in her. Why did he say there was none? And if she *was* poisoned, then why? How? By whom? Jacques must know and dreading the answer, he says,

'My Lord, please explain, I beg you to tell me what you know, what you think. You may imagine that now I am safe, my trials are over. But I have spent long months in fear and extreme discomfort trying to reason with myself. Why would my king, to whom I have always been loyal and for whom I have done so much, abandon me in this way, not protect me against an accusation he certainly knew to be false and which would cost me my life were I found guilty? Sire, now you are telling me that his Lady Agnès, whom I still believe he really loved, was indeed poisoned? But surely without the king's knowledge?'

Following that query from Jacques, King René chews pensively awhile on his second chicken leg, and pauses:

'Alright! Jacquet, we have been friends a long time and trust one another, therefore I will give you my thoughts, though I must warn you that I have no proof, and you will not like what I have to say.'

Both their beakers are filled, and then René sits down opposite Jacques, their knees almost touching, and says slowly:

'I think the king's consuming desire for revenge was noticed by someone close to him. In losing Agnès, he became obsessed with the need to blame someone for taking away from him the greatest treasure in his life; and he could never blame God. It was typical of his character to want to blame. He did so as a child and forever after. This growing abscess of rage in the king was noticed by someone close to him. That person realized he could make use of the king's burning resentment for a cause that would serve both the monarchy and many of the court. The king's envy of your wealth and the weight of his debt – not forgetting the need to satisfy the greed of his avaricious new mistress – added to his anger. I believe a solution to these disparate situations was suggested to him by someone close, perhaps even without his initial awareness, and that the two courtiers who made the accusation were put up to it – for a good payment, I am sure.'

Jacques is even more confused than before.

'But if my accusers were paid, then surely they would have been able to name their paymaster at their trial – to mitigate their own punishment?' he replies with growing alarm.

'And if they did not know who had paid them? If they had received an anonymous letter enclosing money and promising more if they carried out their instructions? Forgive me, my dear Jacquet – I can see I am tiring you. Rest awhile – I must go to speak with my captain in the harbour, where we have a small difficulty. When I return, we can continue.'

That night, however, there is company – old friends of the merchant's and René's, with beautiful music organized for Jacques' pleasure – and by the time they leave, René and his wife have already retired.

Two days pass before they are alone and able to continue their discussion. Two days when Jacques' mind is in turmoil. Who could have insinuated his name to the king as the person to blame for the death of his dearest lady, his best customer, possibly the only member of the court whom it was always a delight for him to see? Her company was a guaranteed pleasure, her purity of soul shining evidence of her love for the king. Naturally Jacques had heard it said that he too was in love with Agnès – why, even Marcée teased him, though she knew their mutual affection was in order to help the king, in the case of Agnès, for the man she loved, in his case, mostly for business. Jacques did help those who needed and deserved his charity – Charles VII did not!

Some days later as they are walking in the garden, beautiful with flowers and lavender even late in the season, Jacques can no longer control his troubled soul-searching. Unable to conceal the anxiety in his voice, he turns to René: 'Sire, please can you help me solve the riddles clogging my brain about the king's behaviour towards me? I am perplexed and deeply disturbed.'

René looks at him with real compassion. 'Of course you are. I apologize for having left you without completing my theory. Listen to me, dear friend, and I will tell you what is in my mind, but what I have to say will shock and distress you. Are you sure you want me to go on? You could leave for Rome, rest content under the Pope's protection and your guaranteed welcome there, a new life waiting, and never have to think of your trials again, your belief in loyalty and friendship, at least of some, intact.'

*I must know,* thinks Jacques. *It is not a question of taking revenge. What would be the point? I have to know for the sake of my dearest friend Agnès Sorel. I owe it to her to discover who might have done this to her. How can I ever forget her dreadful end? How can I forget losing my beloved Marcée, and the ruin of my family and associates in France? The ruin of the life I built from nothing.*

'My Lord, I must know. I must know who could have borne false witness against me, betrayed me with such wicked lies to the king. I keep thinking of the trial of Jeanne d'Arc and her complete innocence, yet no one dared come forward except your splendid mother, tragically too late. With Queen Yolande and the Lady Agnès gone, there was no one left at court to whom the king would listen, who could stand up for me.'

Then comes the mightiest blow, a hard punch to Jacques' stomach that leaves him breathless and reeling.

'Jacquet, tell me true, from your heart,' René says. 'Have you ever considered Pierre de Brézé among your list of suspects?'

He cannot breathe. 'Sire, that ... that is preposterous! Pierre and I are the best of friends. He was very close to the Lady Agnès, who held him in the highest regard, and he was a trusted protégé of your lady mother. He was with you and the king and Jean de Dunois in your youth.

275

He always did your mother's, brothers' and your bidding. He showed his courage time and again for the king. He was chosen by your father as a lad and remained with you all after his death. Your suggestion is simply out of the question!'

'I am not suggesting he poisoned the Lady Agnès, not at the moment. But it was in his interest to remove her, and you, from your proximity to the king.'

'Why? How can you imagine such a thing?' he cries, 'Pierre de Brézé would never act without the king's approval – and we know how the king adored Agnès! I simply cannot believe this – you are mistaken, my Lord, I assure you.'

'That is what Pierre wanted her and the world to think,' answers René grimly. 'I have evidence that Pierre – my mother's protégé, and therefore trusted by you and Agnès – was in league with the dauphin over this.'

Another great thudding kick to his stomach. The dauphin? In league with Pierre de Brézé?

'But Pierre and the dauphin are known to be deadly enemies! Pierre was admitted to the King's Council, a position the dauphin rightly felt he deserved. It was Pierre who even put forward my name and not the dauphin's and who hated him for this preference of his father's – and for other reasons!' Jacques exclaims, jumping up in his agitation.

'Only when it suited them,' answers René. 'With time, they realized they needed one another, and more than they needed you, which made you expendable. Another "*argentier*" could be appointed, and your enormous riches seized for the king. That would make the dauphin an accomplice, and grateful to Pierre. The plot I believe our Grand Sénéschal devised was both dangerous and complicated.'

If there is one man at court who Jacques Coeur thought he knew, even though at times he had had slight misgivings, it is Pierre de Brézé; but with René's words ringing in his ears, he does not know what to think. Is his confusion due to the long months in those cold, uncomfortable cells? Something is not right, he knows that. His calculations over three years in solitary misery have never included Pierre de Brézé. As a protégé of Queen Yolande, in his eyes, Pierre was above suspicion. Apart from his recent dealings with the dauphin of which Jacques' spies informed him at the time, Pierre has never put a foot wrong. Was the dauphin's detestation of Pierre merely a ruse? Or did they both come to the conclusion that it was in their mutual interest to replace the king? Was that the content of the anonymous letters received by the Lady Agnès?

René sees his friend's confusion, his brain working hard, calculating motives, opportunity, searching his memory for evidence.

'Listen to me,' he says as he puts an arm around Jacques' shoulders. 'I will explain.'

They walk on to the terrace and sit to watch the sunset. Jacques feels ill; he must look pale, as René hands him a beaker of wine and motions him to drink.

'First, Pierre removed the Angevin element from the court – I had already left to spend my remaining years with my new young wife in Anjou and Provence. But Pierre was right to do so. The others were merely out for themselves – including my brother, Charles of Maine – and getting in the way of Pierre's excellent plans for the army. He had prepared a number of reforms necessary to modernize agriculture and trade throughout France. You held the monopoly on so many of these industries, making it difficult for others to come in and compete. Without competition, prices remained inordinately high. Many of the growing middle class were finding it impossible to buy the same goods as the court.

'The new members of the King's Council were well chosen by Pierre from among the bourgeoisie, and they made the problem of your monopolies clear to him. As far as good and fair government was concerned, your domination of luxury goods – minerals, wool, leathers – among other trade, had to be broken. But with Agnès as your protector, and she with the ear of the king each night, this was impossible. As you know, Pierre carefully nurtured his own relationship with Agnès. This was done in the hope that he could turn her from protecting you.'

Jacques is aghast. 'Why could my Lord Pierre not have told me, warned me that I had to be more careful and allow others in to share my trade?' he stutters.

'Jacquet, dear friend,' René says gently, 'would you have paid any more attention to his warning than you did to mine about the great house you were building in Bourges?'

Jacques hangs his head. René is right; he understands how his overwhelming pride blinded him to the danger.

'Sire, you are correct. I would not have heard, let alone listened. And my Lord de Brézé would never have spoken to me in such a fashion. You spoke to me as a friend – a king to a commoner. He could never do that – our relative positions made that impossible.'

When René begins to tell Jacques of the growing closeness between the dauphin and Pierre de Brézé, he listens even more intently.

'Brézé surreptitiously moved his true allegiance from Agnès to the dauphin, who hated her.' This Jacques cannot understand. Pierre has consistently worked for the king and his interests – why would he become the dauphin's man? 'He played both sides – not against one another exactly; more as a banker might hedge his investments.

'And he planned carefully. First he had to convince the good Dr Poitevin of his sincere concern for the Lady Agnès's health, and that it was the queen's wish he go to her. He also told the queen that the king would be gravely distressed if anything happened to Agnès; that she would be blamed if she did not allow her doctor leave to go to his beloved.'

René takes a sweetmeat and offers the plate to Jacques, who distractedly puts it down. René continues, munching as he talks: 'Why should there be *two* royal doctors on the road north? Pierre would explain that the queen could use the king's doctor should she have need on the journey. My sister would never risk the king's displeasure, let alone his anger, and she would trust Pierre's judgement.'

Jacques reaches for his beaker – René quickly fills it. He knows he will need it.

'Next, Pierre wrote the letters, and passed them to a trusted page to give to Dr Poitevin to bring to Agnès. His agents in the street in Loches handed her two more letters. Coming as they did from different sources and in different hands, they would convince her that the king was in danger and she had to go to him. Pierre knew her character so well, and that she would make that terrible journey to save the king even if it cost her her life. He also sent medicine containing some of the poison to the doctor as if it came from you, Jacquet.'

René has been pacing the terrace – he often does when he eats and talks. Jacques is frozen to his seat.

'He did that? But what if Agnès decided not to go to the king?'

'Then the medicine would continue to arrive at Loches and slowly poison her there,' says René. It was so simple.

'Yes, it's true. When I saw the Lady Agnès in Jumièges, I was surprised to hear of her gratitude for the medicine I had sent, but I had not sent any. We were all so deeply concerned about her condition that I thought someone had made a mistake – it was when Dr Poitevin was so tired that he replaced himself with a nursing woman. Was she in the plot too? And by then it really was too late.'

René ignores his interjection and continues: 'With the queen and the good doctor convinced they were helping Agnès, the letters did their work as Pierre knew they would. And there was a good chance that the poisoned medicine would kill her – if that terrible winter journey did not – before she even arrived at Jumièges. The doctor went along on that nightmare ride to the north to please both the king and the queen; a journey that almost killed him too.'

Poor Jacques – his head is swimming. 'But why would Pierre want that dear soul dead? What could possibly have been his motive? And after she had gone to Paris on his account and suffered so much to help at his trial.'

'Schemers do not know gratitude, my friend. Their minds are focused on higher ideals.'

'Like what? Murder?' bursts out Jacques in horror.

'No,' answers René with composure, 'the good of the country. Agnès was meddling too much in politics. I have no doubt she felt her interference was in the king's best interest – she had no ambition for herself.'

'I had no idea ...' Jacques almost whispers.

René continues: 'She was, and repeatedly, and during your absences. Frankly, I have always doubted that the king ever paid much mind to anyone, but Agnès was beginning to be all-present at the meetings of the Royal Council and stating her mind in a way that when the king was absent, and you were absent, a number of the other members took her opinion to be that of the king's. Maybe it was, but this was beginning to trouble our Grand Sénéschal. The king was becoming complacent with success while Agnès was enjoying the feeling of her growing power. Did my mother not have power over the Council, and had my mother not trained Agnès? Was not influencing the King's Council exactly what she had implied Agnès should do?'

Jacques is beginning to understand, as if dawn is coming or a cloth has been removed from his blinded eyes. The light of René's reasoning is slowly waking him.

'On several occasions, after spending the night with Agnès, the king changed his mind over an issue he had agreed with Pierre the day before.' It was true; Jacques had heard whispers that she was beginning to meddle.

'But the strongest reason Pierre had for removing Agnès was the dauphin.'

Yes, thought Jacques, there was no doubt about that either. The dauphin hated Agnès, and he terrified her; she could never let his father allow him back into France – she knew he would kill her. *I can never forget the scene at court when the dauphin Louis slapped the Lady Agnès's face in front of his father, and with such force. So not even his father frightened him if he dared do that …*

'Pierre had been dealing secretly with the dauphin – which you know as well as I – and negotiating to bring him back to court and on to the Council. Actually, I thought this was a sensible plan, and I know the king was not as opposed to it as you might think. He wanted peace with his son because he realized the dauphin would have to learn to rule. At the king's age, almost fifty, he could not expect to live more than another five to eight years, maybe less. It would be better for France if his heir was well prepared.

'But whenever he voiced this opinion to Agnès, she simply would not hear of it, out of a mixture of fear for herself and fear for the king. And she had a valid reason: even if the dauphin would not get rid of his father, he would certainly try to get rid of her. No, to her thinking, it was better to keep Louis confined to the Dauphiné. But Pierre was in service to the Crown, not to Agnès. If he had to choose between Agnès and the good of the country, coupled with that of his own career, the decision was not too taxing!'

While Jacques' mind continues to spin in circles, René continues: 'Another factor was Pierre's future. He knew the dauphin would rid himself of his father's Council members once he became king; he has said so often enough. If Pierre could frame *you*, Jacquet, after Agnès's death, then he stood a good chance of being in the next government – though not immediately. He and the dauphin would agree to wait, so it would not look as though they had been on good relations throughout – Pierre is known to be the one to have crushed the dauphin's insurrection, after all. But after a decent interval, he could be recalled. That would not be solely due to ambition on his part either: Pierre is genuinely good at the work of government. Furthermore, he would be in possession of very damaging information on the dauphin, so he would never need to worry that Louis would change his mind.'

*Can I take all this in?* wonders Jacques. *My world is turning upside down. I always thought I was a good judge of character, and I believe I was right in the beginning about Pierre, but how he must have changed following the death of his patroness, Queen Yolande.*

René continues: 'By helping the dauphin with "*this matter of the mistress*" his future was assured, and without any blame falling back on him. Pierre would probably only let the dauphin know of his involvement once the king had died, or else he would have handed the dauphin ammunition against himself.'

Of course! Would Dr Poitevin have been a party to this crime?' Jacques asks. 'Surely not? Or did he kill her by accident, administering far too much of the mercury-based medicine? I am sure you know that it was Antoinette who gave Agnès the last massive dose – there are witnesses. Did someone tell her this would save her cousin? Or was she in the plot as well?' Nothing would surprise him about Antoinette – such a devious beauty.

King René takes another sip of wine:

'With Agnès out of the way, naturally Antoinette would become the king's official mistress, as indeed she did, and quickly.'

'Yes, I heard that even in my prison. But would Pierre de Brézé have been able to convince Antoinette of the strategy he and the dauphin had in mind for France? No, surely they would never expose themselves to her and her venal husband André de Villequier?'

René smiles. 'You will be even more surprised by what I will tell you now.' He has ceased his wanderings on the large terrace and sits down next to Jacques, holding his goblet. 'Pierre encouraged his wife, the innocent Jeanne, to return to Jumièges from Rouen to be by the side of Agnès, her poor friend. He persuaded her that it was you, Jacquet – you, the purveyor of all things to everyone – who had told him that if only the doctors would dare to give Agnès a much larger dose of the medicine, it might work. It was Jeanne de Brézé, the wife of Pierre and a truly loyal friend to Agnès, who asked Antoinette to do this and to add more of the mercury *she had from you, Jacques*. Of course, it did not come from you – but Pierre told his wife it did, and she believed him. Next, he told her, on her return to Jumièges, in her innocence, to tell Antoinette that the medicine was sent by you to your friend Agnès to help save her – even before you yourself arrived in Jumièges; that the doctor was not giving Agnès nearly enough; that only a really large dose would have any effect. This time the mercury Pierre sent to be put in the mixture (as if from you, my friend) would be much stronger than before, and the quantity much greater.

'Antoinette is no fool, and if neither of the two doctors had told her to do it, then she must have known it could not help Agnès. But since it was Jeanne de Brézé who told her, and clearly believed it, then she could blame Jeanne if anything went wrong. Perhaps she even convinced herself she was putting her cousin out of her misery. For misery it surely was. It was Antoinette's idea to rub the medicine into Agnès's legs – just as she had heard from Dr Poitevin himself that the dauphine Margaret had been treated.

'I have even been wondering whether one should ask Dr Poitevin who told him it would help the dauphine to rub the medicine into her legs? Who would argue with the handling given to the dauphine by the queen's own doctor, even though she died nonetheless? There is a tiny worm in my brain that works its way around in my head about the queen's good doctor. He delivered the dauphin; the dauphin will be king; the dauphin hated his wife; the dauphin hated Agnès. Both these ladies died in his hands. He alone did their autopsies. It makes you think doesn't it?' and René paces the room sipping at his goblet, a sweet-meat between his fingers.

'I am only sad for Jeanne de Brézé, but her golden-tongued – or should I say *fork-tongued* – husband would have persuaded her she had done the best she could.'

Jacques is so distressed hearing this story that he feels ill. It is more than he can fully appreciate – so much to absorb. He must think. There will be time enough for him to ponder on these disturbing facts.

But there seems to be still more to this horrifying story, as René continues: 'I believe the Lady of Beauty would have died anyway after that dreadful birthing, but Pierre did not want to take any chances. I am certain he would have indicated to Villequier that Antoinette would be very well rewarded for the excellent care she was taking of Agnès by giving her Jacques Coeur's magical medications.

'After Agnès's death, the king was distraught and it was not difficult for Pierre to persuade him to console himself with the ministrations of his beloved Agnès's cousin. Pierre would also see to it that Antoinette was indeed well rewarded – and he has done, and continues to do so. Each day I hear of more of Agnès's properties passing to Antoinette or to that scoundrel Villequier.'

After some more pacing and nibbling at sweetmeats, René surprises Jacques with something else.

'Jacquet, dear friend, are you aware of Agnès's many enemies? Not just out of jealousy, but on account of her influence on the king's policies – policies that contrasted dramatically with those of some of his closest advisers?'

Jacques is astounded; he has always been of the opinion that the king in his maturity may have listened, but always did what he himself wanted, and not what he was advised to do. René thinks otherwise.

'My dear Jacquet, I think you too were somewhat in love with Agnès and did not see her with the clearer eyes of others. Even if the king did as he pleased most of the time, there were many who believed she *did* influence his policies – and not to their advantage.

'Although he, too, was my mother's protégé, I am curious to see how Pierre de Brézé's career progresses.

Charles VII distrusts him, this much I know, but he also needs him. Knowing our king as I do, I am of the opinion that he will soon give Pierre an even greater position, but one that keeps him away from the court. Perhaps he will create him Grand Sénéschal of Normandy – a magnificent post – rather than just Captain of Rouen, his home city, as he is now. As Grand Sénéschal of Normandy he can make use of his military talents to keep the English out, but at the same time, Rouen is far from the king's favourite palaces where he will keep court.'

Throughout these terrible explanations from René, there is still the burning question in the merchant's mind that he cannot fathom and must ask: 'But why? What would Pierre have to gain from this terrible crime?' The words almost choke Jacques with anguish.

'Ah, my friend, I can feel your distress. You, like my wise mother, have difficulty in accepting that your judgement of someone could be wrong. I will explain. Pierre is a patient man. All his life he has planned his career moves slowly and carefully. I do not believe he has ever made an impulsive decision.

'When the dauphin Louis comes to the throne, he will dismiss all his father's men; he has often said so. If he keeps Pierre, that will be significant. I am certain that Charles VII knows – as I know – that Pierre has been striking deals with the dauphin, looking to his future. What greater test of his loyalty could our dauphin Louis ask of Pierre than to remove Agnès from his father's side? Think on it, my good friend. I am not clever in the ways you are, but I know the secret desires of men just as my mother did before me.'

René fills their goblets and offers his friend a platter of cold meats. Jacques cannot eat; he feels sick with anguish.

'As for Pierre's involvement in the removal of an obstacle to his long-term plan – and you and Agnès constituted that obstacle – think on this: if his material gain from your downfall was too sudden or obvious, might he himself not fall under suspicion as its engineer? However, if he received no immediate advantage at all, there was no reason, no motive to suspect him of any connection with Agnès's death, or your accusation and conviction. Of course, you were meant to die – not even Pierre reckoned with the Pope's intervention. But trust me, Pierre de Brézé's reward will come; you can count on it.'

'How? What do you mean? What more do you know?' Jacques is too stunned to be coherent.

'I would imagine he will have made some bargain with the dauphin. When Louis becomes king, Pierre will be the only one of his father's men he retains on the Council. This bargain will not relate to the death of Agnès, but to your removal from the scene. If the king was obliged to repay what he owes you, his coffers would be empty for some time. Since you had to borrow large amounts on your own credit to lend to him for the war effort, you had the king's surety. To avoid a scandal, especially after honouring you as he did in Rouen, publicly thanking you for the loan to finance his army, he would find himself under pressure from your foreign creditors to repay at least some of that loan.

'Should the dauphin inherit the throne in the next few years, he would still find the royal coffers empty. With you removed, however, that would not be the case. King

Charles would be under no obligation to pay your debts even on his own surety, as it was made out to *you*, not to your creditors. He would also benefit considerably from collecting the money owed to you by your debtors in France. Believe me; he would collect those debts no matter how many courtiers he ruined! The law would be on his side.'

'Surely he would *have* to repay my foreign creditors? He gave his signed surety!' Jacques says in disbelief.

'Jacquet, dear friend, you do not know the king. He would rather make war on the Viscontis or the Medicis or whoever rather than repay the debt. And he would have his victorious army, a far larger one than theirs, to persuade them.'

René is warming to his theme.

'The next part of the payment for such an important agreement with our clever Pierre to have you removed, as well as him acting on his *suggestion* to the dauphin that the Lady Agnès *might* not survive her difficult pregnancy, (and Louis would be under no illusion what Pierre meant by that insinuation), would need to be very attractive. Personally, I think he would demand for it to be sealed with a marriage.

'Pierre has just one son, Jacques, born in 1440, much younger than Louis' own sisters and not grand enough for a marriage with a king's daughter. I would wager that Jacques de Brézé will be betrothed to one of the king's three illegitimate daughters with Agnès, all remarkably pretty and well educated. I am sure our King Charles will legitimize Agnès's girls – an unusual step, but quite possible if he wants them to marry well. He adored their mother, and since he did not allow her to marry – the usual custom for a royal mistress – they have no official father. They are the king's legal responsibility and since they are all three enchanting, I am not surprised that the dauphin is quite taken with them. Such a marriage would be beyond the wildest imagination of a man of Pierre's breeding. It would make him the brother-in-law of the new king, Louis XI – and all-powerful. As I said, Pierre is a patient man, and the dauphin will have great need of his skills when he becomes king.'

Poor Jacques sits speechless and silent, overwhelmed by the devious complexity of the plot – if true – conceived by Pierre de Brézé to remove his two close friends, the Lady Agnès and himself.

King René takes the merchant's hands in his. 'My dear friend – and I have shown you my friendship just as you have shown me yours over the years – I am deeply sorry to have told you what I believe to be the truth of this wretched story. I know you will leave Marseilles in the next few days and sail away to your new life in Rome, and I doubt you will return to France. I beg you, as one friend to another, do not allow what I have told you to become an obsession. Let it go. There is nothing to be done except to warn your patron the Pope in Rome never to put his trust in this King of France or the next.'

## Chapter Thirty-One

Two weeks have passed and Jacques is sailing out of Marseilles on board his ship *La Belle Marcée*, bound for Pisa, and then Rome. How typically thoughtful of Jean de Villages to have chosen this vessel for his departure from Provence; his much missed wife is sailing with him after all. He counts his blessings as he looks back at the shore: yes, he still has his great house there, and he has seen to his staff and warehouses. With the goodwill of his friend King René, his business can continue from his base in Marseilles.

Jean de Villages is at the helm of *La Belle Marcée* as Jacques looks back at two more of his galleys, both armed, accompanying him. *I am safe. I am free. I am safe.* He keeps repeating this and may even begin to sing it like a roundel! Is he mad? No. He is free. He has been blessed with the loyal support of his family, his friends and colleagues. Without this great gift he would have slowly faded away in the prison at Poitiers, the threat of torture making him sweat night and day despite the cold. That was surely the king's intention.

Before he embarked, news reached him that his dear friend Pope Nicholas V has died. Before his death, however, he instructed his enclave of cardinals that whoever succeeded him must continue to protect Jacques Coeur. The new Pope, Calixtus III, has made it known he will honour that pledge. He is well aware – as are the members of the Curia – how energetically and assidu-ously Jacques worked to secure the Rome pontificate.

All Jacques' colleagues from Bourges and his other French bases, together with their families, as well as his son Jean and his other children, have fled to Marseilles and are on board with him – it is better that they leave France. Before they embarked, Jacques bade farewell to his good and dear friend, King René. The two men know they will not meet again, and it grieves them both. The merchant will not dare return to Marseilles as long as Charles VII of France lives, and even if he outlives the king, he has no reason to believe that his successor, the dauphin Louis, will be any kinder to him.

His son Jean returned Yolande's ring to him, and before leaving, Jacques gave it to René. 'My dear friend, this ring was a gift from the late King Charles VI to your mother. He told her she could always reach him with it. As you probably know, she left it to me since she thought it might be of some use. I gave it to my son when he became Archbishop of Bourges as a fitting gift, and now it is time it came home – to Queen Yolande's son; to you, my dear friend.' With that, he slipped the beautiful sapphire with the royal arms on to the smallest finger of René's left hand, and the two friends, king and commoner, embraced.

The sea journey is effortless – it is spring 1455, and the merchant rejoices in this time of year: a time of rebirth, *his* rebirth. Even if they sail into a storm, he would happily endure the worst imaginable, turn his face to the lashing rain and shout into the waves, 'I AM FREE!'

They are blessed with a good wind filling their sails, yet the sea is not rough. Jacques stands at the prow for some time, thinking on his conversation with René. So many shocks and unpleasant surprises, so much to digest, and he weighs it all carefully. His conclusion? René is probably correct. And Jacques has decided to do as he said – to let it go. *I am too tired for revenge*, he thinks.

After Pisa, they hug the coast until they reach Rome's port of Ostia. There they are grandly and most graciously met by several of the Pope's counsellors, who advise Jacques of the situation in their country. The journey to Rome by road is a pleasure, and they arrive in the Eternal City to a splendid reception. Surrounded by the cardinals in purple, the bishops in red, the new Pope himself is there to greet the merchant, dressed in white and seated on his white-draped litter. Jacques dismounts and bows deeply, when, to his surprise, the Pope is lowered and advances, arms outstretched to embrace him.

'Welcome to Rome, our good friend Jacques Coeur, a friend of the Church, a friend to all Christendom.' Overcome with emotion, Jacques kneels to kiss the papal ring and wipe the tears from his eyes as Pope Calixtus continues: 'Know that our predecessor Nicholas V regretted not welcoming you himself, but with his dying breath he asked his cardinals never to forget the debt we owe you. I hereby renew his pledge to guard and keep you safe, and promise that you, your family and your colleagues will always be welcome in Rome and in our lands of the Vatican state.'

The magnificent Palazzo Farnese has been put at the disposal of the merchant of Bourges and his family, and there they settle. After a week or two, it begins to look like home, full of flowers and some of his furniture and tapestries that have arrived from Marseilles. Surrounded by members of his family, Jacques knows that soon more will arrive, as well as his loyal attendants and employees who have fled the French king's wrath to join their master. He is restored to health; he has the energy and the will to begin again. His one wish? If only his dearest wife Marcée was still with him. How he misses her steady, silent support, like the ship bearing her name that brought him here. *I trust she watched me arrive safely from above*, he thinks.

His trading contacts have sent messages of friendship – he knows all will be well. He is not short of money or credit outside France; he has his fleet, his family members are welcome here, and he has his excellent colleagues with him. He decides to forget though never to forgive his king's betrayal; but the loyalty and constancy of so many others more than compensates for his wounded sense of justice.

A year passes. Jacques Coeur is content in Rome, surrounded by his family and his good people. There is no future for any of them in France, and they have all been made welcome here. Progress in his trading business is accelerating as he expected. He has retained his associates in the Levant and will continue to trade from Rome, while his factors spread his goods out from Marseilles. The majority of his connections rightly feel that he has been ill-treated by the king and his judges, and that his punishment was in utter disproportion to his alleged crime of financial misdemeanour.

He does not miss France. What grieves him most is the loss of his wife, his family life and the position of respect he has spent his life acquiring through honest endeavour.

Betrayal is the way of the world, especially in commerce, but at least in Jacques' own business life he has generally been rewarded by the trust he has placed in others. Yolande, that great queen, often chided him for his blind faith in the inherent nobility of knights, yet out of feudal loyalty, he trusted his king.

*Why did I not learn when I had seen so many instances of his contrary nature, and the dishonesty of many of his grand courtiers?* he asks himself. *If my king could abandon the Maid of Orléans, who had done something utterly remarkable for him and his country, why did I fail to imagine he could abandon me?*

*Enough said about betrayal. My trials are over. I am free and have found a home. A new life begins!*

# Epilogue

To the distress of the Christian world, in 1453 the Ottomans conquered Constantinople. It was the wish of Pope Nicholas V to start a crusade to recapture the city, the capital of Eastern Christendom. His successor, Pope Calixtus III, a Catalan, is imbued with the crusading spirit and promises to continue with this endeavour to halt the expansion of Islam in the Mediterranean. He invites the Christian leaders of Europe to join him, but, perhaps tired of war, none come forward. When asked, Jacques Coeur puts himself and several of his ships at the Pope's disposal, especially when in 1456 the Turks occupy Belgrade. The distance on to Rome is not great!

At fifty-six, Jacques Coeur is fit and full of enthusiasm for the crusade. He has always seen himself as having a mission for Christianity, and at the same time he can restore his various ruptured trading links. Then there is always the chance that having received a royal letter of pardon once before long ago in his youth, he might do so again if he aligns himself to the interests of the Pope in a holy war.

The pontifical fleet, consisting of sixteen galleys, three belonging to Jacques Coeur, sails on 11 June 1456, and passes through the Aegean without difficulty. Following their arrival on the island of Chios, the fleet's winter base, a message arrives in Rome: Jacques Coeur became seriously ill and died on the island on 25 November. The distressed Pope calls for a week of mourning for the man who helped to unite Christendom. According to the merchant's testament, made prior to his departure, his family and colleagues should continue as if he is away on a mission.

There is no grave on Chios to mark his burial, nor any reference to him in the island's records. Strange that one of the leaders of a holy crusade for the Pope against the *infidel* should not be honoured with a sizeable tomb.

All that remains of him on the island is a legend:

*One night Jacques Coeur left Chios secretly, sailing for Cyprus with his three ships. There he married a lady called Theodora, who gave him two daughters and no trouble.*

# Afterword

In 1461, Charles VII of France died, and his son the dauphin was crowned Louis XI. As predicted, the new king dismissed the members of his father's Council. Pierre de Brézé, without doubt the late king's most able minister, was also dismissed. He retired to his home in Rouen, having been appointed Grand Sénéschal of Normandy, an important position in the defence of France against the English, though far from the centre of power.

The following year, Jacques de Brézé, only son of Pierre, was married to Charlotte, beautiful and beloved half-sister of King Louis, second daughter of Agnès Sorel and Charles VII. The king chose to be godfather to their son, Louis.

In 1463, Pierre de Brézé was reappointed to King Louis XI's Council in his former position as First Minister. By virtue of his son's marriage, he was acknowledged as a member of the royal family of France. There could be no greater honour for a minor Norman nobleman.

\* \* \*

Following Jacques Coeur's death, Louis XI exonerated his father's *argentier* and restored to his family their position, possessions and wealth. He declared the merchant of Bourges to have been innocent of all charges brought against him, and ruled that he was wrongly condemned and imprisoned. It was decreed that Agnès Sorel had died of puerperal fever following a difficult labour and the birth of a stillborn foetus.

\* \* \*

In September 2004, the tomb of Agnès Sorel in the Collegiate Church at Loches was opened. A toxicological analysis of her hair revealed massive and fatal concentrations of mercury. Tests proved that the poison was imbibed seventy-eight hours before her death, which occurred on 9th February 1450. Agnès Sorel was twenty-eight years old.

# Author's Note

*Quicksilver* is the third volume of The Anjou Trilogy, a work of historical fiction which has absorbed the past nine years of my life. The facts, characters, important incidents are all true; the dialogue, details of decoration, dress, servants, spies, even dogs are based on those of the time but not necessarily true to fact. I have invented much periphery but nothing of significance except in the concluding pages of volume III, *Quicksilver*, where I have suggested the solution to the now accepted killing of Agnès Sorel.

It was a significant shock to me once I had finished researching the biographies of the three main characters – Yolande d'Aragon (The Queen of Four Kingdoms, volume I), Agnès Sorel: Mistress of Beauty (for volume II), and Jacques Coeur for *Quicksilver* – when a reputable pathologist proved Agnès Sorel died following a fatal dose of mercury; too much to have been taken in error.

How could I end my biography with a 'P.S. Now we know she was most probably murdered'? How could I discover who was guilty some five hundred and fifty years later?

The books had to become historical fiction and then my invented solution might not only be feasible, but also acceptable.

# Acknowledgements

For the past nine – almost ten years, I have lived, breathed, existed by day and dreamed by night immersed in the first half of fifteenth-century France. The result of my labours is The Anjou Trilogy consisting of: volume I, *The Queen of Four Kingdoms*, published in 2013; volume II, *Agnès Sorel: Mistress of Beauty*, published in 2014; and now volume III, *Quicksilver*, in 2015, all by Constable in the UK, an imprint of Little, Brown.

I have deliberately released the books one year apart so that readers unfamiliar with the territory will be able to keep up with the unfolding of the story. After all, the action takes place one hundred years before the discovery of America and a sense of time is important.

The Anjou Trilogy is my first break from documented history into part-fiction. Once I had finished all my researches into the period and my characters, a reputable French pathologist discovered through toxicological experiments on the hair of my second heroine, Agnès Sorel, that she was full of poison. Since the mid-fifteenth century, it was believed she died following a difficult confinement in extreme circumstances. Five hundred and fifty years later, how could I find, let alone prove, the identity of her poisoner? I could only speculate and present a plausible and true scenario, but am I right?

Without the help of a number of experts in medieval medicine and poisons, I would not have been able to begin to hazard a guess as to her murderer's identity. It was Dr Philippe Charlier of the Service de Médecine Légale et d'Anatomie/Cytologie Pathologiques in Paris who first made me aware of the crime, with the documentation of the proof reported extensively in the French press. I could not ignore it.

With regard to the technicalities of using mercury in the fifteenth century for medicinal purposes, I am grateful to Wayne Syme of the Royal Society of Medicine for his helpful correspondence. When I research any character, I always try to find their medical history first of all. Much can be learnt in this way. Paul Moynagh deserves my gratitude for his definitive rejection of porphyria being the cause of the recurring madness of Charles VI, father of Charles VII, who is a principal character in the trilogy.

The historian Robert J. Knecht, Professor Emeritus of French Renaissance History, has always been willing to give advice and insight into my innumerable queries, for which I am deeply grateful. The London Library staff also ranks high on my list of people to thank for their help in countless efficient ways. More gratitude is due to Gonzague Saint-Bris for his in-depth explanation of various forms of

QUICKSILVER

behaviour at the court of Charles VI and VII. The historical novelist Philippa Gregory I thank sincerely for her generous advice on the art of writing historical novels. One day, perhaps, I may reach her professionalism and dazzling style. Professor Philip Bobbitt deserves my deep gratitude for advice on the complexities of moneylending and also warfare in medieval France.

I wish to thank Michael Brown for enlightening me on medieval gardens and the flowers and herbs grown for medicine and strewing. I am also most grateful for his insight into the many uses of sugar and vegetables apart from the cuisine of the time. Lente Roode deserves my admiration and gratitude for her advice and information on the life and habits of the cheetah which she bravely breeds to release into the wild in Hoedspruit, South Africa. Thanks must also go to Dr Sheila Kate Maxwell for her initial help almost a decade ago in the research of the most obscure aspects of fifteenth-century France, including lifestyle, clothes, domestic arrangements, all that went on below stairs, bathing and much else. I want to thank Jane Baile for her invaluable information on the horticulture and propagation of plants and vegetables at this time.

I must add my gratitude to the kind assistance of José Baselga, who, together with his father, a professor of Legal Medicine in Barcelona, has been most helpful on the use of mercury compounds as both a medicine and a poison. Another loyal and incredibly helpful correspondent has been Jill Hamilton, whose advice in every area of research and even book promotion, as well as her unfailing encouragement and kindness has been invaluable. I thank her most sincerely for taking the time from her own post-graduate labours.

Again, Jean-Charles de Ravenel deserves my thanks for his help with the trickiness of French syntax and a number of little problems I have encountered with the form of titles and names, as well as his and his wife's constant enthusiasm and support during my writing sojourn in winter. My hostess during my hibernation for many years during Europe's winter months has been my dear friend Sibilla Clark, who allows me the time and space in her guest cottage to devote to my writing. Without her hospitality, kindness and encouragement, my dedication to this long saga might well have floundered.

In my own family, I wish to thank my 'in-house word-smiths' – my ever patient husband, and my word-genius daughter-in-law Sophie Winkleman. Also, my two Freddies deserve unlimited gratitude – my son and my brother to whom in unison this book is dedicated. My banker son has also been most helpful with regard to the currency fluctuations of the time.

It has been said in various media that I write books about my ancestors. Since I do indeed descend from almost every character in the trilogy, that would seem to be true, but it is only through the correspondence of genealogists that I have discovered my connection to the characters – unlike my mother and brother, I am no genealogist myself, and generally have little if any idea of long-deceased relationships. However, for making me aware of them, infinite credit throughout The Anjou Trilogy (as with my three previous books) must go to that incomparable genealogist Leo van de Pas. He has schooled and guided me through the complications of family trees, births – legitimate and otherwise – marriages and deaths contained in this saga. Without his patient help I could not have unravelled many of the genealogical links within the story, particularly since succeeding generations are often given the same name as their forebears.

Geography is another area where I am inept, particularly since boundaries and borders changed often within this story and as a result of wars, treaties and dynastic marriages. Again, it has been my brother Freddy who has solved my problems in this area, as well as calculating the length of time spent travelling cross-country on horseback between destinations in medieval France; judging how long it would take by boat, whether sailing or rowing; the fluctuations of tides and subsequent time loss; the state of the countryside one rode over, and the ever-present danger posed by marauding bands of robbers – all put reckoning the speed of an individual's, a group's or army's movements well beyond my mathematical abilities, both theoretical or practical. This is important since the speed with which news travels often has a lasting effect on the outcome. For example, had the courier not missed Yolande, 'The Queen of Four Kingdoms', in Provence, Joan of Arc would have been saved. My brother never fails me; nor does my husband with his tolerance of my absences spent writing in seclusion, as well as his correction of my English grammar! My gratitude must go to Susan Opie for her expert editorial advice in all three volumes of The Anjou Trilogy.

Throughout my research I have felt that Jacques Coeur's interest and even involvement in 'secret societies' hinted at an early version of Freemasonary. In my search for a connection with established masonic orders in the seventeenth century, I am most grateful to Robert Cooper, curator of the Grand Lodge of Scotland. I still have no proof but if the movement was secret, then there would not be any.

My trilogy is finished and I must leave the characters I have known and mostly loved for almost ten years. It is a sad parting of our ways and I must now surrender them to be enjoyed or disparaged by strangers. I hope they become friends to my readers as they have to me.